PRELUDE: A PREQUEL

GHOSTS OF SOUTHAMPTON BOOK 0

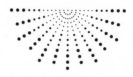

ID JOHNSON

For my Grandma Pansy May

CONTENTS

PROLOGUE

NEW YORK CITY

John Ashton poured three fingers of whiskey into two glasses and sat the decanter down on the side table. Sunlight streamed through a sliver of lace curtains that broke the deep red velvet drapes symmetrically, the only source of natural light that found its way into his study, illuminating a jagged river across the cherry floor and the side of a mahogany bookshelf as it found the face of his long-time friend, Henry Westmoreland, who reposed in a heavily cushioned chair that matched the curtains almost exactly.

"Thank you," Henry nodded as he took the glass, giving it a sip before nestling it between his hands on top of a crossed knee.

John nodded and then found a seat across from his former Oxford roommate. "How was your trip?" he asked, taking a drink and then setting his glass on an end table. "Nothing exciting I hope?"

"Heavens, no," Henry laughed. "I can't imagine anything exciting happening on a trip across the Atlantic. Fairly uneventful."

While John could think of several potentially exciting occurrences, he chose not to list them since his friend would be heading back soon. No need to plant thoughts of mechanical failures or floundering vessels. "Your meetings went well?"

"Oh, yes," Henry nodded, smoothing out his trousers over his knee. "The factory has certainly taken off these past two years. It seems I've finally found a way to get my textiles to the markets successfully."

John nodded. "That's wonderful news. You always knew how to make a quality product. Perhaps this will be just what you need to make Westmoreland Textiles a household name on both sides of the Atlantic."

"Indeed," Henry agreed. At thirty-five, his sandy blond hair should not have been thinning. Yet, when he ran his hand through, John could see much of his scalp. He hadn't seen Henry in almost a year, but he certainly looked different. Thin—gaunt almost. His skin was pale and though he wore a suit, it was apparent he had several lesions near the cuff of his jacket on each arm. "How are things for you?"

It took John a moment to realize he'd been asked a question; he was so distracted by his guest's appearance. "Oh, we are doing well," he finally managed. "Pamela and I are very happy with business. Steel is the future of this country."

Henry coughed rather violently, drawing out a handkerchief as he did so. After a moment, he took a deep breath, and returning the handkerchief to his pocket, he said, "Good. That's good to hear. I really thought you were getting in at the right time, what with the building boom and the expansion of the transportation system."

John's forehead was still puckered, but he overlooked the spell for a moment. He cleared his throat and ran a hand through his own dark brown hair, absently weighing the thickness. "Yes, timing is everything, as you know. If you hadn't made that loan to me a few years ago, I'm not sure...."

"Oh, no need to bring that up," Henry interrupted. "That's ancient history. I was happy to help a friend." He was gazing at John poignantly, and the New Yorker froze in his friend's stare, noticing the glassy look in his eyes. "You've always been a good friend, John."

"Henry," John began, leaning forward in his seat with his elbows pressed into his knees, "is something the matter? You don't seem quite yourself."

Henry took a sip of his whiskey before inhaling deeply, holding his breath for a second and then releasing it slowly. Finally, he said, "I'm dying."

John couldn't believe what he was hearing. He gaped at Henry in shock for a long moment before he stammered, "I'm so... sorry. What is it? What have the doctors said?"

Nervous laughter escaped Henry as he shrugged. "It's all right. We are all dying. Like most things, I'm just more successful at it than others." Clearly, John was not amused, so Henry cleared his throat again and continued. "I've visited quite a few doctors over the last year or so. No one is quite sure what it is, honestly. They haven't found a growth or anything of the like. I have phases when I'm nearly myself, and then the symptoms come back. They are full of theories, but theories don't keep air in the lungs."

John leaned back in his seat, unsure what to say. He finished his drink, considered pouring another, and then decided to wait. "I am at a loss for words," he admitted. "I'm so sorry. Do you think there's any hope? Perhaps...."

"No, I don't think so," Henry interrupted again. He changed positions so that his ankle now rested on his knee and began to absently smooth his trouser cuff. "I have my own theory, though it's nothing I can prove, and honestly nothing I even care to think about."

"What is it?" John asked, leaning forward again.

Henry shook his head, a serene expression crossing his face. He was a handsome man; the women had always thought so. Clean shaven except for a small moustache. John remembered how he'd had his choice of young debutantes to lead around the ballroom at every occasion. Not that John wasn't considered a catch himself. It was just difficult to imagine that this man before him was the same spritely, happy-go-lucky chap he'd spent his formative years with not that long ago. After a lengthy pause, Henry managed to quietly reply, "I'd rather not say."

It was a struggle not to press for information, so John rose and poured himself another drink, offering to top Henry's off as well, but he waved him away. John took a sip and returned to his seat. "What does Mildred think?"

His expression didn't change, nor did his distracted behavior. "She doesn't seem to mind," he finally shrugged out.

John shook his head slowly from side to side. He'd never known what it was Henry saw in the woman. Mildred Truesdale had been a beautiful strawberry blonde vixen, from his recollection. She was quick witted, never shy, and often condescending. But there had been something about her that had captivated his roommate from their third year on, and when he announced his engagement to Miss Truesdale, John hadn't bothered to voice his disapproval. He knew that the marriage was not problem free, not that any of them are, but he couldn't imagine living with someone who didn't support him, someone who seemed to question his every decision, even in business, the way that Mildred did. He knew he was a lucky man to have found Pamela, and he had always wished that his friend could know what it was like to have a true partner in life. Now, to hear that his friend was losing his life and Mildred "didn't seem to mind" was about enough to send him through the roof.

"What can I do?" John asked, biting back the coarse words of consternation that were fighting to break free.

A small smile played at Henry's upper lip for a moment before it faded back to melancholy. "I think my business should be just fine, at least for a few years. I'm not worried about that. It's... Meggy."

Thoughts of his own children, Grace who was twelve and Charlie who had just turned nine, brought a tear to John's eye. "Yes, of course," he replied. "How old is she now? Six?"

The smile broke free this time. "Yes, six—going on thirteen, I believe. She's a little twig of a thing. Always running about. Feisty, full of life." He didn't bother to wipe the tears away that were trick-ling down his cheek. "After losing the other three before we ever even knew them, Meggy has been the breath of fresh air I needed. I can't imagine...." He paused, his voice catching in his throat. "I can't imagine my life without Meggy in it. And my heart breaks for her knowing that soon enough, she will have to carry on without her old Da. That's what she calls me, Da. Must be those Irish nannies," he chuckled, finally brushing the tears from his face.

John realized he was crying as well, but he also let out a laugh as he pictured his friend running around the garden with his little girl, her thin arms wrapped around him. "Little girls are God's gift from heaven." He remembered his Grace when she was that age, how he'd come home from the factory and set her on his knee to read a story each evening.

"So are little boys," Henry replied, and there was a pointedness to the statement that brought John back to the present. "That's what I came to talk to you about, John."

Henry uncrossed his legs and scooted forward in his seat, setting the glass down on the table next to him. With the motion, John could see just how frail his friend had truly become. His movements were not natural; they were forced and calculated, as if each one took all of his concentration. "What is it?" John asked, unsure where this conversation was headed.

"Charles," Henry said. "He's a good boy. You're a good man, a good provider, a good father. I know your son will be, too. I want to ask you to do me a favor. As a friend. I want Charlie to take care of my Meggy. I want him to marry her, to make sure she's taken care of. I can't imagine stepping out of this life not knowing what might happen to her. If I know Charles Ashton will be waiting for her, well, then, perhaps crossing over won't be quite so bad."

John didn't hesitate, not even for a moment. "Of course," he said, nodding with sincerity. "Absolutely. Whatever you need."

Henry nodded, as if he had known his friend would come through for him. "I've put away 50,000 pounds in a safe deposit box at The Bank of New York, along with a very specific copy of my will. Here is another copy for you along with a key to that box," he said as he pulled an envelope out of his jacket pocket. "If Charles marries Mary Margaret before she turns twenty-one, the company will be his. He's to take the money and give half to my wife, the other half to my brother Bertram, who will be running the company in my stead. If he waits until after Meggy is twenty-one, he'll still get the company, but the money will be hers. If he doesn't marry her at all..."

"You don't need to worry about that, Henry. I already gave you my word."

"I understand that, but life isn't always exactly what we expect, now is it?" he asked, managing a weak chuckle. "My Meggy is strong-willed, like her mother. If she marries someone else, or if she turns thirty without marrying Charlie, then the company will still belong to Bertram, but the money will be donated to the charity I've named in the will. I know it sounds rather complicated, but everything is for a reason."

"I've no doubt," John nodded, accepting the sealed envelope and slipping it into his own jacket pocket. "I can assure you that Charles will marry her before she turns twenty-one, as that is your hope, is it not?"

"It is," Henry nodded. "I should like for my wife and brother to have the money, to be pacified by that, and to stay out of Charlie and Meggy's lives so that they can go on about their business without having to worry about interlopers."

John knew he must be missing something, but he simply nodded. He didn't need to know the details of the situation with Henry and his wife and brother. "Charlie is a good boy, that's for certain. I know that he will understand and will willingly accept Mary Margaret as his wife."

"Good," Henry nodded. "It's likely best to start preparing him sooner rather than later."

"Indeed," John nodded. "But here's to hoping you have several more years to spend with us, old friend, and that you are there to give Meggy away on her wedding day."

Henry scoffed, leaning back in his chair as if he could no longer hold himself forward. "That would be lovely," he finally said, his gaze not reaching that of his host. "She does have some money of her own. I've put it away for her. I will make sure she knows. I want her to be... taken care of."

"Surely, Mildred will see that she is," John offered.

"One would think," Henry agreed. "I should hope a mother would look after her only surviving child." His eyes were off in the corner of the room somewhere, and once again, John realized he wasn't getting the full story. After a long pause, he added, "Meggy is a strong girl. Strong in every way. I know she'll be all right, even after I'm gone."

"I will do everything I can to look after her," John assured him.

"I know you will," Henry nodded. "You've always been a good friend, John."

"You're like a brother to me, Henry," John replied, leaning forward and gingerly placing his hand on his friend's knee as if he were afraid any pressure might cause him to shatter like glass or dissipate like an apparition.

Henry covered his friend's strong hand with his frail one. "Do whatever you must, John. Please. Despite what my colleagues might think, my business is not my legacy, Meggy is. She's all that matters."

CHAPTER ONE

SOUTHAMPTON

Meggy Westmoreland loved the toy pram her father had brought her back from New York City. She had snuggled two of her favorite dolls inside, wrapped up tightly in a blanket which had been a gift from her late grandmother. It was a lovely spring day, and she pushed the pram back and forth along the stone path that trailed through the back garden. While she loved all of the beautiful flowers that grew here, the lilacs and oleanders were her favorite. She had even named one of her dolls Lilac, despite her mother's insistence that it was a "ridiculous name." The urge to pick the flowers was overwhelming, but she had learned her lesson the hard way when she was only three, and the sharp slap to her hand hadn't been forgotten. Her mother and uncle sat under a shade tree in the distance now, and the possibility of getting away with even pulling one petal free was simply not worth the risk.

As she walked back and forth, stopping occasionally to check on Lilac and her sister Dolly, who had the loveliest blue eyes, she wondered what her mother was talking about. She couldn't make out many words, but her tone seemed quite serious. She held a fan in one hand and every once in a while, she placed it in front of her face and leaned in next to Uncle Bertram, as if she were afraid someone might overhear or read her lips. Though she was certain whatever they were discussing was likely a "grown up problem" as her da put it, she was still curious by nature and wished she might at least hear enough of the conversation to know if they were speaking about her. From time to time, her uncle looked at her in a strange way, one that made her feel quite uncomfortable, and this made her wonder if maybe they were discussing sending her away to boarding school or making her work at her father's factory. With her mother, one could never tell.

A rustling in the bushes caught her attention, and as she turned to see what the noise might be, a loud voice shouted, "Boo!" followed by the sound of breaking branches and laughter.

Meggy jumped, but upon seeing that it was only Ezra, the gardener's son, she became more perturbed than frightened. "Ezra!" she scolded, looking over her shoulder to see if her mother had heard. "What are you doing? If my mother catches you in her bushes, she'll box both of our ears!"

Still laughing, the slightly older, gawky boy said, "Aw, she ain't heard nothin', Meggy. She's too busy yammering to your uncle. Why don't you come play in the carriage house wi' me?"

Meggy shook her head. "You know I can't go in there without my mother's permission, and if I interrupt to ask her, she'll give me what for."

"You're a silly girl, Meggy!" Ezra shouted. "You should do whatever you like, and see if your mother even notices. She never pays you any mind."

While she was certain he had a point (most of the time, her mother didn't seem to notice what she was doing or where she was) her mother did have a knack for finding her just when she was up to no good. Since her nanny was allergic to flowers, Meggy was only allowed to play in the back garden when her mother was present, which wasn't often. She was more interested in her pram just now than climbing around the dusty carriage house with Ezra, but then, having a playmate was also a rarity. She was torn. Scratching her head, she glanced over at her mother and then at Ezra. Perhaps she could at least ask, and then, if her mother said no, she could continue to play with her baby dolls and Ezra could go off on his own and let her be.

"All right then," she muttered, and leaving the pram behind, she made her way across the yard, her fingers interlaced in front of her.

"I'm just concerned, that's all," her mother was saying, leaning in closely to Uncle Bertram. "It's as if he knows what we're about. And I don't like it."

"Then perhaps it is time to accelerate our strategy," Bertram, who was at least ten years older than her father, with streaks of gray at his temples, replied. "If you're afraid he will find out and change the will...."

"Mary Margaret?" her mother questioned, just noticing her presence. "What in the world are you doing? Why aren't you playing?"

"Beg your pardon, Mother," Meggy replied with a small curtsey, "Would it be all right if I went to play in the carriage house with Ezra?"

"The carriage house?" she repeated, her blue eyes widening in dismay. Her mother was strikingly pretty, but Meggy thought her expression always ruined her face. Why didn't she ever smile? Why must she do her hair up so tightly that she always looked surprised? "You know how I feel about you climbing around in there in your frock! You're liable to get dirty or catch a tear...."

"Now, Millie," Bertram interrupted, "Perhaps Meggy should be off to the carriage house. That way we can speak about... matters... without being interrupted."

He smiled at her, and Meggy felt as if little insects were crawling all over her arms. There was just something about the heaviness of his eyes, as if he could cut her open with a look. She turned away, back to her mother. "Please, Mother?"

She sighed and whispered a word Meggy knew she was never to

repeat before she finally said, "All right then. Off with you. But do be careful. I don't want that dress ruined."

"Yes, Mother," Meggy nodded, holding back her smile so that her mother couldn't see how delighted she was to be given permission to do—anything. She scampered off to meet Ezra who was already headed towards the carriage house which sat at the back of the property. Despite her inability to initially make up her mind, she knew she'd made the right choice. She always had fun with Ezra.

THE SUN HAD DISAPPEARED beyond the horizon as Meggy finished brushing her hair and placed the brush back on her dresser. "Now, say your prayers and off to bed," her nanny, Patsy, directed, giving her a quick peck on the top of her head. Though she'd only worked for the family for about a year, Meggy liked her best of all, and she especially liked it when she was allowed to bring her daughter, Kelly, to play. Most of the time, however, Meggy's mother forbade Kelly from visiting, and she spent most of her time with her grandmother while Patsy carefully tended to someone else's child.

As Patsy put out the lights, Meggy kneeled and said a proper prayer, asking God to look after all those she loved, and as Patsy neared the door, she rose, whispering, "Good night," with a sweet smile.

"Good night, my love," Patsy smiled in return, watching the little girl climb into her bed before she went out, leaving the door open just a crack as she blew a kiss into the darkened room.

"Is she off to bed then?" Mr. Westmoreland asked, meeting her in the hallway.

"Yes, sir," Patsy replied, giving a little bow.

"And you're off too then, I suppose?"

"Yes, sir," she repeated.

"Have a restful evening, Patsy," he said with a smile.

"You, too, sir," she nodded.

Henry approached Meggy's door cautiously so as not to scare her, even though he knew for certain she would be expecting him. He visited every evening when he was home. This night, he felt quite tired and worn down. The trip to New York had been tiresome, though he had begun to feel better physically the longer he was there. Now, back in Southampton for just over a day, he was beginning to feel quite ill again. He did not intend to let his daughter see that, however, and as he approached her bed, she pulled the covers down away from her face, which beamed at him in the moonlight.

"Are you still awake, my little angel?" he asked as he sat down next to her on the bed.

"Yes, Da," she said, still smiling. "You know I cannot go to sleep until I've had a kiss from my da."

He laughed and stroked her hair. "What do you do when your Da is away on business then? Stay up all night like an old barn owl?" He began to make hooting noises until she giggled and then he leaned in and tickled her until she couldn't control her laughter and neither could he.

"Noooo, Da!" she squealed in an attempt to answer his question. "I'm not an owl!"

"Perhaps an alley cat then?" he asked, beginning to meow, while she continued to laugh, though he stopped tickling her quite so much.

"Nooo! I'm not an alley cat either," she reminded him.

"Well, then, what are you?"

"I'm your little girl!" Meggy exclaimed, stretching her arms open wide.

He pulled her into his arms, wrapping her up tightly. "Yes, you are my little girl," he agreed. "You are my little angel, Meggy. My dear, sweet child."

As he released her and she snuggled back down against her pillow, she said, "I love you, Da."

"I love you, too, very much," Henry replied. He leaned down and kissed the top of her blonde silk covered head. "More than anything."

"I wish that you could stay home and play with me forever and ever," Meggy continued, stifling a yawn. "Wouldn't that be lovely?"

"Yes, darling. That would be lovely. Just know that I will always be looking after you, my sweet child, no matter what. You will remember that, won't you, angel?"

"Yes, Da," Meggy replied, nodding off. Her eyes were heavy and her head had lolled to the side as if she were nearly asleep.

Henry leaned down and kissed her once more atop the head and then tucked the blankets in tightly around her. "Good night, my love."

She was clearly sleeping now, her breath shallow and even. He took one more look at her and then quietly pulled himself off of the bed, noticing it took more effort than it should have, and headed towards the door. This time, he pulled it completely closed behind himself, leaning against it for a moment, his eyes closed and his heart heavy.

"Is everything all right, sir?"

He opened his eyes to find Patsy before him, a concerned expression on her face, her voice low.

"Oh, Patsy. I thought you'd gone on," he said, managing a smile.

"Yes, sir. I had just gone back to the nursery to tidy up a bit. Are you feeling well, sir?"

He didn't bother to answer her question. Rather, taking a quick look around to make sure they were alone, he leaned in closely and placed his hand on her arm. "Patsy, you love my Meggy, don't you?"

"Yes, sir, of course."

"As if she were your own?"

"As much as one can," Patsy assured him.

"Good. Then, I need you to know something. If anything should happen to me, will you let her know... when she's older. When she's old enough. Will you let her know that there is a bank account in her name, National Provincial, the one on High Street. It's not my usual establishment. No one should know—unless... unless you tell her. You will won't you, Patsy?"

"Yes, of course, sir," Patsy replied, her freckled forehead furrowed. "Sir? Should I help you into the parlor?"

"No, no, I'm quite all right," he assured her. "I just want to make sure that Meggy is protected, should anything ever happen."

"I understand," Patsy replied.

"Good then," Henry replied, patting her arm. "You're a good woman, Patsy." He smiled at her, and turned to go, leaving her looking after him with a puzzled expression on her face, wondering what had just taken place.

Henry made his way down the stairs to the parlor where he thought his wife might be having tea. His brother was likely out for the evening, as he preferred to frequent the local watering holes. Though Bertram was in line to take over the company should anything happen to Henry, he hoped that he would run it in name only. He knew nothing about running a textile manufacturing company, despite plenty of opportunities to gain an education in that field—or any business field he had wanted. Their parents had been rather wealthy and had done all they could to see that both of their sons were looked after, though neither of them had lived past fifty. His mother had lost a battle with tuberculosis just after Meggy was born and his father had gone on shortly thereafter. The doctors had declared he had suffered a heart attack, but Henry believed his father had died from a broken heart, missing the woman he had loved so dearly.

As he entered the parlor and saw Mildred sitting in her usual chair near the unlit fireplace, a lantern illuminating her embroidery, he wondered what that must be like, to love someone so much you couldn't fathom going on without them. He had been in love with her at one time. She had been a clever, cunning young woman, with beautiful hair and sparkling eyes. He knew almost immediately she was after him for his money and the promise of a prominent life, but they had become involved more quickly than he had planned for, and he'd asked her to be his wife one evening when she'd come to him in tears, carrying the evidence of their indiscretions beneath her ample gown. A month later, after they'd made their vows, the first of their three tragedies occurred, and that evidence was buried in a tiny box in her father's family plot. He had thought at the time their loss would bring them closer together, but that was the beginning of Mildred's emotional rationing; she seemed determined never to care about anyone or anything again. Not even him. Not even Meggy.

"Are you coming in?" she called, not even looking up from her work.

He realized he had been lingering, and holding back a sigh, he replied, "Yes, dear. I was just thinking about how lovely you are, that's all."

She glanced up at him then, a look of skepticism on her face. Without another word, her eyes returned to her stitching and he settled back into his chair across from her, eyeing the newspaper on the side table but choosing to gaze at the portrait above the fireplace instead. He stared into his own painted face, wondering at how different he looked only two years ago when it was made. Meggy was smiling broadly, all of her teeth still present in her four-year-old grin. Now, there were two missing, and her blonde hair was much longer and less curly. Mildred looked exactly the same—her hair done up in the precise extreme chignon she wore every day.

"I'll get you some tea," she said standing and placing her embroidery on a table next to her chair.

"Isn't Tessa still in the kitchen?" Henry asked as she approached the doorway that led to the back of the house and the attached kitchen.

"Yes, she is," Mildred affirmed, pausing to turn to address him. "But you know how I like to bring your evening tea." She managed a smile, and it looked a bit more like a snarl than an expression of happiness to him.

"Very well then," Henry nodded, his stomach beginning to churn. He took a deep breath and leaned his head back against the chair, his fingers digging into the arm rests.

He was not a stupid man. In fact, he was quite intelligent. That's why he wasn't sure why he continued in this charade the way that he had been doing for over a year now. In fact, he could ask himself the same question about their entire marriage, but this farce in particular was not only alarming but deadly. Why would he continue to let her do this when he was on to her? Why not call her out? Leave her? Save himself?

Perhaps it was love. Love for the woman he had met so many years ago, the one he had promised himself to. Perhaps it was doubt. What if he were wrong, and she was not at fault? Wouldn't he seem quite foolish then? Perhaps it was his inability to believe that someone he had once loved so much could do something so innately evil? As he awaited the promised cup of tea, he pondered these options. At last, he decided it was time to do something differently, and he promised himself the next morning he would take action. If not for his own sake, then for Meggy's. She didn't deserve to live with a woman who would poison her own husband.

"Here you go, darling," Mildred said as she set the cup of tea and saucer on the table next to him. She choked on the last word much the same way he was certain he would choke on the first swallow.

"Thank you," he replied eyeing the steaming cup as she forced a smile at him and crossed back to her chair. "I think I'll let it cool a bit."

"I thought you liked it hot," Mildred replied as she picked up her embroidery. "I always bring it to you steaming."

"Yes, I know. It's just that I'm not feeling well tonight," Henry stated, watching carefully for any sort of reaction.

She shook her head and pursed her lips. "I do wish those doctors would come up with something. Some sort of a diagnosis."

"Yes, me, too," Henry agreed.

"Perhaps then they could come up with a treatment that is effective," she continued.

"Indeed."

She glanced up at him and then at the tea. He continued to stare

17

at her, and eventually she averted her eyes. "How was your visit with John? Is he doing well?"

"Quite well," Henry replied, not surprised that she had changed the subject.

"And Pamela and the children?"

"I didn't see them, but John said they are also doing well."

"Delightful to hear," Mildred said, though her tone showed no delight at all. She was quiet then for several seconds, almost a minute, before she reminded him, "Your tea is likely growing cold."

He did not shift his gaze, and after another long pause, she glanced back at him. When his eyes did not falter, she placed her embroidery down again, never losing track of his eyes as she did so, as if daring him to call her out or give in and take a sip.

Carefully, and without looking away, Henry reached for the cup. He brought it up just below his bottom lip and held it there. "Mildred, I think we need to have a serious conversation tomorrow."

"All right," she said, her face cold as steel.

"I think some things need to change."

"Very well then."

"Clearly, neither of us are happy with our current condition," he continued, the tea still poised beneath his mouth.

"It's getting cold."

Despite confirmation of his deepest fear, Henry realized he had little choice but to drink the tea. He could refuse, call her out right now, or he could take a sip, become violently ill for a few hours, and then slowly recover. This would be the last time though; of that he was certain. Tomorrow, everything would change. He would make arrangements. She could have the house, but he would take the one thing that really mattered—Meggy—and she likely wouldn't even argue.

With a deep sigh, Henry Westmoreland slowly raised the cup of tea to his lips and took a sip. As he felt the liquid slide down his throat, Mildred broke into the only true smile he'd seen on her face in nearly a decade. Almost immediately, he realized something was different. He expected to feel like hell, but this—this was something far worse. His heart began to race, his breathing became labored, and the cup slipped from his hand, shattering on the wooden floor.

He began to pull at his collar, hoping that loosening it might let more air into his lungs. When that didn't work, and he felt himself slipping to the floor, he tried to call out. Perhaps Tessa would hear him from the kitchen and could go for help. He collapsed on the floor amidst the shards of China, unable to get a word out, unable to get a breath in.

Mildred walked over, the smile still on her face and dropped to one knee next to him. "Oh, no, Henry! What's happened?" she asked in a quiet voice. "You seem to be having a heart attack! Let me get some help!" She stroked him on the side of his head gently, as if she actually cared for him, though the sneer on her face said otherwise, and without standing or yelling, she began to pretend to call for help. "Someone help!" she said. "Anyone! Fetch a doctor!"

Henry felt his chest constricting. His vision narrowed, and as the darkness closed in, the last image he saw was the grimace on his wife's face as she let him die on the parlor floor. Though he couldn't move, couldn't see, couldn't breathe, he could still hear, and the footsteps he heard entering the room were familiar, as was the voice. "Is he gone then?" Bertram asked.

"I believe so," Mildred said, her voice growing in distance, as if she had left his side. "Now, perhaps, we should fetch the doctor."

"Give it another minute," his older brother replied. "I want to make sure there's no resurrecting him."

"Very well then," he heard Mildred say as he faded into oblivion. Once her voice slipped away, his thoughts shifted to the smiling face of his little girl. In those last seconds on earth, he prayed that John would take care of his sweet angel and remembered Charlie. Yes, Charles Ashton would take care of his Meggy. He knew he would. He had to.

CHAPTER TWO

SOUTHAMPTON

The swing was creaky. Her father had promised to look into it, to see if he could switch out the rope or tie it to a different branch, but he hadn't gotten a chance to, and with every sway to and fro, Meggy was reminded that her father wasn't coming home this time. She would never see him again.

Her mother had said he'd had a heart attack, and when she'd questioned what that meant, she'd been sent out of the room. Later, Patsy had explained that his heart had stopped working, and now he was in heaven with Jesus. Meggy didn't think it was fair that Jesus could just take her Da like that. Didn't he have enough other people to keep him company? Her Da was the only person in the whole world she'd wanted to keep, and now he was gone. Forever.

"Whatcha doin'?" Ezra asked sneaking around the back of the tree.

"Nothing," Meggy replied, still slumped against one of the ropes.

"Want me to push you?"

"No, thank you."

21

He came around to stand in front of her, a solemn expression on his face. He was nine, older than Meggy by a few years, and better understood what had happened. "Sorry about your Da."

She squinted up at him, as he was standing almost directly in front of the sun, and then dropped her eyes back to the ground. "Thank you."

"My papa said that it was fast at least. I suppose that's a good thing. He didn't suffer."

Meggy dragged the toe of her shoe through the dirt. "I would rather not talk about it, Ezra," she replied without looking up at him.

He continued to stand there for a moment. She could feel his eyes on the top of her head, but after a bit, he gave up and sauntered away, leaving her with her sorrow.

She'd cried for the first day or so. The next day had been the service at the church and the cemetery. She hadn't gone—her mother said it was no place for a small child, and she was liable to act out and cause a scene. Meggy knew differently, knew she would have been very respectful. She'd wanted to see him one last time, but her mother had forbidden it. In the end, she supposed it was just as well. The last memory she had of her father would be of him coming in to wish her sweet dreams.

That night, she'd slept remarkably well. No one had woke her in the middle of the night to tell her what had happened in the parlor just below her room. Sometimes she could hear the sounds from downstairs through the radiator. But not that night. It wasn't until after she'd dressed and eaten breakfast that her mother told her in a matter-of-fact tone, "Mary Margaret, your father died last night." If Patsy hadn't been there to comfort and explain, she wasn't sure what she would have done. As it was, she was still having trouble understanding what had happened and that her father would never come home again.

The sun was starting to sink below the horizon, and she decided it was time to go in. No one had paid her much attention lately, not even Patsy, as she had been given lots of other assignments. She had spent quite a bit of time alone, and despite the fact that she was not allowed to go outside unaccompanied, her mother hadn't noticed. Now, as she slipped back in through the side door, she heard voices coming from the parlor, including her mother's, and knew that she hadn't noticed the coming or the going.

She heard her uncle's voice as well and the voice of a man she did not recognize. Whatever it was that he was saying, her mother and uncle didn't seem to appreciate it very much, as the more he spoke, the louder and shriller their voices became.

"You're certain there is absolutely nothing that can be done?" her mother was asking as Meggy took a few steps towards the adjoining parlor.

"No, everything is perfectly legal. He had it notarized just last week when he was in New York," the strange voice explained.

"And it doesn't matter that it took place in another country, for crying out loud?" her uncle asked.

"No, the will itself was written and signed here, in his lawyer's office, in Southampton. It was just the final piece, where Ashton agreed, that took place in New York City. It's legally binding."

Her uncle let go a string of words Meggy was not allowed to repeat, and she jumped back a bit; she couldn't remember ever hearing him so absolutely irate.

"Bertram, calm down!" her mother insisted. "There's no need to lose your head over this now. We have years to figure it all out before any of this goes into effect, right Mr. Steele?"

"Yes, madam. The company will stay in Bertram's name until Mary Margaret either marries Charles Ashton or turns twenty-one," the stranger, Mr. Steele, agreed.

"Let us continue to explore other options. Perhaps John Ashton will reconsider. Perhaps he will make another agreement with you that will supersede this one." Her mother sounded calmer than Uncle Bertram, but Meggy knew that tone, knew that it meant someone was likely to meet with Mildred Westmoreland's wrath in a matter of moments.

"I honestly don't think there is anything that can be done...." Mr. Steele was saying, but Meggy heard the screech of wooden chair legs on the oak floor, and her mother interrupted.

"Thank you, Mr. Steele, for your time. We appreciate your assessment. Now, if you'll excuse us, you can imagine that Bertram and I have much to do."

Meggy took that as her cue to disappear before she was found out, and as she heard three sets of footsteps walking away from her towards the front door, she ducked back around towards the kitchen, hoping not to be found out.

Her prayers went unanswered, however, when her face made contact with the rough fabric of Patsy's skirts. "Miss Meggy, darlin' whatever are you doing?" she asked just above a whisper.

Happy that it was Patsy who had found her out and no one else, Meggy let go a breath she hadn't realized she'd been holding. "Nothin'," she replied looking up into the kind eyes of her caretaker.

Patsy shook her head, frizzy red curls dancing around her mob cap. "Now, I know that isn't true."

"I was just.... Mother and Uncle Bertram were talking, and I wanted to know what they were saying, that's all. I thought maybe they might say something about Da."

Smiling, as if to say she understood, Patsy reached down and took her charge's little hand. "How would you like a cookie?" she asked, leading her into the kitchen.

"Mother says I shouldn't eat cookies. They're liable to make me plump," Meggy reminded her as she was scooped up and deposited on the countertop.

"A little thing you like you?" Patsy asked, shaking her head again. "I don't think one gingersnap is liable to make you anything, except for maybe a little less sad." She produced a cookie out of a jar labeled "Flour" and Meggy's face lit up a bit as she took a nibble, hoping her mother didn't walk in.

"Now, I suspect eavesdroppin' on your uncle and your mother is a good way to get yourself into quite a bit of trouble, little miss," Patsy reminded her, looking sternly into her large blue eyes.

Meggy nodded, knowing she was right. And getting into trouble was the last thing she wanted to do.

"I bet they weren't talking about anything that should concern a little girl like you, anyway," Patsy continued as she straightened up the counters a bit.

"They actually were," Meggy begged to differ. "I heard my name several times. And another name, too, one I'd never heard before."

Patsy glanced back over her shoulder, as if she didn't quite care. But then a few moments later, she asked, "What name was that?"

Swallowing the bit of gingersnap she had in her mouth, Meggy replied, "Charles Ashton."

Her brow furrowed, Patsy turned and looked directly at her. "Who in the world is Charles Ashton?" she asked.

"He's to be my husband," Meggy answered, nonchalantly, brushing the crumbs off of her now empty hands. "He's an American. He lives in New York City."

"Well, you're just full of answers," Patsy said, crossing back over and helping her back down to the floor.

"Patsy, did your mother pick a husband for you?" Meggy asked, peering up at her.

"No," Patsy answered quite quickly. "I picked 'im myself."

Meggy nodded her head. "I don't think I like the idea of someone else picking for me either."

Fighting back a giggle and rolling her eyes, Patsy patted her on the head and said, "Oh, little sprite. You've years to worry about that. Now, off you go. Upstairs to your room, out of sight and out of mind before you get yourself into any trouble."

"Yes, Patsy," Meggy nodded as she made her way out of the room. A few steps into the hallway, she turned to look back at her nanny. Patsy was wiping the counters off, going about her work as usual. Meggy couldn't help but think about how awful it might be if she should never see Patsy again, so before she got too far into the hallway, she spun around and ran back into the kitchen, squeezing Patsy around the hips with all her might, before she turned and took off again, hoping to avoid her mother and uncle as she made her way up to her room where she yearned to be left alone for a bit to ponder this new piece of information.

"Miss Mary Margaret, pay attention. It is vitally important that you learn your sums to one hundred so that we may go on with subtraction. Do you hear me, young lady?"

Meggy looked away from the window, where she could see Ezra running about in the yard chasing butterflies, and refocused her attention on the stern looking face across from her. "Yes, Ms. Strickland," she said, inhaling and beginning her recitation again.

It had been less than a month since her father had passed away, and here she was with a new governess, a mean one at that. Her uncle had insisted that she be schooled properly and had brought in Edith Strickland, a middle-aged, plain-faced, stern-talking governess from London who had come highly recommended from one of the gentlemen Uncle Bertram knew from his new social circle as owner of Westmoreland Textiles. Patsy had been reappointed, and while Meggy still saw her from time to time working in the kitchen or elsewhere in the house, it wasn't the same. She missed her. Everyone she loved had been taken away from her.

"Come now," Ms. Strickland barked, rapping a ruler on the table so loudly that Meggy jumped. "Try your eights again. You must focus. This is not that difficult, Mary Margaret."

"Yes, Ms. Strickland," she said again. She had been focused, or at least she thought she had been. She hadn't been looking out the window. She wasn't wondering why Ezra was allowed to run about and enjoy the sunshine whilst she was trapped in here repeating numbers that meant little to nothing to her.

The next mistake, the ruler was not so polite, and rather than making contact with the table, it met her knuckles. Meggy winced and pulled her hand away, her eyes wide. "You struck me!" she shouted.

"I did," Ms. Strickland admitted. "And I shall do it again if you make another error. Now, pay attention!"

Meggy was outraged. She flew up out of the chair, sending it toppling behind her. "You can't strike me! You're not my mother!" she shouted.

"I can, and I shall!" Ms. Strickland countered, standing. "Now, return to your seat this instant!"

"No!" Meggy shouted, and pushing past her, she ran out the door of the study, shouting for her mother.

Instead, she ran straight into her uncle who was coming around the corner from the foyer. "Mary Margaret!" he shouted, his eyes almost as wide as hers. "Whatever are you doing?"

"Ms. Strickland struck me on the hand with her ruler!" she yelled, turning to see the governess following her down the hallway.

She had her pointy nose in the air, the ruler still grasped firmly in her hand. "That's right, I did. And I shall do it again if she cannot master her sums." Her voice was calm and firm.

Meggy wanted to throw herself at the old bitty and scratch her eyes out. "You cannot! You old bag! You mean, vile old thing!"

"Mary Margaret!" her uncle admonished, grabbing her roughly by the shoulders. "How dare you address your governess in such a manner? She can and she will continue to strike you if you cannot behave like a proper young lady."

He had spun her around to face him, kneeling as he did so, and Meggy found herself looking into those evil eyes. She didn't like when he put his hands on her, and she pulled away now, hoping he would release her. He did not; instead, his grip tightened until her shoulders began to ache. "My mother...."

"Your mother has also given her permission," Bertram explained, his voice tight and bordering on rage. "Now, apologize to Ms. Strickland and return to your studies. If I should hear one more thing about

27

you not following proper instruction... well, I do not think you shall like the consequences, young lady. Do you understand?"

Meggy nodded, fear welling up inside of her gut.

"I said, 'Do you understand?'" he repeated as his fingers dug into her shoulders.

"Yes, sir," Meggy just managed.

"Come along, Mary Margaret," Ms. Strickland ordered, and Meggy pulled herself away from her uncle and followed the stranger back down the hallway, realizing that nothing was the same as it had been before, when her father was alive. He would have never let this happen to her.

Nor would he have let the governess strike her three times on the bottom with the ruler. But it happened just the same. Meggy didn't cry though; she wouldn't let them see her cry.

CHAPTER THREE

NEW YORK CITY

Charlie Ashton always enjoyed walking the floor of his father's factory with him, listening to the owner encourage the workers and comment on their effort. Everyone always seemed so happy and proud to be doing their job. Today was no different, as Mr. Ashton proceeded up and down the rows, patting workers on the back, calling almost every single one of them by name, despite the hundreds of individuals they passed. Charlie wondered how he knew everyone so well, and when he'd asked, his father simply said, "People are important."

The sounds of the machinery made parts of the factory very noisy, and whenever they would approach some of the more dangerous areas, John would always take Charlie by the hand, even though he was nearly eleven years old—practically a grown man—and his head reached his father's shoulder. He said he wanted to make sure nothing happened to his right hand man, so Charlie shrugged and took his father's hand. He pretended like it embarrassed him, but he secretly liked it. He wouldn't mind staying his father's little boy for a few more years if he could help it.

There was one spot that Charlie liked best. A catwalk soared above the factory floor, over by the offices, and whenever they were finished walking through the aisles of workers, his father would drop down and sit with his legs dangling over the edge, Charlie at his side. Usually, he had some sort of treat in his pocket—hard candy or peanuts—and they would share as they discussed important business.

Today, as Charlie dropped down next to his father, John pulled a butterscotch out and handed it over. Charlie's face lit up as he popped the sweet candy into his mouth. His father had one for himself as well, even though Charlie knew he didn't care for sweets quite as much, and they surveyed their empire.

"Someday, all of this will be yours, Charlie, my boy," John said, stretching his hands out to span the width of the factory.

"Yes, father," Charlie replied. He knew all of that, of course. His father had been saying it for years. "I'll know everyone's name, too, Father. Just like you."

"I know you will," John laughed. "And you will be an excellent leader, inspiring your workers to do their best."

Charlie nodded. "I'll never have children working in the factory, either, Father, like some of those other places."

"Goodness, no," John shook his head. "You do hear everything, don't you, Son?"

Charlie smiled. "Yes, Father." He tried to listen to as much as he could whenever his father talked about his business. He wanted to learn as much as possible.

"You know, Charlie, all of this is possible now because of my dear friend, Henry. Do you remember me talking about him?" John asked, looking off into the distance.

"Yes, Father. I remember. Henry Westmoreland. Your college roommate."

"That's right. He helped your mother and I out at a time when we really needed it. If it hadn't been for him, we wouldn't have the factory, wouldn't have... anything. Henry Westmoreland saved us, Charlie. He was a good man." John's voice faltered a bit, but with a deep breath, he managed, "He was the best man."

Charlie was confused, and he couldn't remember ever seeing his father upset before. "Father, did something happen to Mr. Westmoreland?"

There was a pause before John replied, "Yes, Charlie. He passed away. Last year."

Charlie's face fell. "I'm very sorry to hear that, Father," he said. He patted his father on the back, as he had done so many times whenever Charlie was upset. "You must be very sad."

John looked at Charlie's hand and then smiled, though Charlie wasn't quite sure why. "Thank you, Son," he said. "You really are growing up quickly."

"Yes, Father," Charlie repeated, withdrawing his hand and placing it in his lap.

"I was quite sad to hear of Henry's passing, Son. He wasn't very old. He had a lot left to accomplish."

"His family must be very upset," Charlie offered, imagining how devastated he would be if he lost his father.

John snickered and shook his head before saying, "He has a little girl."

Charlie's eyes widened, though he thought he may have heard that bit of information before. "She must be very, very unhappy."

Nodding, John said, "Yes, I suppose she is." He sighed and looked out over the work floor again before turning to look at Charlie. "Son, before Henry died, he came to meet with me. He asked me, if something should happen to him, would we be willing to look after his little girl—you and me. I know I didn't ask you about it, Son, but I thought I knew for sure that your answer would be the same as mine. You'd be willing to look after her someday, wouldn't you, Charlie?"

"Yes, of course, Father," Charlie nodded, knowing that whatever his father thought would certainly be best.

"Good, I'm glad to hear that," John said, finally smiling.

"Do you mean, I'll have another sister?" Charlie asked, thinking of his sister Grace. She was a bit older than him, and sometimes they argued, but for the most part he liked her just fine most of the time.

"No, Son. I mean, someday, she'll be your wife."

Charlie was a bit shocked. He'd never even considered the possibility of having a wife—not now or ever. He ran a hand through his dark brown hair and dropped his father's gaze for a moment, staring off at the workers below. He saw some women working right alongside their male counterparts. They were strong and capable. His father paid them just the same as he did the men because he said that women were just as valuable. Perhaps this Westmoreland girl would be like them—resilient, skillful.

"Charlie?" his father asked, patting him on the back. "Are you all right?"

"Yes, Father," Charlie said, finally looking his father in the eye. "Whatever you think is best, Father."

"I knew you'd agree," John said with a smile. "I knew you'd understand. We owe Henry so much, all of us."

"Yes, Father."

"Such a bright boy," he continued. "It's no wonder your tutors rave about your studies."

"Thank you, Father."

"Come along, Son," John said, bringing himself to his feet and pulling his boy up to join him. "Let's go home and see what's for supper."

Charlie nodded in agreement, following his father along the narrow catwalk. "Father," he called as they approached the stairwell, "what is her name?"

"Oh, yes, of course," John mumbled, as if he couldn't believe he hadn't mentioned it. "Mary Margaret," he answered. "Mary Margaret Westmoreland."

"Mary Margaret," Charlie repeated as they began their descent. It sounded like a suitable name for a wife to him. He hoped that she liked butterscotch.

SOUTHAMPTON

"Time for bed," her mother repeated for at least the third time. Meggy continued to pretend that she could not hear her. She had been playing at reading for nearly half an hour now, not budging from her chair in the parlor, despite the fact that she knew her mother didn't like her to be downstairs. Meggy didn't like her room anymore.

"Mary Margaret!" she shouted this time. "Get upstairs and change this instant or else I shall fetch Ms. Strickland from her chambers and have her put you to bed!"

Meggy took a deep breath, realizing she would have to go now, despite the fact that she would have done almost anything to work her way around it. But without a word of back-talk (which would have gotten her a fat lip at the least) she gathered up her book, dragged herself out of the room, and began her slow ascent up the stairs.

She took her time washing up as well. No longer would Patsy come in and help her count brush strokes or make sure she said her prayers. Most nights, she didn't bother to say them. No one was listening anyway—she was certain of that. Eventually, her mother would come in, or she would send Ms. Strickland by to check on her. Either one was bad, but she would not willingly climb into her bed and attempt to go to sleep because she knew, in a few hours, once the taverns closed, the monster would come. Nothing her mother or Ms. Strickland did to her could equal what the monster would do.

It didn't happen every single night. Sometimes, he was too drunk and would pass out downstairs. Other times, she would hear his heavy footsteps pass by her door and trip their way on down the hallway. But frequently enough, the monster would make his way into her room. Then—well, all she could do was squeeze her eyes shut and wait for him to leave. He said that it wasn't bad, that she was a good girl for being silent. She didn't think that could possibly be true; it certainly felt like a bad thing, a very bad thing.

She had thought about telling her mother, but every time she approached her, she was waved away or told to be silent—that little girls were for being seen, not heard. Once, she had spoken up to Ms. Strickland. She had even gotten the worst part of the story out before she realized that the governess was about to strike her with that awful ruler. She knew immediately that Ms. Strickland was not on her side.

Patsy would have helped her; she was almost certain. But she had taken ill recently and was on leave. She hoped that, once she recovered, her mother would have her back, and then she would tell her everything. She knew that Patsy would help her. The other ladies were all strict and rude, just like the aptly named Ms. Strickland. It would do no good to try to tell them. So Meggy cried herself to sleep each night, hoping to be lucky and not to be awoken in a few hours by the sound of the monster creeping up the stairs. This night, she tucked herself in tightly, hoping perhaps if the blankets were taut enough, he'd give up and go away. That had never worked before, but it was always worth a try. Anything was worth a try—three nightgowns, leaving her school knickers on. Anything. Even begging her father to come back as a ghost and whisk her away. Nothing seemed to work though, and this night she climbed into bed like so many others, hopeful that it would be a good night with no visitors.

She was not feeling particularly lucky, especially since her mother came in and rapped her on the head with her ring to hurry her off, putting the lights out and pulling the curtains tight so that not even the tiniest bit of light could creep in from the street below or the stars in the sky.

She'd slammed the door behind her, leaving the seven-year-old to linger in the dark and await her fate, her eyes shut tight, her pleas sent out to all four corners of the universe should anyone care to hear and save her.

That night, the universe's answer was, "No."

"Meggy?" a familiar voice called from behind the tree. "Meggy, what are you doing out here?"

She didn't bother to glance over her shoulder at Ezra. She knew if Ms. Strickland realized she had snuck out of the study and was out on the swing, and she found Ezra was with her, they would both be punished. Without turning she said, "Go away, Ezra."

"But, Meggy, if she finds you, you'll get a thrashing."

She sighed. "I know that, nitwit," she replied. "But she's gone off to rest and left me to practice my Latin. Unless you wake her. Now, go away."

"Pardon me," Ezra said, his tone indicating that she had certainly hurt his feelings. "I was only concerned for you, Meggy."

"Well, don't be," she said, finally turning to look at him now. "I don't need your help. I don't need anyone's help.

"You've changed," Ezra said, stepping out from behind the tree. "I don't think I like you anymore. Ever since your Da died, you've gone mean."

The words stung, there was no denying that. But she wasn't about to let him see that. Instead, Meggy stood, turning to face him. She balled up her fists and placed them on her hips. "Well, how should you know? Your father's practically a ditch digger! You don't even know how to read, Ezra! Now, leave me be or else I'll tell my mother you sneak into the sugar jar when her lady's not looking!"

Ezra's eyes were wide as saucers as he kicked dirt in her general direction and took off towards the carriage house. Meggy considered chasing after him, wanting vengeance for the filth in her hair and sprinkled across the front of her frock, but she heard her proper name being shouted from the house and knew she was already in enough trouble without running after him and soiling herself more. She realized she'd meet the business end of the ruler as soon as she returned to the study. It was odd how facing the monster had made her so strong that the ruler no longer hurt. It didn't seem like there was much else that the universe could throw at Meggy to hurt her now.

CHAPTER FOUR

NEW YORK CITY

Charles Ashton's study looked out over the courtyard of his parents' estate. The gardens and hedges were gorgeous and a large fountain decorated with cherubs sat directly in the center of his view. He considered himself quite blessed to have the opportunity to take a break from his studies to look out at such a lovely vision.

His father believed that children should stay at home with their parents until it was time to go off to a secondary school to study, so John had hired the best tutors to come into their home to educate both of his children, and despite the fact that she was female, his sister Grace studied just the same as he did, though in another room with a governess instead of a male tutor.

Charlie had always been told he was quite bright and his tutor gave him high marks in nearly every area. He studied hard and paid particular attention to math and business as he knew how important those two subjects would be when he took over his father's business someday. He was also aware that he would be running Westmoreland Textiles by the time he was twenty-four, and he had only ten more years to successfully understand how to lead a corporation. He wanted to be prepared.

He was not yet engaged to Mary Margaret Westmoreland. He had never met her, not that he remembered anyway, and he hadn't so much as written or received a letter from her yet, either, though his father thought that he should begin to write her soon. Yet, he thought of her often, wondering what she was doing, where she might be. He asked his father several times what she might look like or what he thought she would be interested in. His father had recanted several stories that Henry had relayed to him over the years, read from some letters that Henry had written. So, even though Charlie had never met Mary Margaret, he realized she would someday be a very significant part of his life. He even said a prayer for her each night before he fell asleep, hoping she was doing well despite how difficult it must have been for her to lose her father at such a young age. At least she had her mother.

He hoped that somewhere across the sea, she was growing into a fine young woman, that she thought of him often as well, and that she was preparing to come to America someday to be his wife. He could only imagine that she must be sweet and kind, just like her father, intelligent and loving. Surely, she was praised for her grace and compassion as he was. They would make a fine couple someday, he just knew it.

Yes, Mary Margaret Westmoreland must be the lady of his dreams. He was certain of it.

SOUTHAMPTON

The sun was baking the mud into her skin. She could feel the crustiness taking over her legs and arms where it was beginning to dry. Likewise, her hair felt heavy with drying dirt and tangles from the wind. Nevertheless, she spurred the stallion on, taking hedges and gullies as if she hadn't fallen off and landed in a puddle just a few moments ago.

Not only was she straddling the horse, she hadn't bothered to put a saddle on him at all. If she had taken the time to do so, she likely would have been found out, and though she was certain an ample punishment awaited her when she returned to the carriage house, at least she would have her fun first. In Meg's experience, it was always best to have fun first and then be punished. Punishment was bound to happen either way. One may as well have a bit of enjoyment first.

While their estate was located in the middle of Chilworth, there was a wooded area just a few blocks away that backed up to the creek she had jumped—mis-jumped, as it were—and from time to time, she liked to borrow a horse from the stable and take off for a bit. She'd done it several times over the last year or so and only gotten caught half of them. Those were fairly good odds, she thought, and despite the fact that Mr. Bitterly, Ezra's father, the head groundskeeper and overseer of all things horse-related, had been punished severely the last time she had done so, she saw no reason to let that deter her from having a bit of fun. After all, if she could withstand the consequences, so could he. Perhaps he should be a little more careful with where he left the carriage house key.

Meg rode onward and upward until she came to the crest of a hill and pulled the reins, bringing her steed to a stop. She'd reached a clearing, and from here she could see the harbor and the ocean, two of her favorite sights. Both of them smelled of freedom and opportunity. Someday, she vowed she'd board a ship in that very harbor and sail away from here, leaving her mother, her uncle, and all of the ghosts of Southampton far behind.

The sun was beginning to set by the time she led the stallion back towards the gate behind the house. It was still ajar, and she thought, perhaps, this would mean that no one had noticed that she was gone. However, as she dismounted, the horse let out a soft whiny, and it was enough to draw Mr. Bitterly out of the shadows. He stood before her, his arms crossed against his barrel of a chest, his expression saying everything.

"I was just out for a quick ride, that's all," she said as she handed him the reins.

"You're covered in filth, Miss Mary Margaret. You wreak of horse, and your governess has been inquiring about your whereabouts for nearly an hour. I don't understand! Why do you insist on doin' such things when you know it can only lead to trouble?"

Meg shrugged. "Trouble isn't so bad, Mr. Bitterly. Sometimes it's the only way you know you're still alive."

"For a ten-year-old, you sure have a smart mouth," he said, shaking his head and leading the horse off toward the carriage house.

Even though she'd know when she "borrowed" the horse he'd also be held responsible when she returned, she couldn't help but feel a bit sorry for him now. He really was a nice enough man most of the time, though Meg didn't really trust any man. Rather than attempt to sneak back into the house, she made her way to the pump in the back of the garden and began to run the cold water over her legs, splashing it up onto her arms. If she could wash away most of the mud, perhaps she could also eliminate some of the horsey smell, and while she would most certainly be in trouble, she might be able to spare the other party.

"Mary Margaret!"

She would have known that voice anywhere. She turned about, her dress dripping and her boots soaked, to find Ms. Strickland staring at her in horror. "Where in the world have you been?" she asked, stopping quite a way back from her wayward charge.

"Just off in the woods there," Meg replied pointing back beyond the house to the rear of their property. "I went for a walk. And I fell. In a puddle."

"You incorrigible little mite!" Ms. Strickland shouted. "I don't understand why you insist on being petulant—all the time!"

Meg stared at her, blue eyes unwavering as she continued to blast her with insults. Nothing she said could possibly hurt her.

"When you're finished, get yourself up to your room, put on proper attire, and come to the study at once. You will have quite a punishment awaiting you!"

"Yes, miss," Meg said making her voice as sickeningly sweet as she could, which got the reaction of disgust out of her governess that she was hoping for.

"My ruler will be waiting!" she threatened as she turned to stomp back into the house.

Meg held back a snicker and turned off the pump, dripping muddy rivulets of water all over the carefully manicured yard. She had no doubt that Ms. Strickland would find her bottom with that ruler. But she would have to catch her first, and that would take some time, and if nothing else, at least it would be fun. One really couldn't have too much fun, now could one?

CHAPTER FIVE

NEW YORK CITY

Charlie sat in his study staring at a blank page, his pen poised just above his stationery. His initials, CJA, were inscribed at the top in fancy, golden calligraphy. A gift from his mother, the stationery made him feel important. Perhaps that was part of the reason he wasn't exactly sure what to write. What if his words came across as foolish? It would be difficult to be both important and ridiculous at the same time.

Of course, the other idea that made this particular writing task difficult is that it was the first time he was to write to Mary Margaret. He had known for years that she would be his wife one day, but having never met her, he simply had no idea what she was like. He wasn't sure what he should discuss. What if she found his remarks drab and boring? Though he'd written a bit of correspondence before —mostly to his grandparents who lived upstate—this letter seemed important, and he didn't wish to mess it up.

"Charlie, darling, are you quite all right?" his mother asked as she placed her hand on his shoulder.

He had been so absorbed by the task, he hadn't even heard her come in. Pamela Ashton was a diminutive woman. Not even five feet tall, with the type of bone structure that might make one look frail if she wasn't so incredibly healthy, it was a wonder she had birthed such a tall, strong young man as Charlie. His sister Grace was also quite a bit taller than their mother already at seventeen. They did look similar, however. Both women had long brown hair and dark eyes with fair complexions. His mother liked to fashion her hair differently from day to day and this afternoon she had it pulled up on top of her head with tiny curls framing her oval face. Charlie always thought he had the prettiest mother. He hoped one day his own children would look upon Mary Margaret and feel proud that their mother was lovely and kind, the way that he admired his own mother.

"Yes, Mother," he replied, turning to face her and forcing a smile. "I was just considering what it is I might say to Mary Margaret."

"I see," Pamela nodded, sitting in a chair next to her son. "What have you written thus far?"

Charlie shrugged and dropped his head. "Honestly? Nothing."

He thought he saw a hint of a smile at the corner of her soft pink lips. "Well, considering you've been at it for nearly an hour, I would say, you've quite a lot on your mind, my boy."

Charlie looked out at the fountain, which is what he'd been doing for much of that hour. "Yes, Mother. What if...."

"What if—what?" she asked, squeezing his shoulder. "What if you say something silly? Something that makes her laugh?"

"What if I say something that makes me sound—idiotic?"

Pamela laughed then, no longer able to hide her amusement at her son's enthusiasm for perfection. "Charlie, I doubt there is anything you could say to make you sound anything less than the intelligent, kind-hearted young man that you are. However, if you should like, once you've finished, I will read it over and let you know if I think you need to make any corrections. How would that be?"

His countenance brightened. "You wouldn't mind?" he asked, finally feeling as if perhaps he could manage this task after all.

"Of course not," she assured him. "After all, Mary Margaret will be like a daughter to me one day. I wouldn't want her to think I've raised an idiotic son."

He could tell she was teasing, and he couldn't help but laugh. His mother was always so lighthearted. He couldn't imagine having one of those stern mothers who never paid her children any mind except for to scorn them. "Thank you, Mother," he said, patting her hand on his shoulder.

"Anything for you, my love," she smiled. "I shall be in the parlor. When you're finished, bring it down, and I'll have a look."

"Yes, Mother."

Before she turned to go, she bent down and kissed him lovingly on his crown of dark brown hair. Watching her walk out the door, Charlie hoped that Mary Margaret's mother loved her the same way that his mother loved him. It must be awful to lose one's father. Without a proper mother, things would be even worse.

With a deep breath, he readied his pen and began with the only thing that made sense. He quickly wrote the date and the salutation and then began with a bit of an introduction.

April 15, 1902

Dear Miss Westmoreland,

I hope this letter finds you well. It is spring time here in New York City, and the birds are chirping. The buds are blooming on the trees. The air smells lovely. It is as if the world has awoken from a deep slumber. I hope that Southampton is just as lovely this time of year.

I wanted to write to you to let you know that I have been thinking of you. I was so very sorry to hear about the passing of your father these several years ago. I am sure that has been very difficult for you. I hope that your mother is a kind and loving woman like mine. I am certain she must be as my parents speak so highly of your father.

My father will be traveling to Southampton on business in a few months. I hope that I am able to go with him so that perhaps we could meet. I should like to get to know you and form a friendship. I am interested to know what you like to do in your spare time, what you think of your studies, who your friends are, that sort of thing. I believe my father will be contacting your mother shortly so that we might be able to find a time and place to get acquainted properly.

Personally, I enjoy studying math and business, as well as reading. In my free time, I enjoy being outside. I ride but not as well as I might. I enjoy sailing but I have never been particularly fond of the water. My best friend is a young man by the name of Walter Franklin. His father is an associate of my father's. We spend a lot of our free time together.

I also quite enjoy walking around the factory floor with my father learning his trade. I am excited to earn my place in his business some- day. I hope that I will grow up to be a good provider like our fathers one day.

I suppose that is enough of an introduction for now. I hope this letter finds you well. If you are so inclined, I should very much enjoy a letter from you.

Respectfully yours.

Charles J. Ashton

Once he had finished and read it over a few times, Charlie made sure his correspondence was dry and then carefully carried it down to his mother. He found her in the parlor, as she'd promised, working on a needlepoint. When he entered the room, she smiled and laid her piece on the table next to her saying, "Well, let's have a look shall we?"

Charlie waited with his hands folded behind his back, watching his mother's dark eyes scan the document to the bottom. She finished, nodded, and then began reading again. He had suspected she would want to be completely thorough.

"It's lovely, Charlie," she finally determined. "It's quite good. I had no idea you were such a strong writer, my boy."

He couldn't help but smile at his mother's praise. He had never felt like much of a writer, but he truly enjoyed reading, and he thought perhaps some of the words he had absorbed from the classics over the years might have somehow wriggled their way into his unconscious mind.

"May I make one small suggestion?" she asked, her lips pursed just a bit.

"Yes, of course," Charlie replied, stepping forward, nervous to hear what the criticism might be.

"Well, while I believe what you've written is certainly accurate, perhaps we should change this word to 'parents' instead of 'father.'"

She pointed to the sentence he had written that concluded, "my parents have spoken so highly of your father."

"I'm afraid that if we don't say 'parents' her mother might read it and assume we have not spoken highly of her. Now, of course, your father doesn't know Mrs. Westmoreland in the same way that he knew Mr. Westmoreland. Naturally, he doesn't speak of her as highly or as often. But really, there's no need to potentially offend her, now is there?"

Charlie hadn't thought of that. What his mother was saying made perfect sense. He hadn't considered mentioning his parents praising Mrs. Westmoreland because, as far as he could remember, they never had. That didn't mean that she wasn't worthy, however. "Yes, of course," Charlie said, nodding. "That's a lovely idea, Mother."

"All right, then, Charlie. You go make your change and bring it back down. I'll be certain it makes it to the post first thing tomorrow."

"Thank you, Mother," Charlie said, taking the paper. Careful not to wrinkle it, though it was only a draft at this point, he leaned in and hugged his mother, thankful for her thoughtfulness and consideration. He knew he was lucky to have such attentive parents as he knew several other children who did not. The older he got, the more he realized how truly blessed he was.

Charlie made his way back upstairs and corrected his letter. He found an envelope and placed it inside, sealing it, and carefully scribed *Mary Margaret Westmoreland* on the outside. He knew his father would have the address. He hoped that she would be as excited to get a letter from him as he was to send it.

❦

SOUTHAMPTON

"Well of course I'm not going to allow her to read it!"

Meg could hear her mother shouting from the parlor below her. She'd always known that sound travelled up the radiator pipes to her room, but she had only recently discovered that pressing an ear to the pipe (or a glass if one had such a thing handy) allowed even more sound to come through. In this way, she had discovered quite a bit of information that she would have otherwise not been privy to. This evening was no different. Ditching the history textbook Ms. Strickland had insisted she read, she made her way over to the radiator and had a listen, wondering what had gotten her mother so completely bent out of shape.

"Why ever not? It's not as if it even mentions the arrangement," her uncle replied, his voice showing more indifference than irritation.

There was a jolt, as if her mother had tossed something on a table or slammed her hand down. "While Mr. Steele may believe our case to be helpless, that other attorney, what's his name? Marsh—he thinks there might be a chance that we can stop this ridiculous farce from coming to fruition."

"I'm just not so certain that is our best course of action," Bertram replied, his voice still calm. "Business has gone down drastically. Our profit margins are growing narrower each day. Perhaps it would be best if...."

"Perhaps nothing!" her mother shouted so loudly Meg could have easily heard her without the pipe. "This is my company every bit as much as it is yours or was Henry's, and I'm not about to see it shift to someone else simply because my dead husband thinks he found a way to outsmart us!"

To say that she was confused was quite the understatement, but Meg continued to listen while she pondered what she had heard so far, hoping there would be some sort of information to fill in the gaping holes in her understanding.

"I'm just saying, Millie, if we had the money instead, I believe it would allow you be much more comfortable. As it stands, I'm not certain we shall even be able to take that trip to France you've been planning for next month."

Meg's face lit up at the mention of a holiday. It had been quite some time since they'd ventured overseas, and she quite liked those types of journeys. Usually, the monster was so distracted by all of the entertainment and newness of the vessel, he'd leave her alone completely. In fact, she'd spent quite a bit of time off on her own the last time they went abroad. If her mother had any idea the trouble she had caused....

"You must find a way to make the company profitable again, Bert! I will not resort to living off of the Ashton's money!"

Ashton? Meg was certain she had heard that name before, though she really wasn't sure just where. A distant memory began to crawl back into her consciousness, but she couldn't quite place it.

"Mary Margaret is pretty enough. With the proper training, she could find a suitable match...."

"Mary Margaret is a wild animal," Bertram interjected. "Proper training isn't the half of it."

"Well, who was it that wouldn't allow me to send her off to boarding school?" her mother asked, her voice betraying her failed self-control.

"She would only have been sent right back," her uncle insisted.

"In a few years, she'll begin attending balls. She'll need to know how to act properly then, how to dance, how to speak like a young woman."

"You can certainly teach her how to dance," Bertram said, and Meg could picture the detestable crooked smile he likely had on his face, that one eye narrowed. She shivered.

"Oh, Ms. Strickland has tried, but she's gotten nowhere. It's as if Mary Margaret insists on failing, looking daft, and seeming ignorant."

49

"I think that might actually be the case," her uncle offered.

"All I'm saying is, I'm not ready to give in to John and Pamela Ashton. I do not wish to be their charity case!"

"And all I'm saying is...."

Before Bertram could finish his sentence, Meg heard footsteps outside of her door. She scurried back to her work desk, picking up the book and flipping a few pages over from where she had left off the last time Ms. Strickland had come by to check on her.

"Mary Margaret?" the stern voice asked as she threw open the door, as if she intended to surprise her charge and catch her off-task.

Perhaps wearing slippers instead of those clod-hopping boots might make that a bit more feasible, Meg thought as she casually lifted her eyes from the page. "Yes, miss?"

"How is your studying going? Are you able to recite the kings of England from James I to William III?"

"Yes, miss," Meg replied, closing the book. She would have been able to recite all of the ruling monarchs from Egbert to their own Edward IV without ever having opened the book at all. Meg was quite good at memorizing and understanding history and literature. She was even good at foreign language. Maths were what hung her up, but she didn't mind being asked to spend her time working on things she could already do. That way, whenever she was asked to perform there would be less chance of meeting the business end of the switch Ms. Strickland had traded her ruler for last year. While Meg was still careful not to let them see her cry, it smarted quite a bit more than the ruler had.

"Begin," Ms. Strickland insisted, and Meg found a spot on the wallpaper to train her eyes on as she recited the names and dates of each of the rulers that had held the crown these past three hundred years, including the leaders of the commonwealth as well. When she was finished, Ms. Strickland only nodded sharply, never offering any praise or assurance. "I suppose I should find something more difficult to assign next time," she said. "For now, move on to Latin. Review the conjugations from yesterday and then continue with the next list."

"Yes, miss." As Ms. Strickland turned to leave, Meg regained her seat and pulled her Latin book out of the stack of texts on her desk.

While she had more privacy studying here than she had when they used the downstairs study, she had begun to despise this room over the years, and every time the door closed, she couldn't help but shiver, particularly when she could hear her uncle's voice or footsteps in the house.

It had been four years, and not much had changed. Meg pushed those thoughts aside and began to look over the list from yesterday again. She did her best to concentrate, but pieces of the conversation she had overheard came floating back to her. Why was that name— Ashton—so familiar? Why had her mother said the company wasn't doing well? Were they about to be put out onto the street?

She honestly wasn't sure she'd mind too much if they were. Recently, she'd been forced to spend more time with the daughters of her mother and uncle's high society friends, and quite frankly, she wasn't certain she wanted to have anything to do with the lot of them. Sitting about, sipping tea, attempting to outplay each other on the piano or harpsichord, gossiping about others who were not present— it all seemed like a waste of time to her. She'd much rather be out riding one of the horses from the carriage house or climbing a tree.

Though she could play the piano well and embroider, those things were not what interested her. The nearness of the ocean was always tempting; the water seemed to call to her, to promise an escape. More than once, she had considered sneaking aboard a steamship bound for America. It was only fear of what the sailors might do to her if they should find her that prevented her from trying her hand. She knew enough about what unscrupulous men could do to little girls to prevent an attempt at escape under her present circumstances.

But someday, when she was older and wiser, she would do just that—get aboard a steamship and voyage to America. There, she could leave all of this behind and start over. There, she'd find a way to become the young lady her Da had always dreamed she would be.

❦

NEW YORK CITY

"No letter again today?" Charlie asked, a tinge of hope still in his voice, though he could tell by his mother's expression that the answer would be no.

"I'm sorry, Charlie," Pamela said, placing what had come in the post on her husband's desk. "I'm afraid there's nothing today either."

Charlie's shoulders slumped. It had been nearly two months since he'd sent his letter to Mary Margaret, and she hadn't written back yet. "But father's trip is coming up, and if she doesn't answer, then how will I know if it is all right for me to visit?"

Pamela wrapped her arm around her son's shoulders. "Charlie, your father and I have talked about this. Perhaps, this time, it would be best if your father went by himself. He can speak to Mrs. Westmoreland in person, make sure that Mary Margaret received your letter, and then, once they've discussed the situation, you can go with him next time."

"But that may be next year," Charlie protested, turning to face her. "Must I wait so long?"

She sat down on the edge of John's desk, her hand still resting on Charlie's shoulder. "I understand you're disappointed, Son. I would be, too. Try to understand, this is a complicated situation. You are growing into a fine young man, but for now, it's best if adults handle the details. Does that make sense?"

Charlie hung his head and nodded. He didn't want his mother to see that he was fighting back tears. Fourteen-year-old boys were not supposed to cry. He had been looking forward to this trip with his father for a number of reasons. While meeting Mary Margaret for the first time was certainly a priority, he had hoped to have the opportunity to attend some of his father's business meetings, to see how he handled himself in Southampton and London as well. Charlie had traveled to London a few times, but he had never been to Southampton. Traveling with his father would have been a wonderful opportunity to see more of the world and spend some quality time with his father.

"Are you all done with your studies for today?" Pamela asked, lovingly stroking her son's neck.

"Yes, Mother."

"Then, why don't you take the trap over to Walter's? Perhaps the two of you could spend some time together?"

Charlie's face lit up. "You don't mind?"

"You're old enough, don't you think?" she asked, a smile flickering across her mouth.

"Yes, Mother."

"All right then. Be back in time for supper."

Charlie managed a, "Yes, ma'am," over his shoulder as he practically flew out of the room. While he'd been allowed to take the pony trap out a few times, he'd never been granted permission to go so far as to Walter's house. He hurried to the carriage house to ready the trap and his pony, Scout, as quickly as possible, perfectly content to do the work himself.

While Walter's mother had been a bit surprised to see Charlie calling upon her son unannounced, she had allowed him to take a break from his studies and accompany Charlie to the little pond behind their house. Most boys their age were off at boarding school, so they had become quite close to each other, being two of the few left to study at home.

"I can't imagine how it must be to already know who your wife will be," Walter said as he tossed a flat stone across the surface of the otherwise pristine pond. He had a blond mop and despite the lack of a breeze, it still insisted on standing up almost straight on top of his head.

"I suppose it is a little strange," Charlie agreed, skipping a stone almost twice as far as the one Walter had sent across. "But that's how it's been for as long as I can remember."

Walter looked annoyed that Charlie had outdone him, so he tried to throw even harder, which resulted in his stone spinning out of control and sinking before it had even gone a few feet. "What if..." he began, "what if she's hideous?"

"What's that?" Charlie asked, dropping the stone he'd been about to toss and looking at his friend.

"That is to say, what if she's quite ugly? Or plump? Or boring?"

"All right, Walter," Charlie began, shaking his head.

"No, I'm serious, Charlie. What if she's dull or dimwitted? There will be absolutely nothing that you can do about it. You're bound to marry her anways."

"Walter, my father assures me that she is none of those things."

"But how does he know?" Walter pressed on. "Has he seen her?"

"I believe he met her when she was a small child," Charlie argued.

"But a lot could change between then and now—or between now and whenever you actually do marry her. What if you go away to study and meet someone else? What if you fall in love with a beautiful woman? You won't be able to marry her because your father promised you'd wed Margaret."

"It's Mary Margaret," Charlie corrected, "and I highly doubt that will happen."

"Why not?" Walter pressed on, all thoughts of skipping stones laid aside. "You're a fairly handsome fellow, I suppose," he continued, and Charlie snickered at his attempt at a nicety. "It could well happen that you'll meet some other lady—perhaps at a ball or some such thing—and you'll fall in love with her. You'll break her heart."

Charlie continued to shake his head, not willing to hear what his friend had to say. "Walter, I assure you, that won't be the case."

"Or perhaps you shall run away!" His hazel eyes lit up with the idea. "You could elope! Like one of those men in the romance novels my older sister is always reading."

"Walter, you've lost your marbles," Charlie replied. "Listen, I understand our arrangement might seem a bit peculiar, but I will wed Mary Margaret Westmoreland. My father made a promise, and I will always honor my father's word the same way I honor my own. I'm sure I'll meet other lovely ladies, but I will simply have to tell them I'm already betrothed to someone else. If they can't respect that, then they're not the type of honorable young women I'd like to associate with anyway."

Walter stared at Charlie for a long moment before he finally managed, "Charlie, my friend, I think you're wise beyond your years."

"Thank you," Charlie said, nodding.

"I'm not sure that's a compliment. Perhaps you should try being a child for a while. There's quite a bit of fun to have in it."

Charlie considered his words. He had a point. Why was he always consumed with concerns of the grown up world? He was only fourteen. Before much longer, he'd be off to study at a high school and then a university. Then, he'd be forced to pay attention to more important things. So what if Mary Margaret hadn't written him back. Maybe she was too busy being a child. "Race you to the fence line!" Charlie yelled, and without giving Walter a chance to process the dare, he took off sprinting as fast as he could. A bit of spontaneity could actually be a good thing, he decided, as his lungs began to burn. Even if Walter had been ready, there was no way he could catch Charlie. He was fast, and once he'd set his mind to something, nothing could stop him.

CHAPTER SIX

SOUTHAMPTON

"One, two, three. One, two, three," Mildred Westmoreland counted as she traced Meg's steps around the room. "Good, now remember to hold your arm up. It must be stiff. That's it."

The sound of cheerfulness in her mother's voice was not only surprising but refreshing. Ever since her mother had decided that she would teach Meg to dance herself a few months ago, they'd spent quite a bit of time together each afternoon. Though Ms. Strickland had insisted that she knew all of the dances Meg was sure to encounter once she began attending balls on a regular basis, Mrs. Westmoreland had been appalled at the poor quality of her instruction and had taken over the duty almost immediately. She had explained to her daughter that very afternoon, "As a young lady, I was renowned for my dancing skills. No daughter of mine will embarrass herself at a ball."

While it had been odd at first—after all, Meg hadn't spent more than ten minutes outside of a meal time with her mother for as long as she could remember—she had soon learned to enjoy the time spent in her mother's company. Clearly, she was quite the dancer, agile and graceful, and while Meg had never fancied herself being much of a debutante herself, the idea that she could find something in common with her mother was intriguing.

"There, that's it!" Mildred exclaimed as Meg showed off the newest steps she'd learned, this time to the Viennese Waltz. "Splendid! By the time you start attending, you'll be so polished, all of the young men will want to dance with you!"

"Do you really think so, Mother?" Meg asked, coming to a stop in front of Mildred. The smile on her face was so rare, Meg couldn't help but think she actually looked pretty. She couldn't remember the last time she thought her mother anything but stern and stark.

"Oh, yes, most definitely," her mother nodded. "I should hope that Ms. Strickland is better at teaching proper etiquette than she is correct dance steps."

Meg shrugged, not sure how to answer that question. Of course, they'd been practicing etiquette for years, and whenever she accompanied her mother at an event, she always tried to manage to be civil and act like the other girls. But the idea of how one was to conduct oneself at a ball was another thought entirely, and she really wasn't sure how Ms. Strickland would know how to act since clearly she did not attend them herself.

"I will take that improper shrug of your shoulders as a no," Mildred replied, a bit of the stern look back about her face as she clicked her tongue and crossed her arms. "I've been thinking, Mary Margaret, perhaps it is time we found you a new governess. Ms. Strickland has grown a bit... tedious."

Meg's eyes lit up. The thought of being unbound from the wretched Ms. Strickland after all of these years was too good to be true. Perhaps things were finally starting to turn around for her. "Yes, Mother," she said, trying not to show her pleasure too much for fear it might ruin any chance at fruition.

"Do you remember the Tango?" she asked, her eyes twinkling a bit.

She had explained to her daughter that the Tango was a sensuous dance, not one that she would likely be asked to do at any ball in all of England, and yet she had taught her anyway simply because it was the most fun. Mildred explained to her daughter that she and her father had fallen in love thanks to that dance, and when Meg had pressed for more information, her mother had simply giggled and changed the subject. "Yes, Mother," Meg replied. She'd learned it the day before, but she'd been mentally practicing it ever since.

"Good, go through the steps on your own, and perhaps when your uncle returns home he can practice with you. It simply can't be done correctly independent of a partner."

Meg froze. The idea of dancing with her uncle at all, particularly a dance as seductive as the Tango caused her to freeze. "Mother, I'd rather not," she stammered.

Her mother wasn't listening, however. She had already begun to count, doing the steps herself, so Meg went ahead and showed her mother what she remembered, gladly accepting the praise when it was offered. When she had finished, her mother exclaimed, "Yes! Very good! Though it's a pity no one will ever see how well you dance those steps, Mary Margaret."

"Thank you, Mother," Meg replied, wondering why it was so important that she learn them then.

"As soon as Uncle Bertram comes home from the factory, I'll ask him to dance with you. He's not as talented as your father, but he can go through the steps."

Meg swallowed hard. "Must I, Mother?" she asked, her hands folded in front of her, her eyes locked on the floor.

Mildred was giving her daughter her full attention for the first time in her twelve years, and she seemed quite surprised at the question. "Whatever do you mean, Mary Margaret? Yes, of course. What in the world is wrong with you?"

For five years, Mary Margaret had kept her secret. Now, here she was carrying on with her mother as if they were friends, as if she hadn't been discarded and forgotten by the one who should love her most. Perhaps now was her opportunity. She knew her mother was close to her uncle and often wondered at the true nature of their relationship, but surely her mother would listen to her now. Surely, she would understand how it would make her so very uncomfortable to be forced to dance with the man who had misused her so frequently for half a decade.

"Mary Margaret, what is the matter with you?" her mother asked, taking her by the shoulders more gently than she had ever put her hands on her daughter in as long as she could remember.

Meg looked up. Taking a deep breath and swallowing hard, she said, "Mother, it's just... sometimes at night, Uncle Bertram comes into my room...."

Mildred's face changed almost as quickly as the sudden onset of happiness had overtaken her the first time she'd given her daughter a dance lesson. "Mary Margaret," she said, the stern tone resounding in her voice more apparently than ever before. "You shut your mouth right this moment."

Meg's eyes widened. "Mother, it's true. He comes into my room...."

"Shut your mouth!"

Compelled now at putting voice to the secret she'd harbored for so long, Meg's fear morphed into indignation. Now, it wasn't a question of should she dare to be heard but an insistence that she would be. "He does things to me... things that aren't right!"

Before she could comprehend what had even happened, Meg found herself laid out on the floor, her head ringing, the left side of her jaw swelling so rapidly she couldn't even catch her breath. Not only had her mother slapped her so hard she wasn't sure if her mandible was still intact, she had also hit her head on the cherry parquet floor.

"You shut your mouth, Mary Margaret Westmoreland!" Mildred screamed. "How dare you say such evil things about your own uncle. He's raised you! Taken care of you since you were a small child! You horrible, insolent child!"

Mildred stormed from the room, slamming the door behind her, leaving her daughter lying on the parlor floor near where her father's chair used to sit. After a moment, Meg collected herself enough to pull herself up to sitting, her hand clenched against her throbbing jaw. She felt tears stinging the back of her eyes, but they hadn't rolled out yet—not yet. She intended to attempt to make it to her bedroom before she let them fall so that there was less of a chance of anyone seeing them, but she wasn't quite sure she would make it.

Beyond the pain of the blow, the continued betrayal of her own mother, there was the thought that she truly was alone in all of this. Was there no one in the world who could save her? No one who would take her side? She hadn't prayed in years, but since she was already on her knees, she offered up one last attempted plea for mercy. "Please, God. If you exist. If you can hear me. Send me someone—anyone—who will take my side. Even if I am an insolent child. Even though I've done mean and terrible things. Please, send me a friend!"

As she stumbled to her feet, and grabbed onto the furniture to make her way towards the stairs, she put on her brave face again, the one that said nothing they did could hurt her. Beneath that, however, she knew the truth. She was beginning to crumble inside, and if something didn't change for the better soon, she would have to take her chances with the seamen.

NEW YORK CITY

It was a crisp fall morning, and because Charlie preferred to be outside when possible, he had decided to go for a walk about the grounds to clear his head and gather his thoughts.

In a few short weeks, he would be off to attend high school at the New York Preparatory School, not far away in Manhattan. Though he was certain he would see his parents frequently, the idea of going off to school after so many years of being tutored at home was a bit unsettling. His friend Walter would also be attending, so at least he knew he'd see a familiar face. Nevertheless, he was quite fond of his parents and thought he would likely miss them quite a bit, despite knowing they would visit regularly, and he could come home often.

Though he had determined to push thoughts of Mary Margaret Westmoreland out of his head months ago, he couldn't help but wonder if he should write her another letter once he knew his school address, on the off chance that she might finally care to answer his correspondence. After sending four letters and hearing nothing in response, he had all but given up. His father gave him few details of what transpired when he had called upon the Westmoreland residence on his visit to their home after the first letter, and since his father was genuinely an optimistic soul, his lack of detail made Charlie think things had not gone well. Nevertheless, his parents told him he should press on and send Mary Margaret a letter now and again in case she may be curious as to what his life was like in New York.

Charlie was beginning to wonder if Mary Margaret even existed.

After a vigorous stroll that had his heart pounding and his lungs burning, he decided to make his way back toward the house. As he approached the front porch, he heard the sound of piano music coming from the parlor and hurried inside so that he might catch his own private concert put on by his older sister, Grace. She was quite the pianist, and he loved to sit and listen to her play whenever he had the opportunity.

At eighteen, Grace Ashton was the talk of high society. She had her coming out ball earlier in the spring of that year—the first such event Charlie had ever attended—and since then there had been an endless stream of gentlemen callers leaving calling cards at the Ashton home. Having graduated from finishing school and proven herself quite the capable young lady, Grace Ashton would certainly be choosing a suitor soon, and it wouldn't be long until these concerts were no longer held at the family home.

Charlie sat in a leather chair across the room from her where he could get the full experience. The acoustics in the room were wonderful from every seat, but from here, the music seemed to surround him. Grace gave him a quick glance and small smile as she entered a particular difficult portion of Liszt's "Liebestraum No. 3" and Charlie leaned his head back and closed his eyes. Though he had never learned to play himself, he greatly appreciated the art of playing an instrument, especially one as complicated as the piano, and as his sister continued, he absently wondered if Mary Margaret knew how to play and if she did so well.

Just as he was about to drift off to sleep, his sister changed her song and began thrumming out the faster paced, more jovial sounds of a ragtime piece. His eyes flew open, and he sat up to see her laughing at him as she pounded away at the keys. He wasn't familiar with this particular tune and knew it must be something she learned when she went off to school as there is no way her stuffy old piano teacher, Mrs. White, would have allowed her to play such a "scandalous" song.

"You're awake then?" Grace called as she pounded out the last few notes and finished with her hands poised over the keys.

"I certainly am now," Charlie laughed as he strolled over and joined her on the piano bench. "Wherever did you learn that one?"

Grace laughed. "My friend Harriet taught me. Isn't it grand?"

"It's definitely not what I was expecting to hear," Charlie nodded. "I hear that sort of music is becoming more popular though."

"It's wonderful!" Grace exclaimed. "It's so much more interesting to play than those classical pieces Mrs. White made me practice for hours on end."

"Has Father heard it?" Charlie asked smiling up at his sister who was slightly taller than him still.

"Not yet, but I don't think he should mind too much. Father has always been a bit of a progressive. Mother loved it, though. She said I should learn more."

Laughing, Charlie said, "Now that I'm not at all surprised to hear."

"She just cautioned me against playing it for any suitors who might happen by. She said I'd need to make sure I had a good one before I tested out whether or not he should allow me to play popular music."

"I can't imagine she'd like for you to marry anyone who would disagree."

"Quite true," Grace nodded, her fingers tinkling over the keys quietly as she spoke. "I would never marry a man who wouldn't let me play anything I choose."

Charlie nodded and then dropped his eyes to the keys, her last words catching his attention. Grace certainly did have a lot of choices in front of her. He wondered what that must be like.

"Are you all right, Charlie?" she asked. "Have I upset you?"

"Oh, no, not at all," Charlie replied, the smile returning to his face, though it was a bit forced this time. "I was just thinking about how nice it will be for you once you've found the perfect husband, and you can go off and start a family of your own; that's all."

Grace looked at him scrupulously. "You know, Charlie, this whole bit about Mary Margaret Westmoreland—does it bother you?"

His forehead crinkled, Charlie asked, "Why should it?"

Grace pursed her lips, drawing them to one side of her lovely face. "Well," she began, "you're about to go off to school for the first time. You'll have less supervision, less time with parents. More time with your friends. More possibilities of interacting with young ladies. I was just wondering if, perhaps, you might be excited to have the opportunity to see where that might take you, that's all. You're fifteen. Surely the thought of young women excites you. You seemed to enjoy my ball."

Charlie listened intently as she went on, his eyes wide with curiosity, but by the time she finished, he really didn't know what to say. Finally, he shrugged and said, "I don't know, Grace. I've always known I was meant for Mary Margaret. I've never really spent too much time thinking about other young ladies."

"Well, you should," Grace said with a humph as she did a quick scale with her left hand.

"Why do you say that?" Charlie asked, scooting out of her way a bit.

She practiced a few more runs before she answered, "Because—I just don't feel it's very ladylike for someone to ignore several letters, that's all."

While he agreed with her, he was very defensive when it came to Mary Margaret. "You don't know for sure that she's ignored them," he said turning a bit to face her. "There are lots of reasons why I might not have received a letter yet."

Grace rolled her eyes, but she didn't turn to face him, her gaze locked on the keyboard. "Very well, then, Charlie, waste your youth waiting for a young lady who is likely so spoilt she has no idea what she's missing."

"Grace!" Charlie exclaimed. "Please don't speak of Mary Margaret that way. You don't even know her."

"No, I don't, Charlie. That's my point," she said spinning to face him. "Neither do you!"

"I will!" Charlie argued back, sliding off the end of the bench and turning to face her.

"In the meantime, get to know the *world*, Charlie. You have no idea what you'll be missing if you don't!" There was no anger in her tone, just a sense of longing and romance.

Jamming his hands into his trouser pockets, Charlie pivoted on his heels to go. She slammed her hands down on the keys, which caused a bit of anger to well up inside of him. He turned to face her again, and she was sitting with her elbow on the keyboard, her chin resting on it, obviously frustrated. "Grace, I suppose you mean well, but please don't attempt to tell me what I should or shouldn't do. Going off to school is difficult enough without thinking about what I may or may not be missing out on. Father has asked me to do this, and that's what I intend to do. Why is that so difficult to understand?"

She sighed loudly, removed her arm from the keyboard, closed the cover, and slowly rose. Walking towards him, she reminded him more of their mother than the little girl he had run about with in the back gardens not that long ago. "I understand Charlie," Grace replied, placing her hand on his shoulder. "I just don't want you to miss out on anything. You're my brother, and I love you. I can't imagine what it must be like to be in your situation, and I just hope that it works out for the best, that's all."

"While I thank you for your concern," Charlie said with a deep breath, "I assure you it is unwarranted. Everything will work out fine, Grace. Just like it always does."

Nodding, Grace drew him into her arms and hugged him tightly. "I certainly hope so," she said quietly. "I certainly hope so."

As he made his way to his room, Charlie wondered what it was that his older sister knew that he did not. She's always seemed wiser and more worldly than he was. Going off to school had made that particularly true. Still, despite not having heard from Mary Margaret, Charlie was certain that everything would turn out as his father had explained, and he would be betrothed to Mary Margaret and then married. Climbing the stairs, he wondered what he might be able to do to encourage her to write to him. Then, an idea popped into his head. "That's it!" he said aloud. His last few letters had not been as personal as he had intended. He wanted Mary Margaret to feel as if she truly knew him, as if they were friends. He'd send her a likeness. Then, she'd be able to see his kindness and sincerity in his countenance. Surely, that would do the trick. It just had to.

SOUTHAMPTON

Meg had expected a visit from the monster the night she told her mother, but remarkably, that didn't happen. In fact, she had heard him come up the stairs late that night, heard her mother's footsteps in the hallway, and then heard a series of loud banging noises and doors slamming from the other end of the house. Though their home was quite sizable, it wasn't so large that she couldn't surmise that her mother and uncle must be having it out about something. Meg was hopeful that, despite her initial reaction, her mother was both shocked and dismayed at what her uncle had been doing to her. She was not brave enough to get her hopes up entirely, but she was at least hope*ful*—and that was a bit better than having no hope at all.

For obvious reasons, Meg was a light sleeper, and when she awoke to find the sun peeking beneath the heavy draperies that covered her windows, she was startled. Why hadn't Ms. Strickland woken her? She was usually up with the sun, dressed, and downstairs for breakfast quickly so that they could get on with their studies post haste. This morning, the feeling of urgency seemed to only be emitted from Meg herself, and she couldn't quite understand what might be happening.

She dressed as speedily as she could and made a semblance of righting her hair. Her jaw was still sore, but a careful examination in her mirror showed no sign of swelling or bruising. Open hands tended to leave less of a mark, she'd learned. One final straightening of her skirt and she made her way downstairs. As she approached the dining room, she could hear her mother's voice, and from the tone it seemed as if she were giving orders. She did not, however, hear Ms. Strickland at all.

Her mother was sitting in her chair at the dining table, the same one she sat in for every meal, though Meg hadn't actually breakfasted with her in so long she couldn't remember the last time. Tessa, one of the servants who had worked for them for many years, was standing nearby, listening intently as her mother went over a list of items that needed to be done that day. "Make sure that listing gets in the newspaper in order to go out today. Tomorrow at the latest. We will need a replacement soon. You understand?"

"Yes, madam," Tessa nodded, her graying hair tied up neatly beneath her mob cap. "Is there anything else?"

Mildred looked up to see Meg hovering near the door. "Mary Margaret, sit down," she commanded. "Bring her breakfast in, Tessa, before you go."

"Yes, madam," the servant repeated as she went off to the kitchen, and Meg dragged the heavy oak chair out from beneath the table.

"Your hair is a mess," Mildred commented as she took a sip of tea.

"My apologies, Mother," Meg began as Tessa set a bowl of porridge and a plate of dry toast in front of her. There was marmalade and butter on the table, but Meg was not sure what her mother might say if she reached for either of them, so she picked up the toast and took a small bite as Tessa sat a glass of water before her.

"You may have noticed there has been a slight change in our arrangement," Mildred began, setting the tea cup back on its saucer.

"Yes, Mother," Meg replied, once the toast was swallowed.

"Ms. Strickland has been released from her duties. I've found her... tiresome. Tessa will place an advert today for a replacement. In the meantime, I've hired a young lady to look after you, to make sure you continue your studies on your own. You are capable of completing some of your studies independently, aren't you, Mary Margaret?"

Nodding, Meg said, "Yes, Mother," and held back her excitement at the thought of never seeing the nasty Ms. Strickland again.

"Good. You should also know that we've decided to let the other servants go as well. The only ones who will be staying on are Tessa and Mr. Bitterly. Your uncle has determined it would be worthwhile to replace some of the aging servants with younger ones. Of course, I insisted that Tessa stay, as she is practically irreplaceable. And your uncle has no interest in what happens in the yard. Therefore, you can expect to see some new faces here in a few days, once Bertram has the chance to find suitable replacements."

The entire conversation seemed quite odd to Meg, but she said nothing other than the usual. "Yes, Mother," and began to mull over what her uncle might be up to.

"This young lady we've brought on to look after you will do so until your governess is hired, and then she will also go about attending to household chores while you are studying. Since your uncle insists on keeping you here rather than sending you to a proper finishing school, you must have a governess who can ensure you are completely prepared to run a household. However, I also feel it is fitting for you to have your own lady to keep track of you."

"Yes, Mother."

"You must stop this... running away, Mary Margaret. This ridiculous, childish behavior. You are a young lady. You are quite pretty, though you have your father's cheekbones and not mine, and if you tried at all, you could be quite graceful. Digging in the mud, riding bareback, taking things from marketplaces and people's pockets— those things are absolutely revolting! You must stop them this instant. Do you hear me?"

"Yes, Mother," she said again, wondering at how her mother knew all of those things.

"Climbing about in the carriage house with that dreadful Ezra.... You simply must stop, Mary Margaret. While other young ladies are preparing to come out in society, you are sneaking about as if you've been raised by common thieves. It is unheard of."

"I understand, Mother," Meg replied, swallowing back the lump in her throat. She'd done all of those things out of rebellion, to escape, to be... free. Of course, none of them had worked—here she was after all. But when her mother put it like that, she did sound like a vagabond.

Then her mother said the words that would cut her like a knife. "Your father would be very disappointed in you."

Meg's eyes grew wide with dismay as Mildred scooted her chair out and tossed her napkin on the table in front of her, giving her daughter one last callous look as she did so. It had never occurred to her that her father would actually disapprove of what she had been doing. After all, she wouldn't have been driven to do any of those things if he had still been there to protect her, to keep her safe from the monster and her own mother.

She kept her vow of not crying when there was any chance someone might see her and swallowed back her tears. The lumpy porridge looked completely unappealing now, and she was certain any toast she put in her mouth would catch in her throat and choke her to death. Since she'd heard Tessa go out the back a few moments ago, she knew the coast was clear to do yet another thing her mother detested, though it hadn't been on the list, and she took her dishes out into the yard and fed the scraps to her uncle's hounds.

"If my mother knew I had any contact with you, that would be forbidden also," she mumbled as she watched the two dogs lap up the remains of the porridge. Her uncle didn't hunt often, but when he did, he needed to look the part of the capable huntsman, so he had invested in two high-quality foxhounds a few years ago. He had given them some fancy names so that he would sound impressive to his counterparts, but Meg called them Max and Dax because those seemed more fun. She often snuck out from her studies with Ms. Strickland so that she could pat them on the head through their cage or sneak them a scrap of food. The one time she'd been discovered, the governess hadn't hesitated to spare the rod. Hopefully, now that would all be behind her.

When she reentered through the back door, she heard the sound of her mother's voice entertaining in the parlor. The other woman was Mrs. Donaldson. She could tell by the familiar high-pitched tone of her voice. Though Meg thought it was rather early to call on anyone, she knew Mrs. Donaldson to be an odd bird, and since she may have a bit of freedom before this alleged new lady showed up to shadow her, she didn't want to spend that time listening to Mrs. Donaldson drone on about her six Siamese cats or her son who had gone off to war and never returned. Therefore, she decided to sneak upstairs and find something to read that wasn't at all educational.

Meg was very good at sneaking up and downstairs. She had found success on many a staircase while visiting her mother's acquaintances, on ships at sea, attending various events and get-togethers, but most importantly, she was very good at sneaking up these stairs. There was one spot on the fourth step from the bottom that tended to squeak no matter where she placed her foot, so, now that she was tall enough to do so, she simply stepped over top of it and made her way up the rest of the stairs with a light foot and a lighter heart. Today might actually turn out to be a good day at long last.

She was only a few pages into her book when she heard someone at the door downstairs. Mumbling to herself about lost opportunity, she went to the mirror to check her hair. Despite her mother's comment this morning, she really didn't think it looked that bad, but she did poke a few lost strands back into place. By the time she had given up on fixing anything else, she'd already heard the squeak of the tell-tale step twice and assumed her mother was on her way to her room with the new lady-in-question.

The door was slightly ajar, not that her mother would have knocked anyway. (Mildred insisted that she should never have to knock on a door in her own home.) Before she was even in the room, her mother was talking to her. "Mary Margaret, come here and meet your new lady." Over her shoulder, she added, "I really do hope you can do something about that hair."

As soon as Meg looked at the young woman, who couldn't have been more than fifteen or sixteen, she instantly recognized her, though she wasn't sure from where. With her eyes wide, she gaped in silence for a moment before her mother prodded her. "Well, don't just stand there, Mary Margaret. Say something."

"How do you do?" Meg managed, closing her mouth and giving a nod simultaneously.

"Oh, yes, Mary Margaret. You've gotten much taller. It's a pleasure," the young woman said in a fairly thick Irish accent that only seemed to have been watered down from some time spent out of her own home.

"This is Kelly," Mildred continued. "You may remember her mother, Patsy, who used to work for us before she took ill several years ago."

Enlightened, Meg stammered, "Yes, of course. I remember Patsy. And you visited sometimes, didn't you?"

Kelly nodded. "I did. We used to run around the back garden together some." Her smile faded when she saw the expression on Mrs. Westmoreland's face. "Of course, there will be no time for that now. You must attend to your studies, and while I am no governess, I understand that you have work to do until one is appointed for you."

Nodding her head, Meg crossed her hands in front of herself, unsure of what to think of this new arrangement. Kelly had been her friend, every bit as much willing to run and play as she had been. Now, here she was before her, in charge as it were, at least until a new governess was hired. "Yes, you are correct," she said, remembering her mother's harsh words at breakfast. "If I'm ever to find a good young man, I must attend to my studies."

A flicker of confusion seemed to pass through Kelly's eyes for a second, but Meg had no idea why. After a second, she said, "Yes, yes. You should get back to your studies. Perhaps I should put my things away and then come back to check on you?" she asked, looking for permission from Mrs. Westmoreland.

"I will show you to your room since Tessa is still out, and we haven't any other workers just now," Mildred said as she gestured for Kelly to follow her. "Mary Margaret, I do not believe the book on your bed will help you grow any wiser, young lady."

"No, Mother," she called after her, wondering how in the world her mother could tell what she had been reading from this distance when the face of the book was down on her coverlet. Perhaps her mother just assumed she was reading for pleasure and not for educational purposes.

Giving the book another longing glance, she sat down at her table and pulled out her mathematics book. It was by far her worst subject, but she thought, if she wanted to impress a new governess, she should likely study it a bit more. Young women didn't have to know nearly as much about calculations and sums as young men, but she'd be expected to know something about how numbers worked. She felt like such a failure every time she attempted to do a simple long division calculation. Whenever she began to court, she would make sure that all the young men she accepted invitations from could do their computations so that she wouldn't have to.

"That does not look very exciting at all," Kelly said from just behind her. Meg hadn't heard her come in and startled a bit at the unfamiliar voice. "I'm sorry—I didn't mean to frighten you."

"Not at all," Meg said. Being frightened was a weakness, and she had none of those. "I just... I was just looking over my maths."

"I see," Kelly replied. "I have never been too good at that subject, but I do know how to make change when I go to the market and calculate for a recipe. I suppose that's good enough for my station."

She smiled, a facial gesture Meg was not particularly used to, and she wasn't sure if she should smile back or slowly retreat. "You seem awfully young to be looking after me," she finally managed, a bit of defiance in her voice.

"That's true," Kelly agreed. "What are you now? Twelve?" Meg's head bobbed up and down slowly, and Kelly continued. "I'm fifteen. Almost fifteen and a half if you want to do the math." She winked and Meg couldn't help but smile. "But I've been caring for younger children for the past four years, and my mother thought this might be a good opportunity for me. Your mother came by quite early this morning asking if my mother might be interested in returning to her former employment. Since she'd taken a job with another family a few years ago, she wasn't willing to give it up, though she has said many times how much she misses you. She suggested me, and your mother negotiated a fairly small salary which I accepted despite that others may say it is unfair. It will give me the opportunity to strike out on my own and try my hand at something new."

"What of the children you've been looking after?" Meg asked. Hearing that Patsy was no longer ill and that she had waited for re-employment from her mother that never came was both startling and infuriating so she decided not to dwell on that.

"It's been mostly during the summer and nothing for more than a few weeks at a time," Kelly explained. "This, I hope, will be more permanent. I hope that your mother and uncle take a liking to me."

Meg shuddered at that last sentence. "My mother doesn't like anyone, and if my uncle takes a liking to you, well, then, God bless you," she said, leaning back in her chair and crossing her arms.

"What's that then?" Kelly asked.

"Nothing. Never mind," Meg said shrugging her shoulders. If she found she could truly trust Kelly, she might tell her at some point, but not right now, not today. The last time she had told her secret she'd paid dearly for it. Though, in retrospect, at least Ms. Strickland was gone.

Kelly's green eyes were peering intently out the window. "Didn't there used to be a boy as well? The caretaker's son?"

"Ezra," Meg offered. "Yes. He's here sometimes. His father sends him off to school on days when he doesn't need his help. Other times, he's out back working or running around. He's almost your age and still climbs trees and plays in the mud." She said the last part as if the entire idea was completely childish.

"You do those things as well, don't you?" Kelly asked with a coy smile.

Meg's face reddened a bit. "I did. I don't anymore. My mother says it is time for me to grow up and become a responsible young lady. So... that is what I intend to do. So that I may find a husband someday."

Once again, that strange expression crossed through Kelly's eyes. After a long pause, she said, "I see. Well, I shouldn't keep you from your studies and your mother has asked me to help Tessa in the kitchen today until your uncle finds some new help to hire. What happened to the rest of the ladies?"

"I'm honestly not too sure," Meg replied. "I think my mother decided their wages were too high and that if she could find younger workers, perhaps she could pay them less."

"Oh, I shouldn't think she'd be able to pay too little or else she will never find anyone to take the job," Kelly muttered.

"It worked with you," Meg reminded her.

Kelly's lips pursed together. She opened her mouth and then closed it. Finally, she said, "Mine is a special case. Not many will be willing to take what I agreed to. Besides, your uncle owns the textile factory. Surely he can afford to pay a few ladies what they deserve to take care of the household."

While she was tempted to blurt out what she knew about the money—or lack thereof—Meg said nothing. If she mentioned to Kelly that the factory was losing money, she might leave, and Meg was beginning to think that she and Kelly might actually turn out to be friends, a foreign concept but an enticing one nonetheless.

"Do finish your maths and then get on with your Latin and history, won't you?" Kelly said as she stood.

"Yes, Ms...." Meg froze. "What shall I call you?"

"You shall call me Kelly, of course," came the reply.

"Yes, Ms. Kelly," Meg nodded.

"No, silly. Just Kelly will do. I'm not a governess. I'm hardly a miss!"

"All right then, Kelly," Meg smiled.

"I will see you in a bit, Mary Margaret," the redhead said as she started for the bedroom door.

"It's Meg," the younger girl called, turning in her chair.

"What's that?" Kelly asked, turning to acknowledge her.

"Please, call me Meg. All of my friends call me that."

Kelly smiled, her face brightening. "Very well. See you in a bit, Meg."

CHAPTER SEVEN

NEW YORK CITY

The view from his room in the New York Preparatory School was not nearly as appealing as the one in his study at home, which was actually quite helpful when it came time for Charlie to complete his assignments. Despite Walter's constant invitations, he generally chose to stay indoors and do his work, even during the times when the young men were allowed to go outside and have a bit of fun in the yard. Today in particular, he was much more apt to stay inside and finish his history assignment. The temperature was near freezing and there was a thin layer of snow on the ground. However, Walter was persistent, and for some reason, Charlie decided that the only way he was ever going to stop Walter's pestering was to finally give in and head outdoors, promising himself he'd only stay for a bit and would head back in as soon as he possibly could.

Though his school didn't have a football team, one of the other young men was fond of the sport and always had a ball handy. Walter's promise that Teddy was bringing the ball out today was about the only factor that had caused him to change his mind and join them. Nearly a dozen of his classmates were already out in the yard, bundled up with thick coats, gloves, scarfs, and hats to keep out the cold.

"Hey, look who it is!" Teddy yelled as they approached.

"Well, if it isn't Charles Ashton himself!" another boy, Reginald, hollered.

"I want Charlie on my team," came another voice. Though he was difficult to recognize behind the scarf, Charlie realized it had been Tim who had yelled out for him, and despite a bit of a kerfuffle with Teddy, Charlie soon found himself standing alongside Tim with Walter, Reginald, and a few other chaps.

"All right, Charlie," Tim was saying, "You're the fastest. I want you to go long, and I will throw it to you, right down the middle. All right?"

"What about me?" Walter asked before Charlie could even respond.

"You just make sure Charlie gets open," Tim, a lankier boy who was nearly seventeen, insisted.

Though Walter didn't seem to like that answer, he nodded, and the boys went to the line to start the play. Tim shouted a few numbers and then, "Hut! Hut!" and Charlie took off running. He easily skirted past Teddy, past the other boys as well, and then turned back to see if Tim had thrown the ball. He spied it over his right shoulder and brought it down, running until he'd passed the line Teddy had drawn in the snow to show the end zone.

His team cheered while the others groaned, and then Charlie was on defense and lined up to try to protect the other team from scoring.

The game went on for about twenty minutes, Charlie scoring once more and catching an interception. He was having such fun; he'd hardly thought about his studies at all. Tim sent him out for one more long pass. This time, Teddy seemed to know what he was about and attempted to sneak in and get the ball before Charlie could do so. In an attempt to outplay him, Charlie reached his hand out and knocked the ball up into the air. It teetered on his fingertips for a moment before bouncing up again. Teddy got a hand on it but only knocked it free once more. Charlie was certain he could rein it in this time. Just as he stretched his arm up to grab it, another hand shot out of nowhere and plucked it from the sky.

"I've got it!" a high pitched voice shouted, and Charlie turned to see a young lady running with the ball towards the elected end zone.

Teddy and Charlie stared at each other for a moment, absolutely dumbfounded, before they turned to see her run past the line and then raise the ball in the air, cheering.

Once Charlie had regained his composure enough to have a look around, he realized Mr. Founder, one of the instructors, and what appeared to be a potential scholar and his family, stood on the walkway a few steps behind where the girl had apparently come from.

"Stella!" the father shouted in a stern voice. "Put that down and get over here this instant!"

Stella, whose enthusiasm only seemed slightly abated, dropped her hands, cleared her throat, and then, taking a few steps in his direction, extended the ball. "Beg your pardon," she said, her green eyes twinkling. "I believe this was intended for you."

Charlie had never seen a lovelier face. Her skin looked so soft and smooth—it was as if it were made of porcelain. She had long dark eyelashes that matched the tufts of hair that peeked out from beneath her red winter hat. She must have been about his age, he was certain, and when his hand grazed hers, though it was surrounded by a thick, red mitten, he couldn't help but feel as if a pulse of energy radiated from her fingers through his entire body.

"Th—thank you," he stammered.

She smiled, showing perfectly white, dazzling teeth, and then turned around to rejoin her family, who, despite the admonishment, didn't seem quite as put out as many parents he knew might have been.

Mr. Founder continued with his tour, and the family disappeared into a nearby building shortly thereafter. It was only then that the group of gaping boys were able to voice their amazement.

"Who was she?" Teddy finally got out.

"An angel," Tim answered, standing next to the ball-owner.

"The devil!" Walter murmured, though his eyes were like saucers.

Charlie said nothing, but for the first time in as long as he could remember, he was no longer concerned about Mary Margaret Westmoreland and her inability to write letters.

CHAPTER EIGHT

SOUTHAMPTON

"The curtains need to be cleaned," Mildred Westmoreland instructed as she walked through the parlor, Tessa and a new girl, Sarah, close behind her. "Take them all down, take them outside, and beat them until the dust is all gone. Do you understand?"

"Yes, madam," Tessa replied with a nod.

"How do we get them down?" Sarah asked, but a sharp elbow from Tessa silenced her, and if Mrs. Westmoreland had heard, the question was ignored.

"This floor is never clean anymore. Sarah, if you must get down and scrub it, then do so," the mistress of the house continued. "I'm tired of having ladies over for tea only to see them grimace at the floorboards."

"Yes, madam," Sarah answered, learning her lesson from the last time.

"When you are finished with that, come and check with me. I have a few other oddities that need to be attended to. I believe what's-her-name...."

"Blanche," Sarah offered.

"Yes, that's it—Blanche—is still working upstairs. Please tell her to keep a better eye on her daughter. I don't mind you two having your children stay here with you, but they must not run amuck! I wouldn't allow my own daughter to do so, and I won't allow yours either."

"I believe Jessica is outside," Sarah said, clearly a bit offended.

"Yes, madam," Tessa stated, elbowing Sarah again.

"And where did you put the post?" Mildred asked scanning the room.

"Over here, on the desk," Sarah stated as she walked over to where she'd placed the few envelopes earlier that day. "Except for the one that was marked for Miss Mary Margaret. I put that in her room."

Though Mildred had snatched up the mail and was looking through it, at those last few words, she froze. Tessa gasped and took a step backwards as Mildred turned to face the ruddy faced Sarah who was beginning to turn even more red. "You did what?" Mrs. West-moreland asked.

But before Sarah could manage an answer, a voice from behind the mistress shouted out, "Who is Charles J. Ashton, Mother?" and she turned to find her daughter staring at her, a letter clutched in her fist.

"Mary Margaret," Mildred turned to face her, taking a deep breath and attempting to calm herself. "That letter was not meant for you."

"It is addressed to me," Meg continued as she walked forward, "and by the language used, I'm assuming it is not the first such letter this American boy has sent me. Who is he, and why does he seem to think we have a future together?"

Meg was mad—clearly her mother and uncle had been keeping something from her, something important, and despite the possibility of finding herself stretched out on the floor again at her mother's hand, she was not about to let this go. She stood defiant with the letter in front of her, hopeful the tone in her voice would let her mother know just how angry she was at this betrayal.

"I'm so sorry, madam," Ms. Cunningham, Meg's new governess of a few months, said as she scurried up next to the thirteen-year-old. "We took a break in our studies, and she found the letter. I didn't know what it was until after she'd opened it...."

"Go back upstairs, Ms. Cunningham," Mildred said sternly.

"Yes, madam," the young lady replied, nodding and taking off as quickly as possible without running. "Sarah—go to your chambers as well. I shall talk to Mr. Westmoreland about this when he returns. This may mean removal for you, you incompetent fool!"

Sarah said nothing, only nodded and rushed off towards the back of the house and the servant's stairwell. This left Tessa standing awkwardly behind her mistress, and with a jab in the direction of the kitchen with her pointer finger, Mildred sent her away also.

"I'm waiting, Mother," Meg said, dropping the letter down by her side and attempting to regain her composure. This was the first time in her life she'd ever had the upper hand with her mother, and if she wasn't careful, she was liable to have it turned back around on her.

"Mary Margaret, it's nothing, really." Mildred gestured toward the chairs across the room near the fireplace hearth, the one she'd had for years, and her uncle's, which had replaced her father's some time ago. "Let us sit down and have a discussion like two adult women."

Meg couldn't help but feel as if she were being baited, but she nodded and cautiously walked across the room, choosing to sit in her mother's chair rather than her uncle's. The thought of touching something so intimate to him made her shiver.

Mildred's eyebrow arched at Meg's choice but she said nothing about the chairs. "May I see the letter, please?" she asked with a forced smile.

While she had only read it twice and could make little sense of it, there was something about having the letter in her hand that made Meg feel powerful. It seemed like releasing that to her mother would also relinquish the strength she had accumulated these last few minutes. When her mother repeated the word, "please," Meg extended the letter for her to take, though her fingers didn't quite want to unclench it and it took her mother a bit of effort to get it free without tearing it.

Mildred looked the letter up and down just once before she handed it back to her daughter. "It's a lovely letter, Mary Margaret. From a nice boy. From a nice family."

"Who is he?" Meg asked, her teeth grinding in frustration.

"Surely you've heard of John Ashton?" Mildred asked, her expression one of boredom. "He's a millionaire who lives in New York City. Charles is his son."

Meg wasn't sure if she'd ever heard of John Ashton or not. She tried to stay out of the society papers, which also meant never reading them. Occasionally, one of her friends would make mention of something she read in one of them over tea or at a get-together, but Meg was never interested in what other people thought about her and knew most of what those types of people had to say was frivolous and of little consequence. "Why is Charles Ashton writing me, Mother?"

Mildred let out a deep sigh and leaned back in her borrowed chair. Though she was still attempting to look bored and uninterested, Meg could see fear behind her eyes. "Your father and John Ashton were good friends. They were college roommates. I suppose Charles would like to meet you because his father must speak of your father often."

"This letter says, 'I do hope that you will write me back soon. If we are to have a future together, I should like to get to know you as soon as possible. Since you've not answered my first several letters, I am beginning to wonder if I've done something wrong.' What is he talking about, Mother?"

"I honestly don't know," Mildred replied, straightening her back and looking down her nose at her daughter. "I suppose I could have your uncle look into it next time he journeys overseas...."

"You have other letters from Charles to me, don't you, Mother?"

She had to have them. Otherwise, she would not have been so upset at Sarah for giving her this one.

"No, of course...."

"Mother, lying is just as unbecoming of you as it is of me."

Mildred's eyes widened at her daughter's doggedness. "Pardon?" she asked, staring her down, which was usually enough to make her flinch.

Meg felt her resolve weakening. Her mother could cause a grown man to forget himself with those icy eyes. "Mother, if there are other letters from Charles Ashton, you should give them to me. I'm not quite sure what he's on about, but I should like to know. If the Ashton's are so rich and famous, wouldn't it do us some good to know them as well as possible?"

Mildred's face softened, and Meg was surprised that her new line of questioning seemed to be working. Why her mother wouldn't want to cooperate with a rich American family when their factory continued to lose more and more money each month was beyond her. "I do not have any such letters," Mildred continued, clearly still being untruthful. "However, whenever your Uncle Bertram returns from work, I shall ask him if he knows anything about them. If there are more letters, I will give them to you."

"Thank you," Meg said, nodding. "And I should like to write Charles Ashton a letter in return. I would like for him to know I have not received any of his letters until this point so that he doesn't think I was raised improperly."

Again, her mother seemed to consider the request. "I suppose that makes sense."

"I wouldn't want him to think I was raised by a band of common thieves."

Clearly, recognizing her own words, Mildred swallowed hard. "Very well. Write him back. But keep it light. Nothing personal. And I will read it before you send it. Do you understand?"

"Yes, Mother," Meg replied, keeping her face as neutral as possible. "May I go to my room now?" she asked.

With a nod, her mother sent her out of the room, and Meg made her way back up the stairs, the letter still in her hand, the anger left behind. She only hoped her uncle wouldn't come up with some reason to use this against her. For the most part, he had been leaving her alone lately, and she was hoping this new arrangement would continue, though the monster had visited a few times since her mother found out what he had been doing.

Kelly was waiting for her inside of her room, a worried expression on her face. "Is everything all right?"

"Yes," Meg replied, crossing to her table and dropping the letter atop her Latin book.

"I wanted to follow you down the stairs, to see what was the matter, but I was afraid I might make it worse for both of us, especially since your mother sent Ms. Cunningham up and then I heard Sarah crying."

"Poor Sarah," Meg muttered as she sat down at the table. Kelly sat down beside her. "I think everything will be all right. It depends on what my uncle has to say when he gets home."

"So you received a letter from Charlie?" Kelly asked, eyeing the parchment, though not closely enough to read it.

"Yes," Meg answered, her eyebrow shooting up. "How do you know?"

Kelly swallowed hard, pursing her lips together as she did so. "My mother told me."

Gasping, Meg questioned, "You knew about him? Why didn't you tell me?" She and Kelly had grown very close since her mother had brought the young lady on, which was nearly a year ago. Meg was beginning to feel betrayed again, and this time it would be even worse because at least she expected such treatment from her mother —but not from Kelly.

"I wanted to," Kelly began to explain, "but my mother said I should wait. She said things may have changed, and she thought I should wait and see what happened before I said anything to you. When she still worked here, your mother had already hired a lawyer,

PRELUDE: A PREQUEL

and if she had her way, perhaps the arrangement would have been dissolved."

"What arrangement?" Meg asked, her eyes still wide.

Kelly tugged at her apron, clearly uncomfortable. "My mother said that, before your father died, he arranged for you to marry Charles Ashton."

"What?" Meg interrupted. "Marry him?"

"Yes, that's what she said."

"But... why?"

"I honestly don't know," Kelly replied, her face showing that what she said was true. "My mother didn't really know why, either. She just remembered there being a big to-do about it."

Meg was dumbfounded. Why in the world would her father arrange for her to marry the son of a millionaire that she'd never met who may as well have lived on the other side of the moon?

Meg began to contemplate possible reasons, not realizing that Kelly was still talking until she was at least halfway through her sentence, "... newspapers, and he's quite handsome."

"What's that?" Meg asked, returning her focus to her friend, not because of the statement but because she realized she was being rude.

"I said, 'My mother says she's seen his likeness in some of the high society newspapers, and he's quite handsome. Of course, they don't report on Americans much in the local papers, but my mother's new employer does business in London frequently, and he knows how much my mother enjoys looking at the papers."

"Oh," Meg muttered. "Well, it seems to me that my mother might actually be trying to protect me for once—to give me the opportunity I deserve to properly come out and find suitors myself." The words sounded too good to be true, even as she stated them. But otherwise, Meg could think of no reason why her mother wouldn't jump at the chance to marry her off to some rich American. Surely, marrying into a millionaire's family would give Meg the means to properly take care of her mother and uncle, should they play their cards right.

"I could speculate," Kelly replied, looking down at her apron again, "but I don't know for sure. There is something else I need to tell you...."

Before she could get the rest of it out, they heard loud footsteps on the stairs. Meg would recognize those steps anywhere, and she froze. Her heart caught in her chest and she found herself unable to draw in a deep enough breath to even remotely fill her lungs. She couldn't help but repeat the phrase she always did when she heard those footfalls. *Please keep walking. Please keep walking.* She wondered how he'd managed to get in the house without her noticing. She was usually so attentive.

"Mary Margaret," Uncle Bertram called, rapping on the door and stepping in slightly. He looked at Kelly and then stopped in the doorway, as if he didn't want the lady-in-waiting to see him enter Meg's room.

"Yes, Uncle," she called, standing, her eyes on the floor.

"Your mother asked me to give you these."

She glanced up to see several envelopes in his hand. She could tell from across the room that none of them had even been opened.

Kelly jumped up out of her seat and made her way across the room to retrieve them. "Thank you, sir," she said as she took them from him.

While Meg wanted to ask why they were never given to her in the first place and why it was okay for her to have them now, she didn't do so. "Thank you, Uncle," she said, dropping her eyes back to the floor.

She watched as his heavy shoes turned, thankful that he was leaving. But a few steps out into the hallway, he turned again, and returning to his previous position, he said, "You could do worse than an Ashton. That's my two cents anyway."

Unsure what to make of that, Meg only replied, "Yes, Uncle."

This time, he did leave, and once he was down the hall, Kelly pushed the door closed and crossed back over to Meg, who had dropped back into the chair, her breathing finally growing more steady.

"What in the world?" Kelly asked, setting the letters aside and placing a hand on her friend's shoulder. "You're shaking."

"It's nothing," Meg replied. Normally, if her uncle was present when she was downstairs, outside, or at an event, she was able to keep herself calm. But here, in her room, the scene of the attacks, she couldn't control herself.

"Meg?" Kelly said, pushing her shoulder back, "you're trembling. What is going on?"

"Nothing," Meg insisted. "I don't want to talk about it. Now, let me have the letters."

By now, Meg had almost regained her composure, and even though Kelly still had a concerned expression on her face, she complied and handed over the letters.

There were five. Meg looked at the date stamped on each of them and put them in order, resolving to open the oldest one first and work her way forward. It was dated April 15, 1902, which was almost two years ago. Why he continued to write her when she had never answered was beyond her. It's no wonder he seemed both upset and angry by the time he had written this latest letter.

She carefully read through each one, actually going through them twice before moving on. Upon opening the fourth one, a likeness slipped out first, and she picked it up, gazing at Kelly in wonderment. "Is this him, then?" she asked, holding up the picture. "Is this Charles Ashton?"

"Well, it was—last year, I suppose," Kelly shrugged. "Of course that's him. It says it's him. Why would he send you a picture of another fellow?"

"Perhaps he's hideous and wants me to think this handsome young man is him when it really isn't," Meg laughed, holding the picture up in front of her face. "How do you do? I'm Charles Ashton."

"You're ridiculous, is what you are," Kelly giggled, punching her playfully in the arm. "I guess you're in a better mood then?"

"I suppose," Meg replied, placing the picture carefully back on the table next to the unread letter it had fallen out of. "He seems rather nice, though I'm still not sure why in the world he would want to have anything at all to do with me."

"I'm honestly not sure either," Kelly snickered. After Meg returned the jab in the shoulder she continued. "I mean, I don't know what the arrangement is. Perhaps his father has convinced him that you're a fine young lady, one worth marrying."

"But he hasn't even met me."

"Exactly. How else would he be able to make such an argument?"

"Would you stop?" Meg asked kicking her beneath the table this time. "This is serious!"

"I know. I'm sorry. I don't know, though, Meg. Once you've read the rest of the letters, maybe you'll know. Or maybe not. All you can do at this point is write him back, let him know you're sorry you didn't receive the letters, and see if he still wants to meet you."

Meg shook her head. "I have to be very careful. My mother said she would read anything I sent out. I can't make it seem as if she was keeping them from me. Nor can I attempt to make any arrangements she might dislike. Clearly, he's tried to meet me before and my mother kept him from doing so."

"Yes, but the company was doing much better then. Maybe she'd let you now."

"Or maybe I don't want to," Meg offered, still considering her options. She glanced down at the handsome young man in the picture. He must have been about fifteen when it was taken and was probably more like sixteen now. Being only thirteen, she wasn't anywhere near coming out, looking for suitors, discussing marriage. Yet, having the opportunity to experience such activities taken away from her was unsettling. She knew she'd still be able to attend balls and dance with other gentlemen; after all, one hardly ever danced with their own betrothed anyway. But when her friends were trying to decide which man was the right one for them, she'd be boring them with tales of Charlie and his letters. A letter was hardly a suitable escort to the park.

"Meg?" Kelly asked, jarring her back to reality.

"I apologize," Meg stuttered. "I was just thinking about... what I might do."

"Well, I shall leave you to it. Technically, you are still supposed to be working on your studies with Ms. Cunningham, and I have household chores to complete."

"You might check on Sarah and see if Jessica is still outside," Meg called over her shoulder as Kelly approached the door. She worried about Jessica and Blanche's little one, Fionna. They were allowed to stay in the house, but in separate quarters from their mothers, which was odd to Meg. She also found it peculiar that no one truly kept track of them during the day since both of their mothers were always busy with chores. She knew Kelly kept an eye out for them, but there was something quite unsettling about the whole arrangement.

"I'll peek in on her," Kelly assured her. "I am fairly certain your uncle won't dismiss Sarah. He seems rather fond of Jessica."

It wasn't until after Kelly had gone and shut the door behind her that Meg, who had been distracted by the letters, realized what her lady had just said, and the queasy feeling in the pit of her stomach almost erupted. "Oh, dear God!" she muttered. "Surely not!" The weight of this possibility was too much for her small shoulders to carry, and Meg clutched her stomach and stumbled over to her bed, collapsing.

NEW YORK CITY

"Look there, Charlie. You've a letter!" Walter said as Charlie made his way back to their dormitory from class.

He glanced over at his desk but then proceeded to take off his jacket and hang it up, muttering, "It's likely just from my mother."

"If your mother has recently been to Southampton, then I suppose so," Walter sniggered.

"What's that?" Charlie asked, unable to believe his ears. His friend only continued to chuckle, and though he didn't want to seem too eager, Charlie could hardly help but run over to his desk to see if what Walter said was true.

Clearing his throat, he glanced down to see that the letter was, indeed, posted from Southampton, and the penmanship looked very feminine, though certainly not the same as his mother's. He stood staring at the envelope for quite some time, not sure exactly what he should do.

"Well, aren't you going to open it?" Walter asked. He'd been reclining on his bed with an open book, but now that Charlie was acting peculiarly, he came over and stood next to him.

Charlie shrugged. "I suppose I should."

"You've only been waiting for it for two years, Charlie," Walter reminded him.

"I'm aware," Charlie snapped, turning his head to give Walter a scowl.

Walter raised his hands and took a step backwards. "Hey, you do whatever you need to, old chap. I just thought you'd be happy. That's all."

"I'm sorry," Charlie said, pulling the chair out from under his desk and tossing himself down. "It's just... I was finally starting to think perhaps you were right. Everyone was right. Maybe I am spending too much time thinking about Mary Margaret. Maybe there are other girls out there that would appreciate my attention."

"Like Ralph's sister, Stella?" Walter asked, now back on his bed.

Despite his best effort not to, Charlie felt himself blush at the thought of the beautiful brunette they'd met on the football field last winter. Now it was spring, and since Ralph Pettigrew had come to be their classmate, all of the boys were constantly asking if Stella, who attended school in Boston, had sent a letter. Charlie never asked, but he always wondered what she was doing and where she learned to catch a football like that.

"Possibly," Charlie managed, not surprised to hear Walter snigger again. "I suppose I'm just afraid I'll open it and the real Mary Margaret will be nothing like the one I've imagined."

"I don't think she's stuffed herself inside that envelope, Charlie my boy," Walter teased.

Fighting the instinct to glare at him again, Charlie managed, "No, of course not. But one can tell a lot by the way a person writes a letter. What if she is brash or inconsiderate? What if she doesn't ask after my family? What if she's written to tell me she'll never marry me despite what our fathers decided?"

Walter was back at his side again, patting him on the shoulder. "There's only one way to find out."

Charlie shrugged. He plopped his elbows down on the table, the envelope between them, and rested his head on one fist.

"Do you want me to open it for you?"

"No, of course not."

"All right then. I'll give you some privacy. Teddy said I could come by and help him study for his physics exam."

"Bully for you," Charlie replied, raising an eyebrow.

"I know, but at least if I help him study, we're more likely to get invited to the next game of catch."

"Unless he doesn't pass," Charlie called after him as he approached the door. Walter stopped and narrowed his eyes at him playfully, and Charlie couldn't help but laugh. It would break Walter's heart to know that Charlie was always invited but seldom went because he was so busy studying whereas Walter was seldom invited but always went because he was so terrible at football.

Returning his attention to the letter, Charlie finally decided to have at it and carefully pulled it open.

MARCH 25, 1904

DEAR MR. ASHTON,

I HOPE *this letter finds you well. I apologize that there seems to have been some problem with the post. It certainly has not been my intention to give you the impression I am ignoring you. I have very much appreciated reading your letters. New York sounds like an exciting place, and you seem to be quite the student. I would like to hear more about your friends at school. Walter seems like a particularly interesting fellow.*

I attend lessons daily with my governess, whose name is Ms. Cunningham. She is my second governess. I am learning English diction, Latin, history, and maths—which I think you Americans call "math" instead. I like most of my subjects but am not particularly fond of calculations. I am also learning all sorts of etiquette and that sort of thing. My governess says I am very polished for a thirteen-year-old.

I enjoy riding as well and am quite good at it, though I do not have a horse of my own. I am allowed to use my mother's from time to time. I also enjoy reposing in the back garden. My mother has quite the green thumb. Her lilacs are particularly lovely, as is the oleander. Not many can grow the type my mother tends, but she is quite skilled at horticulture.

We have taken a few trips to Europe, particularly France and Italy, but I have yet to visit America. I should think it would be remarkably different than what I am accustomed to. I have met a few Americans that are business associates of my uncle's, though I'm afraid I've yet to meet your father. I've also met Lucille, Lady Duff Gordon. Though she is not an American, I'm sure you must know of her as she spends quite a bit of time in New York and Chicago. She is the most interesting of all of my uncle's associates I've met thus far.

I apologize that I do not have a current likeness of me that I can send, though my mother promises to send one soon. I had one made about a year ago that she will send if I do not make another one soon. I appreciate being able to put a face with your name. I personally try to avoid the newspapers and do not read them either, though I suppose I would have known what you looked like if I had checked the society section there.

I suppose I am rambling now. Again, I apologize for the delays, and I hope this letter finds you well.

Sincerely,

Miss M. Westmoreland

CHARLIE READ the letter over twice, not sure what to think. Though it was a lengthy letter, there truly wasn't too much personal information about Mary Margaret. It almost seemed as if someone else had written it. He thought that couldn't possibly be the case. She had even signed it in a peculiar way. He wondered if she might be nervous since either this was the first letter she'd written to him, or she knew he was upset that none of her other letters had actually made it to him. If she had mailed other letters, where could they be? Or was someone in her household preventing her from sending him correspondence? The whole thing seemed a bit fishy to him, but since he had no more information to go off of, he decided to wait a few days then write her back. Perhaps, if she wrote again, the next letter would be a bit more personable.

CHAPTER NINE

SOUTHAMPTON

Meg had found solace beneath the lilac bushes in the backyard. She hadn't come here for years, though when she was smaller, on occasion, she would hide here. The sound of shouting from the house had driven her outside, and even though she knew it was for a good cause, the idea that someone else was being punished for what she had done was enough to make her sick to her stomach.

She was fairly certain Kelly would find her soon, though she was still supposed to be studying with Ms. Cunningham. The sound of her uncle berating Wilma downstairs, and then obviously striking her, had sent Meg running down the back stair case. Ms. Cunningham was young and inexperienced—nothing like Ms. Strickland—and whenever Meg ran or hid from her, she never bothered to go hunt her down.

A few minutes later, Meg watched as Wilma came through the back door, her tattered garment bag in one hand, the hand of her young daughter, Angelina, in the other. Even from this distance, Meg could see that Wilma's nose was bleeding and she had tears streaming down her face. In a few days, Meg would return her uncle's favorite cufflink to his drawer, but he would never call Wilma back to work or apologize. He had found one in Wilma's pocket this morning after he'd searched the house and likely accused her of selling the other. She had, of course, claimed innocence, sworn on her life and that of her daughter's that she didn't take it. He didn't believe her, and now out she went, Angelina questioning why she was crying and where they were going.

Anywhere was better than here.

At first, Meg had tried to do the right thing. Last year, when she'd discovered what was happening with Sarah's and Blanche's daughters, she had attempted to talk to them. Neither of them wanted to hear what she had to say. They both said this was the only work they could find. They were unskilled young mothers, with little children to care for. Meg understood that, but surely they must appreciate exactly why her uncle wanted them there, wanted their daughters in the adjoining maids' room and not with their own respective mothers. Deaf ears had pleaded ignorance, so Meg had done the only thing she could. She had gotten each of them fired.

First, Sarah ruined her mother's favorite ball gown, and then Blanche broke the glass in her uncle's portrait above the fireplace. Of course, neither of them had actually done anything, but after her mother and uncle had lit into them, and in Sarah's case she'd been given a black eye, both ladies had been sent away. After that, there had been Eunice and her daughter Tildy. Then, Kathleen and Belle. Then there was Gretchen, who had actually listened to what Meg had to say. Last week, she'd taken her daughter Clara and left of her own accord. Meg was thankful that Clara had a good mother who cared for her.

Some of these women were actually married, but their husbands were employed elsewhere. Some were unwed, and some were young widows. She'd made the argument that perhaps their daughter would be better off with their fathers or their grandmothers if they were available (as Patsy had done with her Kelly) but the mothers wanted their daughters close by and refused to believe what Meg was telling them, even when their little ones confirmed it by wetting the bed and hiding at bedtime. Meg knew what those signs meant. She knew all too well.

She had been left alone for the most part. At first, she'd worried about Kelly, but she soon realized that her friend was too old for her uncle's liking. She wondered if that was the true reason he rarely entered her room anymore or if it was because of whatever her mother had said to him that night, after the dancing lesson. She didn't spend too much time trying to figure it out. As long as he stayed away, she didn't really care why.

Meg heard a stirring in the branches and looked to see familiar muddy boots entering her private space and then a familiar face. "Whatcha doin'?" Ezra asked, dodging a low hanging vine to settle down next to her.

"Nothing," she replied, her hands still grasped tightly around her folded knees.

"Ms. Wilma sure didn't look good when she lit out of here," he continued.

"I wouldn't know," Meg replied. She glanced up at him, and Ezra looked a bit skeptical. "Fine. I was scared." Lying was better than telling the truth sometimes. If Ezra thought she was hiding because she was scared she might get hurt, instead of because she felt guilty for getting a woman's face smashed in, well, then, that would shift the blame back to Wilma and away from her.

"I see," he said. He pulled a rambling vine out of the ground and snapped it, placing part of it in the corner of his mouth as if it were a stalk of straw, something she'd seen him do lots of times when they were younger and ran around the dusty carriage house.

"Why are you here anyway?" Meg asked. "Shouldn't you be at school?"

"Shouldn't you be with your governess?" he countered.

Meg looked up at him for the first time. She couldn't remember the last time they'd been together at all, though sometimes she saw him in the back garden helping his father. He was nearly seventeen now and quite tall. With light, wavy hair and blue eyes, some girls might even think him handsome—if he weren't covered in muck and didn't smell like horse or automobile oil. Of course, Meg didn't think he was handsome at all. He was Ezra—nothing more than the caretaker's son. So she didn't understand why her stomach felt all queasy when he smiled that crooked grin at her. It wasn't the same type of topsy turvy her stomach felt when she thought of her uncle or what she'd done to Wilma. This was different, and she thought she might actually like it.

But she wouldn't let him know that.

"I think I should go back inside now," she said, realizing she didn't want to be sitting beneath the lilac bushes with Ezra anymore.

"All right," he shrugged. "I wish you came outside more often," he added as she began to make her way out of the bushes. "I miss you, Meggy."

She glanced back at him, and though she could barely see his face through the branches, she could tell he was smiling at her and his blue eyes were twinkling. Butterflies began to dance in her stomach. "I'll... I'll see you later, Ezra."

She hurried off to the house then, wondering why Kelly hadn't found her and why Ezra suddenly made her feel so different than he ever had before.

When she entered the parlor, she found Kelly on her hands and knees with a bucket of soapy water. She could hear her mother and uncle in another room, and though it seemed they were trying to keep their voices low, they were obviously arguing. "What are you doing?" Meg asked, just above a whisper.

Kelly glanced up but then returned her concentration to her work. "Trying to get Wilma's blood stain out of the rug."

Meg's eyes widened. "Oh, my," she said, her hands covering her mouth.

"I don't understand why these servants keep stealing and breaking things," Kelly continued as she scrubbed, her voice showing the strain. "Is it just the caliber of people they're tending to employ these days, or is something else amiss?"

"It is peculiar," Meg agreed. "I should go check in with Ms. Cunningham." Though she scurried past Kelly as quickly as she could, she couldn't help but think the slightly older girl was giving her a look that said she knew more than she was willing to speak.

As Meg approached the stairwell, she could more clearly hear the voices coming from the room across the hall. Her mother was shouting, "Perhaps we could pay better if you hadn't insisted on purchasing that ridiculous automobile."

"I must have an auto," Bertram shot back. "Everyone in our circle has them. If I didn't, I should look like a penniless fool."

"I don't know how much longer we can keep this charade up," her mother replied. "We must find a way to increase income or cut expenses!"

"I'm doing everything I can...."

Meg chose not to hear any more. Her mother was clearly doing her best to keep them at the level of accommodations they were used to whereas her uncle continued to spend money like nothing was wrong. The automobile, the telephone, the brand new radio—all of those things seemed like luxuries they could not afford to Meg, and as she continued on her way up the stairs, she wondered how in the world her uncle was able to pull this off. "He must have one very long line of credit," she mumbled.

Ms. Cunningham was no longer in her room, and though Meg didn't usually enjoy being in there at all, she decided to duck in and take a few moments to read a book she'd started a few days ago. Reading for pleasure was something she enjoyed greatly, and she was lucky that her mother had amassed a bit of a collection of novels when she was younger and they could still afford such items. Now, if she asked her mother for a new book, she likely wouldn't even bother with a response.

As Meg reclined on the bed, book in hand, movement outside of the window caught her eye. Her room was on the side of the house so she could see both the front and side yard, which was connected to the back garden. She liked that she could see the street outside, see who was coming and going, and also liked that she could see some of the flowers, though the view of the back gardens wasn't nearly as lovely as it was from the study. Today, however, it wasn't the gardens that caught her eye; it was Ezra. He was with his father working on something, she couldn't quite tell what, but it looked as if he was swinging an axe. She hadn't noticed before the broad muscles in his shoulders or the way his hair glistened when the sun caught it just so. Before she realized what she was doing, she had set her book aside and was standing at the window, peering around to get a better view.

"Are you ready to get back to work?"

Meg jumped, nearly slamming her head into the glass before her. Once she had calmed herself a bit, she turned around. Of course it was Ms. Cunningham, and she hadn't seemed to notice anything as she had pulled a chair out at the table and was flipping through the pages of Meg's new French textbook. "I should think you ought to be able to master at least these next two verb conjugations before lunch."

"Yes, I believe I can," Meg replied, sitting back down. Her heart was still racing, but at least Ms. Cunningham didn't seem to take any notice of what she had been doing. As the governess began to give her instructions, Meg took some deep breaths and attempted to concentrate on her studies, not at all sure what in the world was going on inside of her own body.

NEW YORK CITY

With high school nearly at an end, Charlie was glad to be back at home for one final weekend before his end of term exams. Then, he'd have the summer off before he attended Harvard in the fall. Though it had been a difficult decision for him to make, his father assured him that Harvard's business program was one of the best in the country,

PRELUDE: A PREQUEL

and if he wouldn't be attending his father's alma mater, then Harvard was the next best thing.

Walter would be attending New York City University, and Charlie was a bit concerned about not having any friends at his new school, though he did know of a few others from his school who would be attending. It wouldn't be the same not having Walter around, but his mother had recently taken ill, and he wanted to stay close to home. Charlie had also considered NYCU but in the end, he just didn't feel there were many schools in the same league as Harvard, and NYCU certainly didn't meet the mark.

Grace and her husband Peter were also visiting, and he was looking forward to having an opportunity to spend some time with his sister. It had been quite a while since they were able to visit, though they did correspond from time to time, and he had telephoned once when he was visiting home. She lived upstate now, and her social circle kept her very busy. While Peter had been given the opportunity to work for his father's shipping company, he had taken on his own challenge and decided to open a factory working on an invention that would allow the air inside a home to be cooled via electricity, a concept he wasn't familiar with but that intrigued him. Charlie was interested in new inventions and experimentations, so spending time talking to Peter was never a waste.

Charlie had just returned from a stroll around the grounds, something he missed while studying in the city. He spied Peter sitting in a chair in the parlor, open newspaper in hand, and his father seated across from him looking over what appeared to be a business magazine.

"Charlie, old boy! How are you?" Peter asked when he noticed Charlie had entered the room and sat down nearby.

"I can't complain," Charlie replied. "Anything exciting in the paper today?"

"Nothing to write home about," Peter replied, setting it aside. He had a nice looking moustache that Charlie was more than a bit envious of, though he'd never tried to grow one himself. He never

103

thought it would look quite right on him. Now that he was seeing Peter's again, however, he thought he might give it a go. "How's life at Prep?"

"Same old, same old," Charlie shrugged, crossing one leg so that his ankle rested on his knee. "It's been a wonderful experience, but I think I'm ready to move on."

"Harvard—those are big digs," Peter laughed.

"Yes, we finally decided that was the right school for Charlie," John chimed in, setting his magazine aside and joining in the conversation. "Not an easy decision, I assure you."

"I should say not," Peter agreed. "There had to have been hundreds of proper universities vying for your attendance, what with your excellent grades and family legacy."

"Charlie might be an Ashton, but his acceptance to Harvard was due to his hard work," his father assured his son-in-law with a smile.

"I've no doubt," Peter nodded. "Grace is always saying what a studious young lad you are, that you'd rather be reading a textbook than out running about with the other young men."

"I do enjoy studying," Charlie admitted, "but I also try to get some exercise and fresh air regularly. I feel I can study better when my head is clear."

"Good point," Peter replied. "Wonderful attitude to have. I find I do my best thinking after a good, brisk walk."

"Indeed," John agreed. "There is something to be said for fresh air."

"You must have plenty of fresh air in Buffalo," Charlie said. "Surely there isn't the type of polluted air up there that you'll find down here in the city."

"Oh, it's lovely," Peter agreed. "There are a number of manufacturing facilities there now, including my own, but it's not nearly as dense as what you're used to here. Not nearly the people, the movement, the noise. I quite like it."

"I imagine it's more peaceful," John agreed. "Grace seems to be enjoying it."

"The people have certainly embraced her," Peter nodded. "She is the toast of the town. It seems everyone wants to have brunch with Grace Ashton Buckner."

They all laughed, though Charlie wasn't quite sure why that was so funny. His sister had always been good at entertaining. It shouldn't matter where she was living; he was certain she would always love to throw a celebration of some sort. "Tell me more about your factory."

"Well, right now, we are mostly producing pieces for existing coolant machinery—ice boxes, fans, that sort of thing—not really that exciting, but we have in development some very exciting innovations that may actually allow one to cool their home to whatever temperature they like, even in the summertime," Peter explained, leaning forward with his lanky arms on his knees. "It's really quite exciting."

"It sounds fascinating," Charlie admitted. He continued to ask questions about how the new product would work, and Peter did his best to answer them though there were times that Charlie's questions stumped even him, the owner of the factory. John sat and listened for the most part, only chiming in to express his amazement periodically. After a lengthy discussion, Charlie finally managed, "Well, I'm very impressed. And I think it says something that you didn't feel pressured into running your father's company. Going out into the world and making your own mark really speaks volumes about your character, I think."

"Why thank you, Charlie," Peter smiled. "I appreciate the sentiment. But I'm sure you'll do the same. I'll still take over my father's company whenever he is ready to retire, but in the meantime, I may as well find my own interest and do my own thing. I'm learning a lot about business, probably more than I would if I was solely under my father's tutelage. Though he knows a great deal about running a business, having my own factory allows me to do everything for myself, to take my own risks and learn my own lessons. It's really the way to go, I feel."

"Charlie will always be able to start his own business if he so chooses once he's graduated," John interjected "I believe he knows that."

A bit surprised to actually hear these words from his father, Charlie decided to mask his astonishment so as not to offend him. "I have always been interested in taking some risks, looking at some cutting edge technologies. I hope to have the opportunity to do so someday."

"And you will also have Westmoreland Textiles," John reminded him.

Though he was aware of this condition in the agreement his father and Mr. Westmoreland had come to so many years ago, it wasn't something Charlie was looking forward to. The textile industry simply didn't interest him, and it seemed as if this particular company was not doing well from what he could gather in the business pages if and when it was even mentioned. "Yes, Father," Charlie replied. "Another venture I'll need to be sure I'm prepared for while I'm at Harvard."

"How is Mary Margaret?" Peter asked. "Have you met in person yet?"

Charlie wasn't sure why Peter was asking since he was fairly certain this is something his sister would have discussed with her husband. Perhaps he was trying to make a point, though Charlie wasn't quite certain what it might be. "Not yet," he answered. "Though we do correspond rather regularly. She sent a likeness the last time she wrote."

"Oh, how lovely," Peter nodded. "I'm sure she's breathtaking."

Though the picture Charlie had received was a few years old, and therefore he wasn't certain what the young lady might look like at her present age, he decided it would be better to avoid that entire discussion. "Yes, she's certainly very pretty. Of course, she's not reached her majority yet, so only time will tell."

"Her mother was quite a striking young woman," John offered, the look in his eyes revealing faded memories at play. "I can't imagine

Henry and Mildred Westmoreland's daughter being anything less than beautiful."

"Indeed," Charlie nodded. "At any rate, I should like to go and visit her at some point, but that will be difficult with me going off to school in the fall."

"Couldn't you go this summer?" Peter asked. The question seemed innocent enough, but Charlie wasn't exactly sure, again, what he might be getting at.

Before he could formulate a response, John replied, "I've decided not to go to England this summer. I was there in the winter, and Charlie couldn't go because of school. I have several meetings lined up with business associates who will be visiting the city this summer, and I intend to concentrate on them."

"I see. And Bertram Westmoreland isn't one of them?" Peter probed.

"Not at present," John admitted, "though it would be nice if he were to drop by. We honestly don't do much business at all with Westmoreland Textiles anymore, but it would be suitable to know how business is as we approach the shift."

"We have a few more years to worry about getting that all straightened out, though," Charlie reminded them.

"Yes, of course," Peter replied, perhaps realizing he was nearly stepping out of bounds. "Well, I do hope you know what you have to look forward to. Married life is so much better than I ever thought it would be. To come home from work each day to your sister's smiling face and to know that the house is in perfect order because of her tireless efforts—it's really not something one can understand unless he lives it."

"Now that, she gets from her mother," John laughed. "Pamela has always done a wonderful job of making my home my solace."

As the other two gentlemen continued to ramble on about how important having a good wife was to one's sanity, Charlie's mind began to wonder. He hoped that Mary Margaret would have those skills, but he had no way of knowing, and since he hadn't even met her, it was likely he wouldn't find out until after they were married. Times like this made him wish he had some sort of a say, a choice in the matter. But since he knew he did not, he briskly brushed those thoughts aside and put his faith in his father and his college roommate. Surely, they knew what was best for their children. They just had to.

CHAPTER TEN

SOUTHAMPTON

Meg pulled up to the large estate in her uncle's motor coach, which he insisted on driving himself despite her mother's embarrassment at having Mr. Bitterly sit beside him in the front seat as if the auto was his, and stared at all of the finely dressed people.

She had never been to a ball before, but now that she was fifteen, she would be allowed to attend, though there were certain rules she had to follow as she had not yet had her own coming out party. She absently wondered what the point of that might be since she was already promised to someone, but as she took the offered hand of a young man dressed in high-fashioned servant's clothes and made her way out of the backseat of her uncle's prized possession, her focus was on the people, the lights, the music, and the dancing.

She could hear the musicians from outside. The house was lit so spectacularly, one might think it was daytime. Though the majority of the lighting was finely crafted gaslights, Meg noticed that some of them appeared to be electric, and she wondered how long it might take Uncle Bertram to try to convince her mother that they needed electricity in their own home.

Forced to place her hand on her uncle's arm out of respect for high society's rules, Meg entered the ballroom where they were announced by a regal sounding man who was later identified as the master of ceremonies. Her mother, who was on her uncle's other arm, instructed him to escort Meg to an area of the room where several of her friends and acquaintances were seated, and once they had ensured she was where she belonged, they went about their own ritualistic greeting ceremony which Meg had only read about in books.

"Good evening, Mary Margaret," Beatrice Townly said with a smile as Meg took her seat.

"Mary Margaret?" her younger sister Alise, who was only thirteen, and in Meg's opinion shouldn't likely be there, questioned. "Why aren't you calling her Meg like you do every other time you see her?"

"This is a formal," Beatrice scolded. "We should be more proper."

Meg couldn't help but laugh at both sisters. "Good evening, Beatrice; Alise," she stated, straightening her gown. It was by far the loveliest dress her mother had ever allowed her to own, and she had spent half the night before wide awake thinking of all the awful things that could happen to it like if she spilled something on it or tore the train.

Meg spoke pleasantries to several other young ladies, many of whom she had known for years. There were others that she hadn't met yet, but all of their names sounded familiar. Some of them had come from as far away as London and even New York City for the event, including Madeline Force and her family, whom Meg recognized as one of the socialites she actually recognized from the papers. When Meg had a chance to talk to the young debutante, she found her quite clever and interesting, and they'd hit it off right away. Unfortunately, she'd been asked to dance almost immediately and Meg wondered if she'd get another chance to speak to her again that evening.

Christina Edgebrook, the girl whose womanhood they were celebrating that evening, proved herself to be quite the catch. Otherwise, surely no one from as far away as New York would have bothered to come. As she watched the young woman flutter from suitor to suitor, in the back of her mind, Meg thought perhaps she shouldn't bother to have a coming out after all. What if no one attended?

She spent most of the evening in her seat. She wasn't allowed to go anywhere without a proper escort, and since she was one of the younger ladies there, the gentlemen were not inclined to ask her to dance. Like Alise and some of the other younger girls, she was only there to be seen and to observe. Nevertheless, when one young man, who she'd been introduced to earlier that evening, asked her if she should like refreshments, she did let him lead her to the table in the adjoining room where Mrs. Edgebrook had supplied her guests with an endless array of fruits, desserts, and finger foods. Meg didn't want to overstuff herself since she knew dinner would also be served, but it was late and she was hungry, so she indulged a little more than she probably should have. When she realized her escort, Marcus Hayworth, was staring at her, she asked, "What is it? Haven't you ever seen a young lady eat before?"

He smiled, and though his cheeks were a bit round and his eyebrows a bit bushy, he had very straight, white teeth. "Not quite as jubilantly as you, I believe," he replied.

Meg wasn't sure if she should be offended or complimented, but since he didn't seem insulted at her enthusiasm, she laughed. Finishing her refreshments, she allowed him to escort her back to her seat. "It's been a pleasure, Miss Westmoreland," Marcus said as he delivered her back to her chair.

Giving a little curtsy, Meg smiled and sat back down. For a brief second, she wondered what it might be like if Ezra were the one escorting her back to her seat. Would he have any idea how one was to behave in high society? Likely not....

Her thoughts were interrupted by a comment from over her

shoulder. "I guess one can eat whatever she likes when she doesn't have to worry about impressing anyone."

Meg turned to see that the speaker was Samantha Fairweather, and though she was speaking to another young lady, Connie Mercer, she had obviously kept her voice up so that Meg would overhear, even over the noisy giggles of Miss Mercer who sounded a bit like a donkey in Meg's opinion.

Her mouth open in shock, it took Meg a moment to gather her thoughts. She had thought Samantha a friend. Why would she say something so ugly? Before she could even consider censoring her reply, she found herself saying, "Fairweather seems an appropriate last name for you. I shall remember that when Mr. Ashton and I are writing our wedding invitations."

She heard both girls gasp in shock, but she swung back around to face the dance floor, pretending that she couldn't care less about what they had to say about her. Though she could hear them continuing to whisper, she could no longer hear what they were saying, and she decided that if they were talking about her, it really was no longer her concern.

Though she didn't dance herself, Meg quite enjoyed watching the others spin around the room. Alise was asked to dance by her own father, which was a bit of a faux pas in some stricter rule books since she was so young, but Meg found it endearing. She was hopeful that some of these ridiculous rules would begin to change. After all, she should be able to get up and use the ladies' room without having to wait on an escort. Watching her young friend spin around the dance floor with her loving father was both joyful and melancholy. How she longed to have the opportunity to dance with her own father once more.

She watched her own mother dance as well, though she had no idea where her uncle might have gone off to. She assumed he would be getting his fill of the spirits and other alcoholic beverages Mrs. Edgebrook had on offer. There were not too many times in her life when she could actually remember being proud of her mother, but watching her twirl so gracefully around the dance floor, regardless of the skill of her partner, was breathtaking. Meg wasn't the only one who noticed as others began to comment on how elegantly her mother danced. One day soon, Meg hoped to have the opportunity to show some fine young man everything her mother had taught her. She wondered if she would ever have the occasion to dance that way with Charlie.

Or with Ezra.

The night was much longer than Meg had expected, and after dinner, she found herself struggling to stay awake. She couldn't remember ever having been out this late before. It was a wonderful experience, but she was ready to go to sleep. Even the thought of her own bed seemed inviting, and she couldn't remember the last time she felt that way.

Just as she began to nod off, there was a bit of a ruckus from back by the ladies' lounge, which was out of the ballroom and around the corner a bit. She could hear the sound of a man shouting and what sounded like a woman screaming. Though the music was loud, she was seated nearby enough that it had awoken her, whereas people on the other side of the dance floor likely didn't even know anything was happening.

"What's all that commotion?" Meg asked Alise, who looked as if she had either just woken up or was about to fall asleep herself. Most of the other girls around them were also peering off in that direction, though some of them seemed not to have heard.

"I don't know," Alise replied, "and the only way we are about to find out is if some gentleman decides to escort us back there to see. Let us hope the building isn't on fire."

Meg couldn't help but giggle. Alise was sharp and witty. She reminded her a bit of herself.

The laughter stopped, however, when Meg noticed a man she did not recognize rushing across the dance floor to her mother, who was sitting with a group of ladies. He stooped down and whispered something in her ear, and her mother's already pale face turned ashen. She took his arm and hurried off in the direction of the noise which had died down a bit now, but Meg could tell, whatever it was, it wasn't over.

She heard another voice then, a familiar one, and braced herself. Whatever her uncle was up to, it couldn't be good.

A few moments later, he was escorted around the corner, one large gentleman on either side of him, his elbows gripped tightly in their hands. They were attempting to be nonchalant, it was clear, but she could tell by their strained expressions that they were upset.

"Isn't that your uncle?" Connie asked, leaning down next to Meg's ear.

"It looks like the Westmorelands have decided to put on a second act," Samantha chided, causing Connie and a few of the other girls to giggle.

Meg stood, though she wasn't supposed to, her face red. How could she possibly compare her consumption of a few too many canapés to her clearly inebriated uncle being escorted out? Though Meg wanted to turn and give Samantha a stern talking to, she could see her mother, accompanied by Mr. Edgebrook this time, rushing over to collect her.

"Mary Margaret, it's time to go," her trembling voice said, and Meg quickly said goodbye to Alise and a few of her other friends before grasping Mr. Edgebrook's other arm and hurrying out of the room. Her legs were not as long as his, and she was not used to walking in these fancy shoes at all, so she stumbled a few times, but he did nothing to right her, and she hoped that no one noticed how clumsy her exit must appear.

Her mother directed her into the backseat of the motor coach as she turned to address Mr. Edgebrook. Once Meg was in, she realized her uncle was nearly passed out in the front seat and Mr. Bitterly, who had likely spent all these hours sitting in the car, was in the driver's seat.

She couldn't quite hear everything her mother was saying, but it seemed as if she was apologizing. Mr. Edgebrook looked very unsympathetic and appeared to cut her off before spinning and heading back into the house. The other two gentlemen, the ones who had escorted her uncle out, stood nearby, and as one helped her mother into the seat beside her, the other made sure the path was clear for Mr. Bitterly to make a speedy departure.

Having no true idea what had just transpired, Meg looked at her mother and then her uncle to see if either of them might give her a clue. Her uncle's head was tipped back, and after a moment she could hear him snoring. Each time Bitterly took a corner too quickly, his head would flop around, and Meg was hopeful that it might smack into the glass window or at least the side of the door. When she returned her attention to her mother, she could clearly see tears on her cheeks, and for a brief moment, Meg began to feel compassion for the woman. She reached out her hand to place it on her mother's shoulder, an attempt to comfort her, but she literally slapped it away, so Meg put her hand back in her lap and silently hoped that, whatever it was that her uncle had done, her mother was equally as shamed for it. That's what she got for feeling compassion towards someone who had never felt anything for her at all.

Since Mr. Bitterly had nearly carried her uncle out of the motor coach and deposited him on a sofa in the formal living area, Meg was fairly certain she could rest easy for what was left of the night, as could the other little girls upstairs in the attic. She fell asleep that night hoping that the two gentlemen who had escorted her uncle out had made him pay for whatever it was he had done before they forced him to leave. It was about time he got a taste of his own medicine.

CHAPTER ELEVEN

CAMBRIDGE

"It's not quite like a ball; it's more like a dance," Charlie's roommate, Quincy, insisted. "There aren't so many of those ridiculous rules like you're used to. You have to experience it to believe it."

"Why would anyone allow their daughter to attend a ball without following the formalities we're all accustomed to?" Charlie asked, still unable to fathom precisely what his friend was describing.

"Why not? Are American gentlemen so unruly that we can't be trusted? Besides, most of the girls will be from Radcliffe, and their parents are far away. Listen, Charlie, just come for a bit, have a drink, and if you don't want to dance, that's fine. You've just got to liven up a bit, old boy. You live like an old married man, and you're not even formally engaged yet!"

While Charlie had a scathing response ready, he bit his tongue. Perhaps Quincy was right. Maybe he did need to get out more. He had spent most of the first semester sequestered in their dorm room, making sure his grades were all that they should be. Even though he was a bit afraid of what this so-called dance might be like, he knew that things were different in Cambridge than they had been in New York City, and rules seemed to be changing so far as what was acceptable and what was not. He finally reluctantly gave in and followed his friend out into the night to make their way the few blocks over to where the get-together was being held.

The first thing he noticed was how informally everyone was dressed, including himself. While he still had on a three-piece suit, it wasn't the tails he would normally wear to a formal event. The ladies were dressed in long gowns, but they were not nearly as elegant as what he was used to. There were several full-fledged adults in attendance, and they also seemed to be enjoying themselves. He noticed that the ladies were attending to their own needs, getting drinks, disappearing off to what must be the ladies' lounge, etc., with no escort.

"Wow—this is certainly something," he muttered, taking it all in.

"I told you," Quincy replied, nudging him in the shoulder.

Quincy was quite the handsome young man. Tall, like Charlie, well-built, with sandy blond hair and a charismatic smile, he had told Charlie many times of his exploits at these types of events. Charlie didn't believe everything he said as he couldn't imagine a young lady agreeing to most of what he had to say, but now that he was in this new setting, he was having an easier time accepting some of it might be true.

A moment later, Charlie found himself standing alone as Quincy rushed off to the side of a beautiful young lady with light blonde hair pulled up on top of her head in a nice chignon. He must have known her because her eyes were sparking before he even reached her, and Charlie wondered which of the girls he had heard Quincy speak about this one might be.

Though Charlie noticed several young women smiling in his direction, he felt very uncomfortable and decided to have a drink rather than try his hand at asking one of the young ladies to dance. He approached the punch bowl cautiously as several unaccompanied young women were standing nearby, and he wasn't quite sure what to make of their presence. One of them said, "Good evening," to him, and he nodded at her before getting his drink and stepping away, hoping to find a seat in the corner somewhere. Observation might be best at first lest he embarrass himself.

He hadn't been sitting for more than a few minutes when he heard a voice beside him. "First dance then?" she asked, and while he couldn't quite place it, Charlie knew for certain he'd heard that voice before.

He turned to see familiar green eyes smiling up at him. Though it had been years since he had seen her, he would recognize that face anywhere. "Stella?" he asked, and then catching himself, he corrected, "I mean, that is to say, Miss Pettigrew...."

She laughed, and despite the loud music, he couldn't help but feel as if he were hearing the tinkling of angel's wings. "Please, Charlie. You can call me Stella."

"How do you know my name?" he asked, shocked.

"How do I know your name? How do you know my name?" she joked playfully nudging him. "Don't you think I asked my brother who you were just as soon as I had the chance? Besides, it's not like the newspapers ever go a day without writing something about you or your family." Leaning in closely to his ear, she whispered, "You're famous."

She pulled away laughing, and Charlie couldn't help but smile, though he wasn't sure what to think of her forwardness. He was beginning to wonder what was in the punch. But then again, this was the young woman he had met catching a football and running it into the end zone, so it wasn't as if she were a rule follower. "Why are you here?" he asked. "Do you attend Radcliffe?"

"I do," she nodded. Her long brown hair was tied up neatly atop her head, and she was wearing red, as she had been the first time he saw her. In the soft glow of the gaslights, she looked exquisite. "This is my first year."

"What are you studying?" Charlie asked, sipping his drink, still afraid it might contain copious amounts of alcohol.

"Physics," she said with a straight face.

Charlie laughed, almost spitting the punch out. However, almost as quickly as the fit of humor attacked him, he realized that she was quite serious. "Physics?" he repeated. "I had no idea that was even an option at Radcliffe."

"You mean you had no idea women were capable of studying the sciences?" she asked, leaning back in her chair and crossing her arms.

"No, not at all," Charlie protested. "My sister is quite intelligent, as is my mother. I honestly don't doubt for one second you're fully capable. I'm only surprised that the coursework is available to you."

"It's a new program," she replied, and he began to think perhaps she wasn't as offended as she was at first—as she rightly should be. "But quite successful. I'm certain you'll be hearing about it soon enough."

"Remarkable," Charlie muttered, shaking his head. "I am very interested in that sort of thing—making new discoveries that could lead to important inventions and the like."

"Well, I'd love to tell you all about our work sometime, but I hardly think a party is the place for such discussions. Wouldn't you like to dance?"

Charlie was confused. He wasn't sure if she was commenting on the fact that he was not dancing or if she was actually asking him to dance—something so forward he couldn't even imagine a college-attending, football-playing, female scientist daring to do. "I do like to dance, though I've never been too good at it."

Stella stood and gestured to the dance floor. "Then, after you!"

Though he was still having trouble grasping this strange world he had entered into, Charlie led Stella onto the dance floor and was at least somewhat assured by the fact that the dance, a simple waltz, was familiar and expected. Stella was a wonderful dancer, and it was clear by the number of eyes following her around the dance floor that he was not the only one interested in sharing her time. Once the song ended, he barely had a moment to thank her before another gentlemen was extending his hand, asking her to dance. Being a well-mannered young man, Charlie excused himself and soon found another young woman whose soft brown eyes seemed to implore that she wouldn't take no for an answer.

Before the evening was over, he had danced with more girls than he could count, and a number of them had approached him, though Stella was the only you who was so bold as to actually ask him outright. The others only made demure faces at him until he asked them himself. For the last song of the evening before the musicians packed their instruments and the host and hostess sent them on their way, Charlie found himself face to face with the graceful brunette, and without a word, he took her hand, leading her around the dance floor as if they both knew they were meant to be together.

When the song ended, Stella squeezed his hand "Good night, Charlie," she said.

"Good night, Stella," he replied, holding her gaze.

"I had a lovely time. I hope we'll run into each other again soon."

Charlie wanted to respond, but by the time he'd worked out an appropriate phrase, she had already gone, off to join her friends across the room who were gathering together to make their way back to Radcliffe no doubt.

He felt a slap on his shoulder as Quincy brought his hand down and rested it there. "Well, my friend, what do you say? Did you have a memorable evening?"

"I'll say," Charlie replied, his eyes still following the disappearing silhouette of the girl in the red dress.

"Good. Let's get back to the room. Perhaps next time I make a suggestion, you won't doubt me, old man."

Once again, Charlie had no response, and he followed Quincy out into the night. Though he was slightly attuned to the realization that his life may have just become a lot more complicated than it had ever been before, he decided to push those thoughts aside and concentrate only on the memory of twirling Stella around the dance floor. It had been a night to remember.

CHAPTER TWELVE

SOUTHAMPTON

Meg entered her room and noticed an envelope on the desk, something she hadn't seen for several months, and was a bit surprised to see that Charlie had finally written her back. The last time he had corresponded he had seemed quite distant. He'd discussed his classes at Harvard and a few of his friends, but the letter was short and not very personal. She wondered if it was in response to the sort of letter she was forced to send him, but she couldn't imagine what it might have been that had changed his tone.

She picked the letter up and was about to open it when she heard footsteps behind her. Setting it back on the table, she found Kelly approaching her bed, the expression on her face quite serious. "What is it?" Meg asked, sitting down next to her.

"I have something important to tell you, and I'm not quite sure how you're going to react," the redhead said with a heavy sigh.

Meg was quite concerned, her mind jumping all over the place. "Has my mother let you go?"

"Oh, goodness, no. Nothing like that," Kelly assured her.

"Well, what is it then? It isn't my uncle is it?"

Kelly's eyes grew quite large. By now, everyone in Southampton seemed to know that her uncle had nearly forced himself upon a young lady at Christina Edgebrook's coming out, an act that had him banned from every social activity ever since and had lost the factory quite a deal of money in contracts pulled away by outraged individuals, friends of the Edgebrooks and the young lady in question.

"Do you honestly think I wouldn't have told you immediately if he were to try something like that with me?" Kelly nearly spat.

Meg considered the question and then shrugged it away. She still had never told Kelly, so yes, she could understand. "What is it then?"

"I've met someone," Kelly said, a small smile pulling at the corners of her mouth.

Confused, Meg asked, "What's that now?"

"A man. I've met a man," Kelly clarified.

"I've met dozens of men," Meg replied, leaning back against the headboard. "Each time I attend a ball, I meet half a dozen more. So what?"

"So what? Oh, Meg, you are truly ridiculous," Kelly said picking up a nearby pillow and tossing it at the younger girl. "I mean to say, I've met a man and fallen in love, Meggy!"

This had her sitting bolt upright. "What? You've fallen in love? How is that possible, Kelly? You're only..."

"Nineteen!" Kelly reminded her. "I'm plenty old enough to be married. You're nearly there yourself, though one wouldn't know it from the amount of running about you still do. At any rate, I've met a man and he's proposed, and we are to be married soon."

Meg leaned back again, taking it all in. The thought of Kelly getting married.... Before she knew it, she'd be having babies and then going off and leaving her. She really couldn't think of much to say. She was happy for her friend, but at the same time, she hated the thought of losing her. At last, she finally replied, "Well, congratulations. I hope he is a nice fellow."

"Oh, he's wonderful," Kelly answered, dreamily. She tossed

herself back onto the bed and interlaced her fingers behind her head. "He has strawberry blonde hair and gorgeous eyes. His laugh is so robust, yet he's just the gentlest man you could ever imagine. I really do love him, Meg," she said, turning to face her.

Pursing her lips, the closest thing to a smile she could muster, Meg asked, "What's his name?"

"Daniel," Kelly sang. "Daniel O'Connell. He's a carpenter. He has his own place, a little one, over by my mother's. He does quite well for himself. I met him a few months ago when I went to visit my ma."

"Why didn't you ever say anything?" Meg asked, crossing her arms.

"I don't know," Kelly shrugged, returning her gaze to the ceiling. "I wasn't certain how he felt about me at first. And then, well, I was afraid I might ruin it if I spoke about it to anyone else. Then, when he asked for my hand yesterday, well, I couldn't wait to get back here to tell you. You're the first person I thought of to tell, Meg, though I did see my mother first so she knows."

Meg let out a loud humph and managed, "I suppose I should be happy for you. And I am. I truly am. I'm just... surprised. I had no idea. And you honestly think you'll stay on here, then?"

"Oh, yes," Kelly assured her. "We've talked about it. I'll stay on here for as long as need be—at least a few more years, I'd say. Then, when we've saved up enough money, Daniel and I have decided to go to America."

"America?" Meg repeated, her eyes like saucers.

"Yes. I know it's far—and a very expensive endeavor—but I have a cousin there, and Daniel and I have decided that we're just the sort of adventurous people who could really make it work."

"Adventurous?" Meg repeated. "You've never even left Southampton except for the few times you've traveled to the mainland with me or home to Ireland with your mother. I'd hardly say you're adventurous."

Kelly sat up, looking at her sharply. "That's not true, Meg, and

125

you know it. I love a good adventure. I just haven't had the means to explore much, that's all."

"Well, I know you about as well as anyone does, and I certainly wouldn't call you adventurous."

"Now you're just being mean," Kelly said, crossing her arms. "Just because I don't steal horses and ride about in the muck...."

"I haven't done that in years!"

"Still, I may not have the means you have to make my wanderlust known, but it's there nonetheless."

"And I think you'll go to America and miss your mother and be on the next boat back!"

"I can't speak to you when you're in one of your selfish moods!" Kelly practically shouted as she jumped up off the bed.

"Selfish? I'm selfish? You're the one who just said she's going to leave me here with these... these monsters!"

"I never said that!" Kelly retorted. "Good grief, Meg! Why does everything have to revolve around you? Why can't you just be happy for me for once?"

"Perhaps you should go find a pot to scrub or a stocking to mend!" Meg shot back, ignoring the question because she knew in her heart she was being selfish, but she couldn't face that just now.

"You really can be horrid sometimes, Mary Margaret Westmoreland!" Kelly yelled as she approached the bedroom door.

All she could think of to say was, "Get out—and stay out!" and when Kelly slammed the door behind her, she flew out of the bed and ran over, grabbing the doorknob and pulling it open. "Only I get to slam my door!" and forced it to again as loudly as possible.

Turning away, she took a deep breath. Clarity began to sink in, and she couldn't help but hope that her mother was out for the day or else she'd likely be upstairs giving them both the what for. She knew she needed to be happy for Kelly, but it was so difficult when it seemed that Kelly was realizing everything Meg had always wanted for herself. She'd fallen in love with a good man—one she'd chosen for herself, and even though he was a simple carpenter, he was a hard worker who loved her back and wanted to do whatever she needed to be happy. Now, she was talking of going to America, and even though that had always been Meg's dream, she hadn't bothered to tell Kelly that she hoped one day they would both go off to America together, to start again, as sisters, to find love and happiness together. Now, here she was, all alone again, wondering if she had the strength or courage to defy her parents and run away to America on her own.

It crossed her mind that it should actually make it easier to do so if Kelly were there waiting, but what if she and Daniel weren't ready to go when Meg was? What if they had a child and decided to stay so that they'd be near Patsy? What if... there were a lot of what ifs, and thinking about them made Meg's head hurt and her heart ache.

She crossed back over to the table where Charlie's letter sat, still unopened. She knew by now that her mother wasn't coming to yell at her or else she'd have already made it up the stairs. Picking up the envelope, she noticed it was a bit heavier than usual and she decided it must contain a picture. With a sigh, she pulled it open, thinking perhaps hearing from Charlie would bring about some normalcy.

AUGUST 28, 1907

DEAR MISS WESTMORELAND,

I HOPE that this letter finds you well. I apologize that it has been several months since I have written. My coursework at Harvard is quite demanding. I've also made a number of friends, and we've been enjoying the new freedom college life allows. I don't know how things are in Southampton, but over here, things are changing. I see it all around me. New inventions are making lives easier. New ways of thinking are allowing more independence. New music, new modes of transportation. It's all rather exciting.

127

My father has mentioned the fact that you are nearly sixteen now and that a formal announcement of our engagement wouldn't be unheard of at this point, though you are still a bit young. I should like to know your thoughts and feelings about this. It would be wonderful if we could meet in person before the announcement, though I'm not exactly certain how that may work. I've enclosed a recent photograph of myself. It would be lovely to have something current of you. You certainly do a nice job of staying out of the newspapers.

I'm afraid my time is up, and I need to get back to studying. I hope you are doing well. Would love to hear from you soon.

Sincerely,

Charles J. Ashton

MEG PLACED the letter on the table and picked up his photograph. He certainly was a handsome young man, but she couldn't help but feel sorry for him. It was difficult to tell through a letter—one that perhaps someone had also read before he sent it, though she doubted it since it was post-stamped Cambridge and his parents were still in New York—exactly how he felt about this entire arrangement. Meeting him in person would be nice. It would give her the opportunity to discuss the entire situation with him and see if he truly wanted to marry her or if he was just going along with what his parents had to say.

After all, she might have done a good job of staying out of the papers, but he did not. There were articles about him spending time out and about the city with his friends, the philanthropic endeavors he partook in and helped to organized, even discussion of his pristine academic career. Surely, while he was out and about enjoying galas and events, driving around in his new motor coach, he had met a girl or two. Wouldn't one of those lovely ladies be a better option than marrying someone he'd never met who lived across the ocean and honestly wasn't nearly good enough for him by society's standards?

"By society's standards," Meg mumbled. Who was she fooling?

She wasn't good enough for him by anyone's standards—even her own. If he had any idea the things she'd done, the problems she'd caused, the things that had happened to her, he'd certainly be just as happy to go on with his life without her in it as she would be to have the freedom of her own choice.

Nevertheless, this was the predicament they were in. She couldn't possibly send him a letter to let him know that she was dreadful, nor could she even consider letting him know that her mother and uncle had ruined the company he was supposed to take over. If he was just looking to make some money through her father's business, he'd be in for a rude awakening. Attempting to tell him anything about herself or her family would absolutely not make it through the scrutinizing eye of the house police. Meeting in person, however, now that was different. If she could have him to herself for a few moments, perhaps she could manage to explain a few things to him that would certainly have him scurrying for the exits as quickly as his athletic legs could carry him.

Glancing at the photograph one more time, she decided to go downstairs and see if she could find her mother and ask her if it would be possible for her to meet Charlie at last. After all, her mother should be excited about this match. She had the opportunity to look important in front of society again and possibly take some of the light off of the scandal her uncle had caused nearly a year ago.

Her mother was nowhere to be found, but when she walked into the kitchen, she found Kelly there scrubbing a pot, and she couldn't tell if the beads of liquid running down her face were tears or perspiration. She instantly felt awful for how she'd treated her friend.

Noticing her entering the room, Kelly shouted over her shoulder, "Don't worry. As soon as I finish this pot, I'm off to find a stocking."

Leaning on the counter next to her, Meg said, "I'm sorry, Kelly." She ignored her, still concentrating on the pot, scrubbing so viciously, Meg thought she might tear a fingertip off. "I only said those things because... because I was afraid of losing you. That's all."

"I already told you that will never happen," Kelly replied, setting the pot back into the sink and turning to face her.

"I know, but you can imagine, from my perspective, how worrisome that might be, can't you?"

"Yes, and that's why it was difficult for me to tell you. But I was honestly hoping that you would be happy."

"I am happy," Meg assured her. "I'm very happy for you. I wish you nothing but a lifetime of happiness."

"You do?"

"Yes, of course."

"You're certain?"

Meg held out her arms, and despite the drippy soap bubbles clinging to her hands, Kelly threw her arms around her. "You're the closest thing to a sister I've ever had. We may not look alike, or talk alike, but we are family just the same."

Kelly took a step back so she could look into her eyes. "You will always be my family, I promise. Whether we go to America ahead or behind you, nothing will keep us apart. Not the widest ocean or the holiest boat."

Meg giggled, as that was not exactly what she was expecting to hear. She put her head on Kelly's shoulder and embraced her even tighter, hoping that what she said was true. She honestly couldn't imagine her life without Kelly in it.

A noise at the front door drew her attention, and Kelly pulled away. "If that's the mistress, I best get back to my pots."

Meg nodded and stepped away, absently brushing at the back of her dress, which was slightly wet from the suds. She entered the foyer to see her mother taking her gloves off, speaking to Tessa about something that seemed rather important. All she heard was, "If that price doesn't work for that baker on Tenth Street, then go to the one on Fourth. I don't like that one nearly as much, but I won't be overcharged either."

"Yes, madam," Tessa said as she approached the door, clearly on her way back out again.

"Oh, Mary Margaret. Just the person I needed to see," Mildred said, as if she were stepping into a place of business.

"I needed to speak to you as well, Mother," Meg replied.

Her mother began to walk into the parlor, and Meg followed, not sure if her comment had even registered. Mildred sat down in her chair and gestured for Meg to sit across from her where he uncle used to sit. Lately, he did not spend as much time in the parlor as he once did. Now, most nights, he left work and went straight to the pub, and they didn't hear from him until around midnight. Of course, Meg only assumed he was actually going to work. There was really no way to tell for sure.

"Mary Margaret," Mildred began, "Your uncle and I have decided to go ahead and have your coming out party this year, for your sixteenth birthday."

"What?" Meg asked, hardly believing her ears. "But why?"

"Well, while we know that many young ladies are waiting until they are eighteen or nineteen, your circumstances are slightly different, so we've decided to go ahead and have it done now. Then, whenever the Ashtons determine it is time to announce your engagement, we'll be ready."

"So you've decided to go ahead with the arrangement then?" Meg asked, leaning forward in her seat, still doubting her own understanding.

"Your uncle and I have discussed it at great lengths. It does seem that it would be the most appropriate choice."

"You're just willing to hand over father's company to them?" Meg asked, a bit outraged at the thought.

"Meg, you know very little of what has transpired between your father and Mr. Ashton and between your uncle and I and the Ashtons," Mildred replied, sighing as if speaking to her daughter was exhausting.

"Please, enlighten me," Meg insisted, leaning back and opening her arms wide. "I've got plenty of time."

"Actually, you don't. We're due over at the Townly residence in just a bit. They've invited us for tea."

Meg couldn't help but shake her head. Even before her uncle's reprehensible action, she'd never felt a part of the group, never felt comfortable with others of her "social standing." Of all the families to have to endure, at least Beatrice and Alise were tolerable. She even quite liked Alise from time to time, though now didn't feel like one of those times.

"You should change your gown. Get Kelly to help you."

Her mother's voice cut through her thoughts, and Meg wanted to throw something at her for being so dismissive. "I want to meet Charlie," she blurted. That wasn't at all what she had practiced saying over and over in her head as she had made her way down the stairs early, but nonetheless, that is what had come out.

"Beg pardon?" Mildred asked, her eyes wide in astonishment.

"I said, 'I want to meet Charlie.' It's only fair that the pair of us get to meet each other before the entire country—two countries—begins congratulating us on our engagement."

"Oh, absolutely not," Mildred replied. "I know what you're on about, Miss Mary Margaret. You think that if you can get him alone, you can convince him not to marry you, don't you?" Meg said nothing, only stared at her mother in shock, unable to understand how she could guess such a thing.

Mildred laughed, but it came out more like a cackle than anything sounding remotely like pleasure or merriment. "You seem to forget, Mary Margaret, I know you. I know more than you give me credit for, young lady. You will meet Charles Ashton when your uncle and I decide that it is time and not a moment before then. Now, go upstairs and get ready for tea."

Meg stood, a defiant look in her eyes, her fists clutched at her side. Every part of her wanted to scream at her mother, "If you know what I'm on about—if you know my secrets—why did you do nothing while I was tortured? Why do you stand by while others are harmed under your own roof? Why do you look at me like an insect you'd like to step on instead of as your child, the only semblance of my father you have left?"

Instead, she said nothing, and fighting back the tears she would never allow to fall, she made her way upstairs to change her dress as instructed.

CAMBRIDGE

Though it was still rather hot outside for a late September day, Charlie didn't mind the temperature so much as long as they sat in the shade. Visiting the park in the spring or late fall was always more appealing—even the winter was generally better than the summer—but this was the best place for him to meet Stella without anyone of consequence taking note, so he waited on their park bench for her now, his thoughts darting back between the conversation he'd recently had with his father and the letter he'd sent to Mary Margaret a few weeks ago.

The last year and a half had been a whirlwind ever since Quincy introduced him to a new sort of social life he'd never experienced before. While part of him wanted to blame Quincy for being a bad influence, Charlie knew that his friend had only been the catalyst. A young man with money, influence, a new set of wheels, and eventually, alcohol, along with a few girls with coy smiles, and it didn't take a scientist to know that things were bound to erupt. He was thankful that things had not gotten out of hand enough to embarrass his family or get him into serious trouble. His grades hadn't even suffered, which was also remarkable.

Charlie had spent most of the summer out with his friends, rarely seeing his parents and not abiding by any sort of a curfew. Right before the fall semester started, his father asked to speak with him and reminded Charlie that he had a duty and a reputation to withhold. It was time to start taking things seriously again. It was time Charlie remembered that he and his father were both bound to a promise from many years ago.

At first, Charlie wanted to argue and tell his father he no longer wished to uphold the obligation. But the longer John spoke, the more Charlie began to remember what it felt like to be truly close to his father. He had looked up to him so immensely as a child. When his father pulled out a butterscotch and handed it to him, Charlie realized he needed to turn things around. He had renewed his promise to his father that day. He would marry Mary Margaret Westmoreland, just as his father had promised hers. He would concentrate on his studies again and stop wasting his time out with his friends.

Now, he just needed to convince two girls that this was the best course of action.

While it would be more difficult to get a feel for Mary Margaret's convictions, he knew that Stella would certainly speak her mind. Though Charlie hadn't been spending his time with her exclusively, and they certainly weren't an item, he knew she had strong feelings for him, and he had for her as well. He had realized, however, even before his father reminded him that he was already spoken for, that Stella truly wasn't the one for him. While he loved her daring spirit, he wanted a wife who was a bit more traditional, a bit more relaxed. Stella would make a very good wife to someone one day, but it wouldn't be him.

"Sorry I'm running behind," Stella said, breathing heavily as she sat down on the bench about a foot's distance from him. "I had trouble getting out of the dorm."

This happened fairly often considering how closely the girls at Radcliffe were watched, particularly in the daytime during the week, so Charlie just shrugged. "It's all right. Gave me a few moments to collect my thoughts."

"I haven't seen much of you since school has been back in session. Is everything all right?" she asked, leaning a bit towards him.

He noticed her hair looked longer, as if it had grown over the summer and he hadn't yet noticed. She had it down—a style she'd been wearing a lot lately, one his mother would never have approved of—and it flew about her face in brunette wisps with the breeze. "I've been attempting to concentrate on my studies."

"I'm sure they've missed you," she giggled, alluding to the fact that he certainly hadn't spent much time studying in the most recent semesters. "Is everything all right, Charlie? You look... anxious."

There was really no point in being elusive, so Charlie decided to just have at it. "I had a conversation with my father a few weeks ago, and it's been weighing on my mind quite heavily lately."

"Is he well?" she asked, clearly concerned.

"He's fine," Charlie assured her, watching her relax a bit. "Stella, we've spent a lot of time together over the last year, year and a half, and there's something I want to make sure you are aware of. You see... I have a prior arrangement...."

"Mary Margaret Westmoreland?" Stella asked, sitting up straight, her hands folded in her lap.

Charlie looked at her, his eyes wide. "How did you know?"

"Everyone knows, don't they?" she asked, shrugging. "I don't think it is a secret, is it?"

"Well, no, I suppose not," Charlie mumbled. "But I thought you must not be aware or else...."

"Charlie, just because you're promised to some girl who lives an ocean away that you've never met doesn't mean that I can't enjoy a bit of time with you, does it?" she asked, leaning back against the bench.

"So you've known all along?"

"Of course."

"Well, why didn't you ever say anything?"

"What was I supposed to say? How's your soon-to-be fiancée? Oh, that's right. You wouldn't know because you've never met her. It's all a bit of fluff, isn't it, Charlie?"

Charlie could feel the heat rising in his face. He wasn't sure if he was simply embarrassed or if she had actually offended him, but he was bound to find out. "No, it isn't, Stella. It's real. She's real. Just because I haven't met her doesn't mean she doesn't exist."

"Funny, I remember saying the same thing about Saint Nicholas when I was three," Stella muttered.

"What is that supposed to mean?" Charlie asked, turning to face her, his inner question answered.

"Nothing, only that I don't believe that you will marry her, that's all."

"That's all?"

"Yes, that's all. And I'm not the only one, Charlie. Surely, you must know. Everyone thinks it's a farce. Especially since her uncle has made quite a name for himself as nothing more than a dirty old man. The business is washed up, and so is her family, Charlie. Why in God's green earth would your father honor a promise he made to a man that's been dead these ten years to marry you into a family that isn't anywhere near a proper match? It just doesn't make any sense."

Charlie had done his best to keep his temper under control, but the longer she spoke, the angrier he felt. "Stella, my father is a man of his word—and more importantly, so am I. I've promised Mary Margaret Westmoreland that we will marry someday, and I intend to keep that promise."

Stella's eyes grew wide, as if she couldn't believe what he was saying. "I've never seen you so upset before, Charlie," she managed after a moment.

"I'm not upset—I'm angry," he replied, pounding his fist down on the bench on the side away from her.

They sat there in silence for a few moments. Charlie took deep breaths and tried to control his temper while Stella looked about in confusion. After a while she finally said, "Well, Charlie, why is it that you've brought me here today? You've been intended to Miss Westmoreland for a very long time. What's different now?"

His response was slow and calculated, and he did not turn to look at her as he spoke. "I don't think we should spend any more time in each other's company."

She was silent again for a very long time, and he could hear her breathing heavily, as she had when she'd first sat down. "I can't believe you're saying that, Charlie," she finally managed to say.

"I'm sorry..."

"No, don't," she cut him off, spinning to face him. He turned to look at her for a moment but then looked away again. "I don't want you to be sorry for my sake. You will be sorry—but only because you've made a horrible decision, Charles."

She only used his given name when she was particularly upset, and he hated to hurt her like this. But given the revelations of their conversation, he was quite confident he was making the right choice. If she couldn't understand the importance of upholding his word, of honoring his father's wishes, then she certainly wasn't the girl for him.

"I suppose I'll see you around then," Stella muttered as she stood.

He stood, too, as it was the polite thing to do, absently thinking he probably would not see her around as he intended to avoid any such event she might be present at, though he did see her on campus every so often. "Goodbye, Stella," he said as she turned to walk away.

She didn't respond, nor did she look back as she slowly made her way towards the edge of the park and back to Radcliff. In all of the time they'd spent together, he'd seen the gamut of emotions from elation to anger. This was the first time he could ever remember seeing her so crestfallen. He truly hoped that, in a day or two, she would recover and be back to her happy-go-lucky self, and while he hated being the cause of such lamentation, he knew he had done the right thing.

Now, he only had to prove her wrong, prove everyone wrong it seemed, and actually marry Mary Margaret. Of course, it would be easier to do so if he actually had the opportunity to meet her first. He anxiously awaited her response, hopeful that she would agree to find a way to visit or at the very least consent to him traveling to Southampton on his next holiday. Seeing her face would put aside all question of whether or not she really did exist, and he had to admit that he had even begun to wonder about that himself.

CHAPTER THIRTEEN

SOUTHAMPTON

Meg had never liked playing the piano, though she reputedly did it well. Now that her coming out party was over, and no suitors had begun showing up because they felt it was a waste of time, she decided practicing piano could possibly keep her mind off of what was—or was not—happening. After all, the purpose of coming out was telling the world she had learned everything she'd ever need to know. So why keep up the pretenses of studying with a governess who wasn't any more qualified to give instruction than Meg herself?

Her mother had agreed and sent Ms. Cunningham off just a week after Meg's ball. The event had been a lovely affair, though crowded. Her house wasn't made to hold so many people, and even though the crowd wasn't what it might have been if her uncle hadn't soiled their reputation, there were still nearly a hundred people present.

Meg honestly didn't care, though. None of it mattered, and the more she dwelt on the fact that none of the gentlemen who had asked her to dance or had looked at her longingly would ever drop his card at the door, the more disheartened she became. Her mother had insisted that she write Charlie back and say she would not meet him in person until after they were engaged—which made little or no sense to her—and when his father had attempted to contact her mother to see if they could make the formal announcement, she had put him off again.

Her mother either had something even more vile up her sleeve than even Meg could imagine, or she honestly had lost her mind.

She was willing to bet on the second.

As she sat plunking the keys, she heard the front door open, and since she wasn't expecting her mother back for an hour or so and the servants were all busy in the kitchen, she decided she had better go see who it was.

Pushing the bench under the piano, she approached the foyer. She could smell the alcohol before she even rounded the corner, and she froze in her tracks, hoping he wouldn't notice her and she could sneak away.

"Mary Margaret, is that you?" Uncle Bertram called, his speech slurred.

Her first instinct was to try to do an impression of Tessa or one of the other girls, but before she could say anything at all, he was standing in the doorway before her. "Yes, Uncle," she said, hoping the fear wasn't still evident in her voice. She'd be seventeen later that year and he still evoked a terror in her the same way he had that first night he'd forced himself into her room a decade ago.

"Seen the paper have you?" he asked thrusting it at her, losing his balance and nearly falling as he did so.

She took it, wondering what in the world could possibly be in the paper that would bring him home drunk in the middle of the day, hoping it wasn't another scandal that might embarrass her, too. She didn't see it at first, but then, on the bottom of the front page, in the portion that usually highlighted society news, she saw what he was referring to. "Ashton, Westmoreland to Marry," she read aloud.

"Yep, that's the one. Keep reading," Bertram ordered, stumbling backwards.

"Mr. John Ashton of New York City announced earlier this week that his son, Charles, 19, will marry Miss Mary Margaret Westmoreland, 16, of Southampton, daughter of the late Henry Westmoreland and Mildred Truesdale Westmoreland. Though no date has been set yet, Mrs. Westmoreland reports that her daughter is beside herself with joy over what will surely be a marriage founded on wedded bliss." Meg wasn't sure if she should be more outraged at the announcement appearing in the papers before she was aware that the engagement had taken place or the fact that the paper had written about her life as if it were a sappy romance novel.

"She's done it now," Bertram shouted, swaying. "She thinks she can do whatever she wants, and there's nothing I can do about it."

Meg could only assume he was talking about her mother, and while she was confused because she had been under the impression that he wanted her to marry Charlie, she didn't dare ask why.

"This is my company," he spat, continuing to slur his speech. "My company. My house. My money!"

Seeing that he was growing angrier and out of control, Meg took a step backwards towards the stairs. He looked up at her as if he just realized she was in the same room. "And you're mine, too," he said, his eyes narrowing in on her. Just as she placed her foot on the bottom stair, he lurched for her, knocking her off balance. She fell hard, onto the uneven surface of the stairs, her uncle on top of her.

Meg began to panic. The weight of him on top of her brought back memories she had worked so hard to force into the deepest crevices of her mind. She could feel his hands begin to crawl up her body, but this time she knew she could fight him off, could get away. "No!" she shouted, and as he reached up with one hand, she kicked him, hard. He fell backwards, taking some of his weight off of her, and she took off up the stairs as fast as she could.

Her body ached from the fall, and with tears streaming down her face, she was having trouble with her footing. She slipped, and as she went down hard on her right knee, her left leg went flailing behind her. It was enough. He grabbed her ankle and began to pull himself up toward her. Meg began to kick and scream, but despite his inebriation, her uncle seemed much stronger than her. Just as he regained his grip on her, a voice called out from the adjoining parlor, "Miss Mary Margaret, are you all right?"

Knowing that Tessa was on her way into the room must have been enough to startle him. He let go of her, and Meg scrambled to her feet, fixing her gown, just as Tessa entered the foyer. "Goodness, what happened?" the servant asked, seeing Bertram still sprawled on the stairs.

"Uncle Bertram... fell," Meg stuttered. "I think he's all right, but I'm not certain."

"Oh, my," Tessa said, rushing over to see if he was okay. He was starting to pull himself to his feet, and once she saw that he was all right, the servant returned her gaze to Meg, who was still standing a few steps up. "Did you fall as well?"

"I was... trying to help him," she replied. "I think we're all right."

Tessa's stare told Meg that she wasn't quite buying the story, but she could see no reason to get Tessa involved in the situation. She'd gotten enough women hurt over her situation in the past. There was no reason to do it again now. "Well, so long as you're both unharmed."

"Yes," Meg, stammered. "Yes, thank you, Tessa."

Tessa picked up the newspaper off the floor and handed it to her uncle, and as she began to ask if there was anything he needed, Meg retreated to her room, the irony of hiding from the monster in her room not lost on her.

Once she was seated on her bed, she began to take some deep breaths and felt better. Though she knew she'd have to worry about attacks again that evening, and perhaps every evening until she left Southampton, she felt relatively safe for the moment. Thank goodness that was over.

Except it wasn't.

"Meg? Is everything all right? I was outside, and I thought I heard you scream."

It was Kelly, and one look at the concern in her face and Meg couldn't hold back the tears any more. Ten years' worth of pent up anguish came flooding out. Kelly rushed to her side, wrapping her arms around her, hushing her, reassuring her everything was all right.

Even if she'd wanted to, Meg couldn't have managed to tell Kelly what had happened, what had been happening. She didn't have to, however. A few minutes into Meg's break down, Kelly pushed her back so that she could look her in the face. "Meg?" she began, "What's happened? Has someone hurt you?"

Meg couldn't speak, so she shook her head "no" furiously, afraid that Kelly might do something they would both regret if she knew the truth.

Suddenly, she did.

"It's your uncle isn't it?" she asked, her face turning almost as fiery red as her hair. "Oh, my God! That bastard!"

"No, Kelly," Meg cried out. "Please, calm down."

"Calm down? Calm down! All these years—he's been hurting you, the way he did those other little girls, hasn't he? That son of a bitch!"

Before Meg could stop her, Kelly was up and flying out of her room. She screamed after her to stop, but Kelly was infuriated, and even if Meg hadn't been sore from the fall and blinded by her tears, she wouldn't have been able to keep up. A few moments later, she heard Kelly yelling from the parlor, and then her uncle shouting back. Meg hurried to the staircase, hoping she could stop him before he hurt her friend, but a few seconds later, she heard the loud, unmistakable *thunk* of fist hitting bone, and Kelly began to scream.

Meg rushed down the stairs in time to see her uncle rushing out the front door as quickly as a drunkard could go. She ran into the parlor and found Kelly lying on the floor, her hands grasping her face.

"Oh, my God! What did he do?"

Kelly said nothing, only stared at her as blood gushed through her fingers. As Tessa came in, Meg realized her face wasn't the only place that was bleeding and shouted, "Get the doctor!"

NEW YORK CITY

"I can't make heads or tails of it," John Ashton was saying as he sipped a whisky in his study, Charlie and Pamela seated nearby. "She swears she's not the one who contacted the newspapers, but if she didn't, then who did?"

"Why would she make a declaration in the press—in Southampton, London, and New York—and then deny it? It honestly makes no sense at all," Pamela agreed, shaking her head.

"Well, what did she say when you asked her if she intended to honor the content of the newspaper article?" Charlie asked. Though he thought it was ridiculous of Mrs. Westmoreland to deny making the announcement of his engagement to her daughter public, when clearly she had to have done it since his parents had not, what really mattered was whether or not this meant he was, in fact, engaged to Mary Margaret, and what should happen next.

"She said it would be difficult to take back now. It really is a struggle carrying on a conversation with someone via telegraph. I am not exactly sure what that meant, but I suppose it means that you and Mary Margaret are officially engaged," his father explained, setting his glass down on the side table.

"And will I be allowed to travel to Southampton to meet her then? Have we set a date? She's not quite seventeen yet, is she Father?" Charlie asked, a million questions burning in his mind.

"She will be seventeen in September," his mother confirmed. "What did she say about a visit?"

"She didn't answer," John replied with a shrug. "Likewise, Mrs. Westmoreland ignored my question of a date. As soon as she stopped responding to my telegraphs, I went to meet with my lawyer. He said that she had not formally removed her inquiry into the will, and as far as he knew, she was still disputing it."

"Maybe she had to leave the telegraph office, and she'll answer in a day or two," Charlie offered, hopeful that she would give some sort of a response to the two most important questions.

"Possibly," John agreed.

"Perhaps she just hasn't given word yet that she'd like to withdraw her attorneys from the case. It has been nearly a decade since she started looking into the possibilities of getting the will revoked. Maybe she's forgotten she even hired an attorney to begin with," Pamela reasoned aloud.

"I think you give her too much credit, darling," John said, smiling fondly at his wife. "I think Mrs. Westmoreland can't decide what she wants. The company is failing, her brother-in-law is ruining the family reputation and dragging her name through the mud. And then there's the question of losing her daughter. It's possible the thought of sending her only child to live thousands of miles away amidst strangers is too much. She may worry about how much she would miss Mary Margaret."

"You should offer Mrs. Westmoreland a place here," Pamela replied, realizing her husband might be right. She couldn't imagine what it would be like to have an ocean separating her from either of her children indefinitely. It was difficult enough to have Grace upstate.

John nodded, scratching his head through thinning dark hair. "That's a lovely idea. Perhaps if she knows she will be able to come to New York with Mary Margaret she'll feel more comfortable."

"What of her uncle? Do we want him here as well?" Charlie asked. He wasn't exactly sure what all the man had been accused of, but he did know he had a less than stellar reputation.

"I should hope he would want to stay in Southampton and continue to oversee the day-to-day operations of the factory, though I'm certain you wouldn't want him to truly be in charge of anything," his father replied.

145

Charlie considered that response. He certainly wouldn't want Bertram to continue running the plant if this was the best he could do, but he also didn't want to completely take the Westmoreland out of Westmoreland Textiles, especially since he didn't really want to take over the business at all. "It's worth an offer," Charlie shrugged.

"I will bring it up the next time I send word," John agreed. "In the meantime, I suppose this doesn't change things too much. There's no sense in planning a wedding when we have no timeline or date. There's not much else we can do until Mildred responds to my inquiry."

"We should go there."

"What's that?" Charlie's father asked, as if he hadn't heard his son correctly.

Charlie was certain he had heard, but he repeated the phrase again, giving his father the opportunity to let his declaration sink in. "We should go there. She hasn't agreed to a meeting, but if we were to just show up at their doorstep, surely she'd let us in."

"Your father tried that once before," Pamela explained. "Several years ago. He went to their home, and Mrs. Westmoreland said she only had a moment, didn't even invite him in."

"Yes, I spoke to her on the front stoop. It was... humiliating at best."

"I wasn't aware of that," Charlie said, hanging his head, his hopes dashed.

"If I had other business to take care of in Southampton, it would certainly be worth it, but at present I don't," John said, though his expression said he was thinking about any potential prospects.

"What about Dexter Townly?" Charlie asked, a recent conversation he had had with his father coming to mind. "Didn't you say that you were considering partnering with him to do some of your manufacturing in the London plant?"

"Dexter Townly..." John repeated, scratching his chin. "That's right. I met him at a gala downtown a few months ago. Nice enough fellow. I'm not sure if his company can do what I need it to...."

"What better way to find out than to visit for yourself?" Charlie asked.

John considered his son's recommendation, continuing to stroke his chin as if pulling on an invisible beard. After a few moments he said, "I suppose that wouldn't hurt. I've got some free time coming up in July without a lot in my schedule. I could go then."

"We," Charlie corrected.

"What's that?" John asked.

"I'm coming with you."

SOUTHAMPTON

Two long days passed between the incident between Kelly and Uncle Bertram without Meg being allowed to see her friend. As soon as the doctor had arrived, he'd assessed the situation and moved her to the sofa in the parlor. After the bleeding was controlled, she'd been moved to her room. Daniel and Kelly's mother had been allowed to visit, but the doctor explained he thought it best if everyone else allow her to rest. She'd overheard him explaining to Mildred, "If she isn't allowed to get some sleep, she'll lose the baby for sure."

The baby. Kelly was carrying a child, and she hadn't told Meg yet. Now that she was allowed to speak to her friend, she wasn't sure if she should say anything about it at all for fear of upsetting her, but how could Kelly keep such a secret from her?

Patsy was sitting on the end of Kelly's bed when Meg came in, and when she realized who had interrupted their conversation, she smiled, patted her daughter's hand, gave Meg a hug, and then left them alone. Meg took her place, gently sitting down for fear of shaking the bed and making Kelly uncomfortable.

"How are you feeling?" Meg asked?

Kelly had a bandage over her broken nose but the bruise spread out from under the white across her cheeks beneath her eyes. She also had a lump on the back of her head and her mother had been bringing her ice packs consistently to try to keep the swelling down. One was poised behind her head now. "I'm much better today," Kelly replied, readjusting and wincing a bit.

"You gave us a bit of a fright," Meg said, managing a small chuckle, as if it was all harmless.

"I'm sorry," Kelly replied, smoothing the blanket over her lap. "I didn't mean to."

"No, it's okay," Meg interjected. "You've no reason to apologize."

Kelly smiled meekly. "I've always had a bit of a temper."

"You have," Meg agreed. "You're just... spirited. Which is a good thing. Most of the time."

"I wish you would have told me...."

Meg cut her off. "How's Daniel? Did he go back to work?"

Kelly sighed, as if she realized Meg was not going to let her discuss the horrible secret that had brought about the argument with her uncle to begin with. "He did," she said. "His overseer said he could come back at lunch time and check on me. I told him not to bother. I'm fine, but he's worried."

"About the baby?"

"Yes."

Meg shook her head and looked down at the quilted blanket. She absently wondered if Patsy had made it. It must be nice to have a mother who would make you a quilt, who cared enough about you when you were injured to leave work for several days to take care of you.

"I didn't know," Kelly said, bringing Meg back to the conversation.

"What's that?"

"I didn't know about the baby," Kelly clarified. "Before your... I mean, before I fell, I didn't know I was carrying a child."

"Oh," Meg nodded. That explained it. She couldn't well tell her if she didn't know.

"My monthlies have always been sporadic, and I wasn't sure. I had an idea that maybe... but I'm not far enough along to feel anything—any movement or what have you. So I was waiting. I hadn't even mentioned it to my mother or Daniel. I wanted to be sure."

"I understand," Meg said, also concluding that this must mean she was now third on the list of important people when it came to knowing secrets. She reconsidered all that Kelly had said and then, clearing her throat, asked, "What do you mean your monthlies have always been sporadic? What does that have to do with anything?" She wanted to know because hers had been as well, and if that meant she could potentially be pregnant, that could be a problem.

Kelly's eyes widened and then receded, a knowing expression on her face. "Your mother hasn't told you anything, has she?"

"About what?"

"About babies—where they come from."

Meg was sixteen—and a half. She felt like, perhaps, she should know something of how that worked, but she really wasn't quite certain. She hesitantly shook her head.

Kelly smiled, and at first, Meg thought it was because she found her response humorous, but then she realized that she was smiling about the process—the baby making process. And as she began to explain everything to her, in fairly non-specific terms, Meg didn't know what to think or how to feel. She asked several questions, and Kelly answered all of them. Meg was thankful to know there was no way that she could possibly be pregnant, despite having irregular monthlies. When Kelly was finished, she asked, "Why are you smiling?"

"Because—it's wonderful, Meg. When you're with the man who loves you, and that you love with all of your heart—there's nothing quite like it in all the world."

Meg silently hoped that someday she would know what that felt like, though overall the entire description had her both a little nauseated and nervous. It sounded a bit uncomfortable to her. Deciding they'd talked enough about married life, she asked, "Do you think you'll return to duty soon or will you be done now?"

"Oh, no. I should be back in a few days. The doctor said that the bleeding was likely from the fall. He said the baby seems to be strong and healthy and that I have at least another six months to go. Of course, it's hard to tell by listening and an examination. But he feels that the baby will be just fine so long as I take it easy."

"That's good to know," Meg said, relieved that the child should be okay, as well as to hear that Meg would be coming back to work. She had thought she might be gone for good now.

"Your mother said I can stay on so long as I feel comfortable. Apparently, when your uncle finally came back yesterday, he denied everything. He said he wasn't even in the parlor that afternoon and that I must have fallen and hit the corner of a table. Naturally, I chose not to argue with your mother. She knows the truth."

"And... you feel comfortable staying despite what he did to you?"

Kelly held her gaze for a moment and then nodded. Finally, she said, "How could I go and..."

"Leave me here?" Meg finished her sentence for her.

"Yes."

"But if you feel threatened, or in harm's way, you don't have to stay here just for me."

"Meg," Kelly said, leaning forward slightly, careful to keep the ice in place, "I would never leave you. Never. Besides, I don't feel as if your uncle will bother me again. Daniel said he saw him at the tavern last night and made it perfectly clear that if he should so much as look at me sideways, Daniel doesn't care what his last name is or how much money he has."

Meg only nodded, hoping that Daniel's threats were enough to keep her uncle at bay. There was not much anyone could do if he had his mind set on hurting them, at least not in her experience. Daniel was young and strong, though. Surely, he could protect his wife. Though that didn't help her any.

"If he ever touches you again, Meg, you let me know. Do you

understand? Daniel will make sure that he never hurts either of us again."

"All right," Meg said, nodding. There was no way she would ever tell Kelly anything about her uncle, not after what she'd witnessed two days ago. From now on, Meg's secret would stay her secret and hers alone.

"He hasn't bothered you since, has he?"

Meg really didn't like to fib to anyone, particularly not her best friend. But in this case, she couldn't help it. If she told Kelly the truth, that the monster had attacked again the night before, angered by the newspaper and Kelly's attempt to hold him accountable for his actions, Kelly could find herself in harm's way. "No," she managed, praying for forgiveness for her dishonesty.

"Good," Kelly replied, leaning back, seeming to believe her. "He deserves to have his entrails eaten by ants."

Having spent hours and hours imagining all of the different possibilities of punishment for her uncle, Meg neither agreed nor disagreed with the statement aloud; she could think of even worse fates he deserved to suffer, and she knew that one day, he would. But that was for another day, and right now, she needed to let her friend rest. "You should go to sleep. Take care of that wee one."

Kelly was already nodding off, and she simply shook her head, a small smile on her face as her eyes began to close. Meg stood and kissed her lightly on the forehead. "I love you, Kelly. Like a sister," she whispered. Her friend murmured something in response that Meg thought was an agreement, and she smoothed the bed before she made her way out the door, hopeful that this was the last time Uncle Bertram hurt someone she loved.

As the months passed, Kelly recovered nicely, and by late spring she was showing. Though Mildred struggled with displaying kindness to others, she was willing to give some leniency, and Kelly's duties lightened after the incident. Clearly, she had a soft spot in her heart for Patsy, though Meg was a bit surprised to see any evidence that her mother had a heart at all.

When Meg questioned her about the newspaper, Mildred insisted she knew nothing about the article or who had posted it. She said she would inquire to see if the Ashtons had released the information, but whenever Meg brought the subject up again, she would simply change the topic of conversation to something else or pretend not to hear. Meg was certain her mother must have been the one to make the information public, but she couldn't understand why she would do such a thing and then not take responsibility for it. Was she just trying to see how far the Ashtons were willing to go?

Meg continued to make appearances at social get-togethers, quite enjoying herself, considering there was no pressure of having to look or act a certain way in order to gain the interest of suitors. She got plenty of attention from the gentlemen, and after having heard Kelly's explanation about conception, she had grown rather curious about the euphoria her friend described. She certainly wasn't willing to go there, but when Marcus Hayworth had snuck a kiss at a formal last month, she hadn't denied him. She wasn't interested in him romantically, however, and a reminder that she was already spoken for had caused him to cease his amorous advances—or at least to retreat. She still spied him looking at her longingly from time to time, him and a few other young men. She wasn't interested in any of them, though. No, whenever she let her mind explore the possibilities of what Kelly had described to her, it was not Marcus's face that smiled down upon her. Nor was it the stranger in the pictures tucked away in a box in her closet.

It was the strong, blond-headed boy who worked alongside his father in the back garden, and though she had done her best to keep her fantasies to herself, every now and then, she knew he had caught her staring at him through the upstairs window or peeking at him from behind her fan as she climbed into the motor coach.

The more time Meg spent thinking about Ezra, the more she began to dream of running off to America with him by her side. Such thoughts invaded her mind almost nightly, especially after her uncle began to visit her again. Though it was not nearly as frequently as it had been before, it was still happening, now that Charlie Ashton had officially spoken for her. Bertram said she needed to remember who she really belonged to. While Meg was no longer the weak seven-year-old girl, her uncle was amazingly strong for someone his age, and the fear that engulfed her the moment she heard his footsteps at the door paralyzed her, as did the possibility that he might hurt someone she loved again. Though it had crossed her mind that Ezra may well take it upon himself to protect her if she let him in on the secret, she couldn't bear to see anyone else she loved suffer in her name.

One afternoon in June, she sat sipping tea, looking out the parlor window as Ezra weeded one of the gardens, listening to Alise Townly ramble on about her studies and how she was looking forward to going away to boarding school in the fall, when Alise's mother, who was sitting nearby talking to Mildred caught her attention.

"You must be looking forward to seeing the Ashton's next month," Roberta Townly said, placing her teacup back on its saucer delicately.

Mildred looked at Meg, whose eyes were wide with inquisition, and then returned her attention back to her guest. "Next month?" Mildred questioned, as if she had simply lost track of the calendar.

"Oh, yes. Dexter has an appointment with John to discuss working together. I'm not sure exactly what it is about—business talk is so boring, you know—but I just assumed that, if John Ashton is coming all the way to Southampton, surely he'll stop by to visit with you. I believe Charles will be coming as well." With that last bit, she turned her head and smiled at Meg, her eyes twinkling a bit.

"I can't wait to meet him," Alise interjected. "Can you imagine? Charles Ashton at our home?"

Meg looked at the girl as if she had insects crawling out of her nose. "No, I honestly can't imagine," she replied.

"Well, I'm not exactly sure what our plans are," Mildred replied, matter-of-factly. "Mr. and Mrs. Ashton and I correspond frequently. Perhaps something is caught up in the post."

"That's why we always telegraph nowadays," Roberta informed her. "It's so much quicker than waiting on a letter."

"Yes, indeed," Mildred said, her expression guarded and stone-like.

"Someday, perhaps we will have telephones that can call all the way across the ocean. Wouldn't that be something?" Alise chimed in, taking a bite of a biscuit.

"I doubt that will ever happen," Roberta said. "Can you even imagine?"

Wiping her hands on a napkin, Mildred responded, "No, I can't imagine. It seems the world is beginning to close in on us."

As soon as the words were out of her mouth, Meg knew there was no chance she was actually going to meet Charles Ashton next month; her mother would make sure of that. Thinking the Ashtons had actually intended to surprise them, and Alise and her mother had unwittingly sold them out, Meg shook her head. Though she still had no idea why her mother wasn't simply carting her off in exchange for a sum of cash from Charlie and his parents, she was thankful that she was still being used as a pawn in whatever scheme her mother had up her sleeve. The longer Meg could avoid meeting, and consequently marrying, Charles Ashton, the better her chances were at escaping her fate altogether.

JOHN ASHTON HAD FOUND himself in a bit of a predicament. He had to arrange a business meeting with Dexter Townly to ensure his calendar was clear and that he would be in town. Yet, he planned to surprise Mildred Westmoreland while he was in town. Coming out and directly telling Townly that Mildred knew nothing of the visit wouldn't do; it would seem odd and suspicious. Likewise, he couldn't lie and say that he was certainly visiting the Westmorelands or else Townly might feel compelled to bring it up, should he see Mildred or

Bertram at an event. Therefore, he decided to leave the entire topic alone and hope that everything turned out for the best in the end.

As he sat in the Townly home, Charlie at his side, across from Mr. and Mrs. Townly and their two daughters, Beatrice Townly Huxton and Alise, his mind began to wonder. He'd already met with Dexter earlier that day, and while he'd allowed Charlie to have a hand at the negotiations, which had taken slightly longer than it would have taken him to do it himself, an agreement had been reached. Mr. Townly had insisted that they return to his home to meet his family. He said that his younger daughter in particular was looking forward to meeting Charlie.

Now, he was in a rush to get over to the Westmoreland residence and see if he could catch them at home. They had only planned on being in Southampton a few days, and he realized it might take them that long to actually arrange a meeting. Something told him he may have to catch Mildred coming or going in order to find his way into her house and not be left outside on the porch again.

As if reading his mind, Mrs. Townly offered, "It's a shame you won't be able to see Mildred and Mary Margaret while you're in town."

"What's that?" Charlie questioned, nearly choking on his tea.

"The Westmorelands," Mrs. Townly clarified, as if she thought Charlie didn't know who she was referring to. "They are overseas."

Though he was shocked to hear that information, John attempted to steel himself, not wanting to look uninformed. "Yes, it was bad timing on our parts," he managed to say.

"Mary Margaret certainly is a lovely young lady," Mr. Townly offered. "You must be quite pleased about the engagement."

Before Charlie or John could respond, Beatrice made a noise that could only be described as a guffaw or a cluck, and all eyes turned to her. "Pardon me," she said.

"Are you quite all right?" her mother asked.

"Yes, of course," she replied, setting her tea cup aside.

"She only did that because she doesn't think you'll actually marry her, that's all," Alise explained.

"Alise Constance Townly!" Dexter scolded. "Mind your manners."

"That's not true," Beatrice exclaimed. "I've never said such a thing."

"It's quite all right," Charlie replied. "I understand why you might say that."

"Charlie..." John began.

"No, Father, it's no secret that Mary Margaret and I have had a long distance relationship with very little contact. I can imagine it must be difficult for others to understand."

"It's not our place to judge," Mrs. Townly offered, looking at both of her daughters as if she wanted to shake them.

Charlie smiled at her attempt at nicety. "Nonetheless, I understand that people are curious. You can be sure, however, my father and I both are men of our word. Mr. Westmoreland and my father had an agreement, and that agreement shall be fulfilled."

"Well, I certainly hope you aren't married before my coming out," Alise began, her immaturity bubbling to the surface once again, "because I should be ever so happy to have a turn around the ballroom on your arm."

Charlie laughed, and soon the rest of the party had joined in. "I promise you, Alise, when you have your coming out party, I shall be there. And I would be ever so honored to dance with you." He knew she was still young and hadn't even started finishing school yet, but he couldn't help but wonder if he would have even met his fiancée by then. It seemed that fate was bound and determined to keep them apart. Fate—or Mildred Westmoreland.

CHAPTER FOURTEEN

SOUTHAMPTON

From the moment Meg laid eyes on Ruth Ann O'Connell, she was in love. Though she'd never spent much time thinking about what it might be like to be a mother, holding the angelic creature against her heart made her think that she would very much like to have children of her own someday. Ruth was born in the fall of 1908, and now, at nearly six months old, she was beginning to be very active. Though Mrs. Westmoreland insisted that Meg not take time away from important activities—like piano, embroidery, and socializing—she spent as much time with Ruth as she possibly could, particularly since Kelly's duties had increased.

The staff had been cut to just Tessa and a new girl, Charlotte, who wasn't even Meg's age and had very little idea how to take care of a household. This left much work for Kelly and Tessa, and Meg absently wondered why Charlotte wasn't let go, but she thought, perhaps her uncle had taken a liking to her; however, she thought Charlotte was too old for his preference, though she was nearly eighteen now, and that didn't stop him from shadowing her door.

Mr. Bitterly still handled all of the outside work, even though he was getting up in years, and Ezra was around much more frequently now to help him. Meg did her best to ignore him; even if she wasn't already spoken for, it would never do for her to let the servant boy know she had eyes for him. It was difficult to pull those eyes away sometimes, however, particularly if he was working in the sun, which illuminated the golden streaks in his hair and caused him to glisten like a knight in shining armor.

"Meg, are you even listening to me?" Kelly asked, taking Ruth from Meg's arms. "I said, 'Daniel will be home from work soon, and Tessa is almost finished with supper.'"

"Oh, yes," Meg muttered, trying to pull her head out of the clouds. "I'll head downstairs then." She made one more silly face at Ruth, who laughed, and kicked her legs, and then headed down out of the attic.

Her mother had allowed Daniel to move in once Ruth was born, another shock to Meg as she didn't think her mother could show that sort of compassion. She wondered if her mother secretly harbored some guilt about what had happened to Kelly when she'd tried to protect Meg, something her mother had never been brave enough to do.

"There's a letter from Charlie in your room," Kelly called after Meg as she approached the door of the small attic space that now housed an entire family.

Meg stopped for a moment before turning to acknowledge that she had heard and then headed back on her way. It had been a very long time since Charlie had written. She knew he must be upset that her mother had whisked her away to France last summer when he had come to visit. It certainly wasn't Meg's doing—or even her preference—but she could hardly argue with her mother. She had attempted to discuss the situation with her mother so many times, she couldn't possibly count them, but she may as well have been speaking a foreign language because Mildred wouldn't even acknowledge that she was talking.

She found the letter on her pillow, and hesitated to open it. On the one hand, she hoped with each letter that Charlie would say he refused to be her husband and they could call the entire arrangement off. On the other hand, she hated to disappoint her father, and while she wasn't sure whether or not God was looking down on her or not most of the time, she was fairly certain her father was. With a shrug and a sigh, she tossed herself down on the bed and tore the envelope open.

APRIL 9, 1909

DEAR MISS WESTMORELAND,

I APOLOGIZE that it has been quite some time since I have written. I wish that I had an excuse, but in all honesty, it has been out of aggravation more than anything else. I will apologize for my frustration, since I'm certain there was no way you could have guessed that my father and I were planning to pay you a visit on our trip to Southampton, but I was sincerely looking forward to meeting you at last, and when you were not available, it was quite disconcerting.

Mary Margaret, I know that this situation could potentially be frustrating for you, whether or not you have voiced your feelings to your mother and uncle or not. I can understand that. However, our fathers have made a promise to each other, and I feel in my heart that it is our duty to uphold that promise. Regardless of the time we have spent not knowing each other, I believe that we can learn to admire—perhaps even love—each other. I hope that you feel the same way and that you have accepted this path we walk together.

I am sure you are aware that the newspapers have announced our engagement to the world. From time to time, I see an article about myself where your name also appears. Though the world may have *already declared that we are betrothed, I should have liked to have had the opportunity to ask you myself, in person, for your hand. Regardless of how that announcement came to be made, I have not quite considered our engagement official these past months because I was not able to ask you myself. Since a great deal of time has passed, and I still have not been afforded that opportunity, I must ask you in writing. Mary Margaret, will you consent to honoring the promise our fathers made to one another and become my wife at such time our parents deem appropriate? If your answer is yes, then I should like to move forward with planning the wedding. You should know that we are more than happy to have your mother and uncle accompany you to New York City and should be pleased to have them as guests in one of our estate homes for as long as they should like to stay.*

Please answer quickly as I am eager to fully move forward with our arrangement. If your answer is something else, it is quite important that I know that soon as well.

Sincerely yours,

Charles J. Ashton

MEG READ THE LETTER TWICE, the last full paragraph making her sick to her stomach each time she read it. She had always hoped that if her plan to run away didn't work and she was somehow forced to marry Charlie, at least she would be able to escape her mother and uncle. Now, it seemed that she would never get away.

She wanted to crumple the letter, to tear it to a thousand pieces and toss it in the fireplace. However, just as she was about to rip it apart, she heard footsteps behind her.

"Mary Margaret, what did Charles have to say?" her mother asked approaching her bed.

Hating for her mother to see her cry, Meg attempted to snuff her tears out and somehow pull them back from whence they came. Of course, she couldn't manage that, so she wiped them away on the back of her hand. By now, her mother had taken the letter from her and was reading it. Once she'd finished, she handed it back to her daughter, a thoughtful look on her face.

"Well?" Meg asked. "What shall I say?"

"You should say, 'yes.' Of course you plan to follow through with the arrangement."

"I do?" Meg asked.

Mildred folded her arms across her chest. "Mary Margaret, you know this is legally binding. There is nothing either of us can do to prevent it."

"But I thought you didn't want me to...."

"What I want is for you to say yes. We'll worry about the rest later."

"But—you wanted to keep the company. Uncle Bertram...."

"Mary Margaret," Mildred began, clearly losing patience with her daughter, "this will be a long, drawn-out engagement. We shall see what else the Ashtons intend to promise in exchange for your hand. If they're willing to give us a house, perhaps they will be willing to give us more."

Meg wanted to say, "So now you're using them for their money?" but she bit her tongue, listening, as her mother went on.

"While there are pros and cons to any business deal, this one is particularly complicated."

"Because it involves my hand?" Meg asked, thinking perhaps her mother was feeling a bit motherly all of a sudden.

"No, because it involves a potential way to save the company. As you know, we are nearly at our end, Mary Margaret. I could scarcely afford to keep the lamps lit this month. Every penny, every credit extension, is maximized. If the Ashtons can keep us afloat, perhaps we can manage to keep our heads above water a bit longer."

"Why not just move to New York City then and let them take care of us?" Meg asked, dumbfounded.

"Because—I've worked so hard to build what I have here. Despite your uncle's best attempt at ruining our name, in Southampton, we are high society, Meg. In New York, we'll be nothing. No one will know us. Any invitations we get will be out of pity for the Ashton's in-laws."

"But—people will invite you because you will be related to the Ashtons," Meg argued.

"How can I entertain in someone else's estate house?" Mildred shot back, looking down her nose at Meg.

"I'm sure they will find you a suitable home, Mother," Meg countered. Then she realized, she actually seemed to be arguing in favor of moving to New York City—with her mother. Had she become so bitter that she was willing to say whatever it took to prove her mother wrong?

"Mary Margaret, you simply don't understand," Mildred said, a sigh of exhaustion.

Well, that much was certainly true. "All right, Mother," Meg replied. "So you do want me to accept Charlie's official engagement?"

"Yes, and we must ask for part of the bride-price upfront. Now."

Meg was shocked. How could she possibly write Charlie a letter asking for money? "Mother? What in the world will I say?"

"Leave that up to me," Mildred said, her eyes narrowing and a cunning smile pulling at the corners of her mouth.

CAMBRIDGE

Charlie was on his way to the dining hall for the evening meal when he bumped into Quincy. Though they no longer went out together socially, as Charlie had been able to stick with his resolve to stay focused on his studies, they still had several classes together and remained friends. A few months before, when Quincy had feared he'd gotten a young woman pregnant, he had rushed to Charlie for help and advice. Though it turned out to be for nothing, the incident had brought Quincy back to earth a bit, and Charlie noticed that he was not spending as much time at parties as he had been before. It had also brought them closer together.

"How's life?" Quincy asked. "Have you heard from Mary Margaret lately?"

There was a time when Charlie would have assumed the question was asked in ridicule, but not anymore. When Quincy realized that Charlie was serious about his obligation, he had begun to take his side, even though he had been unable to understand why Charlie didn't give up after Mary Margaret dodged his visit.

"Yes, I received a letter today," Charlie replied, his hands buried deep in his trouser pockets.

"Really? What did she have to say?"

Charlie wasn't about to share the entirety of the letter, since parts of it were a bit embarrassing. If he told his friend Mary Margaret had hinted at needing some money for a proper engagement party she would like to throw at her next birthday—a party he certainly couldn't attend because of his studies—and money for a motor coach so that she could be escorted about Southampton properly, he would think she was nothing but a gold digger. Rather than revealing all that, he said, "She only said that she is excited about our engagement and looking forward to spending time with me."

"Wonderful," Quincy said, patting him on the back. "And is she planning on coming over soon?"

"She said that her mother was considering a trip soon, though she wasn't sure when that might be," Charlie replied. What she had actually said was that her mother would consider Charlie's offer to permanently move to New York City and live in one of his family's homes, but again, he didn't feel that Quincy needed to know all that. "What about you?" Charlie asked as they approached the dining hall.

"Oh, I'm doing well," Quincy said, stepping inside. He cleared his throat and looked a little uncomfortable. Charlie stopped in his tracks and turned to look at his friend, a questioning look on his face. Finally, Quincy said, "Charlie, I need to tell you something."

"What is it?" Charlie asked, moving out of the way of another pair of young men entering the hall.

Quincy cleared his throat again, still looking quite uncomfortable. "Charlie, I've asked someone to marry me as well."

Unable to believe his ears, Charlie beamed, patting his friend roughly on the shoulder. He never thought Quincy would settle down, and now here he was engaged to be married. "That's wonderful, Quin! I didn't know you were seeing anyone seriously."

"Well, it's sort of been off and on..."

"I'm so happy—I don't even know what to say," Charlie exclaimed. "Quincy Cartwright, finally becoming a proper gentleman...."

"It's Stella."

Charlie caught himself, thinking perhaps he misheard. His hand froze in midair, just about to pat Quincy on the shoulder again. "What's that?" he stammered.

"It's Stella," Quincy said again, his eyes focused on the ground between their pristinely polished loafers.

"Stella?" Charlie choked. "Pettigrew?'

"I wanted to tell you, I really did..."

"No, it's fine," Charlie managed.

"It's just, we were afraid you'd be upset."

The use of the word "we" when it came to Quincy and Stella—or Stella and anyone, for that matter--made Charlie feel queasy. He took a few deep breaths and tried to pull himself together. "No, I'm not upset. I'm just surprised, that's all. I didn't realize you were seeing each other."

"We haven't been for long," Quincy replied, "but I've always liked her. And well, things just sort of... happened."

Yes, that seemed about right. Things did just sort of happen when it came to Stella Pettigrew. "Quincy, I'm not upset, believe me," Charlie replied, though he really wasn't sure if he was troubled or not. He wasn't certain what he was feeling, other than shock.

"Stella and I were never formal. It's perfectly fine that you're going to... marry her. I'm happy for you. Honestly."

"Are you sure, Charlie?" Quincy asked, hesitantly. "Because your friendship means so very much to me...."

"Yes, I'm sure," Charlie nodded. "Congratulations, old man."

Quincy let out a sigh of relief. "Oh, thank you," he said, pulling Charlie in for a quick embrace. "We are intending to wait until after graduation, so it will be a year or more before we actually wed."

"That seems like an ideal plan," Charlie said, though he was having trouble listening to his friend go on about marrying the girl he once thought he might love.

"I would be honored if you would stand with me when we make it official," Quincy said as they began to walk again.

"Yes, of course," Charlie nodded. "It would be my privilege."

As Quincy thanked him and continued to ramble on about their plans and how he was so happy that Charlie wasn't angry, he had to tune him out. His thoughts went back to the letter and the odd tone Mary Margaret had taken. Though she wasn't outright demanding money, she was beginning to ask for a lot of expensive items. It had never crossed his mind to think that she might only be interested in marrying him because of his money, though it probably should have; she wouldn't be the first woman to want a piece of the Ashton fortune. Still, he had thought she was different. Perhaps it was the fact that she had always known she had no choice that made her press forward now. If she had been imagining spending his money all along, now would be the perfect time to begin spending it in reality. He intended to write her again as soon as he returned from dinner so that he could get a better feel for exactly what she wanted with his money and how much she thought she might need. If nothing else, focusing on Mary Margaret would take his mind off of Stella and Quincy.

CHAPTER FIFTEEN

SOUTHAMPTON

The change in her mother's disposition since Charlie had agreed to begin sending them a bit of money was unbelievable to Meg; it was as if she had transformed into some sort of happy-go-lucky girl. It wasn't what Meg would consider a fortune, but it was enough to make sure necessities were accounted for and the lights stayed on at least.

Mildred had instructed her daughter to describe a party she wanted to have and to ask for enough money for an auto in the first letter. Of course, the money would go to neither of those things. Meg didn't even need a motor coach of her own anyway. She would much rather ride on horseback if she had to go somewhere close by, and her uncle was rarely home anymore, but his own auto was often parked in the garage where she could get Bitterly to drive her if she needed.

In her last letter, she'd asked for enough for a new dress and some proper jewelry, and Charlie had sent it, asking for a picture of her in the dress with the jewelry in exchange. When she'd asked her mother if she could afford to sit for a photograph now, her mother only laughed. Charlie obviously wouldn't be getting the requested item.

Meg felt awful about lying to Charlie and taking his money. However, she had little say in the matter. If she refused to write the letters, her mother would simply do it on her own. And Mildred insisted that Charlie was worth millions. What was a few thousand pounds to someone who could afford anything his heart desired?

The thought of money had Meg dreaming of running away again. She'd been doing her best to save as much as she could ever since she was a child. Any time she found a coin or her mother gave her money to purchase something, and she had some left over, she'd put that away. There'd even been a few times when she'd taken loose change off of sideboards—and not always in her own home. The thought of money and freedom made her heart begin to race, and since her mother was down the street visiting Mrs. Donaldson, she decided perhaps it was time to have a little fun like she used to when she was a young girl. She quickly changed into riding clothes and headed off to the carriage house.

There were not nearly as many horses as there had once been, and part of the carriage house had been transformed into a garage for her uncle's motor coach. Still, Meg's favorite stallion, Lancelot, met her gaze as she entered the building, and his expression seemed hopeful. He was clearly ready to breathe in some fresh air as well.

She took a quick look around and did not see Mr. Bitterly anywhere. He was likely off in his quarters taking a nap, an activity he seemed to do more and more of these days. Ezra was probably in school, she thought, or off with his friends. She wasn't quite sure what his educational arrangement happened to be. She only knew that from time to time when her mother asked for him to complete a chore, his father would say he was at school. Since Ezra was slightly older than Meg, it seemed to her he should be finished with his studies by now. It wasn't as if Ezra were attending university.

Meg pulled a saddle down off the shelf where they were kept and approached Lancelot's stall. However, a noise behind her caught her attention, and she turned to find Ezra there, nearly right beside her, a curious expression on his face. She jumped, frightened by his sudden proximity, and nearly dropped the saddle on the ground.

Grabbing the heavy device, Ezra took it from her so that it didn't fall and land on her foot. "Sorry, Meg. I didn't mean to frighten you," he said as she relinquished the saddle to his stronger grasp.

"Oh, no. It's just... I thought I was alone. I didn't see you."

"I was in the loft," he replied, gesturing above them.

"I see," Meg said, nodding. "I just thought I'd take Lancelot for a quick ride." The building was rather dark and dusty with fine particles of straw floating in the air, but as Meg looked into Ezra's eyes, she couldn't help but think he looked quite handsome despite the debris and his sweaty appearance.

"Why take one horse for a ride when you can take twenty?" he asked with a crooked smile.

Meg was confused. They only had two horses left in their stable. "Whatever do you mean?"

Without answering her, Ezra took the saddle and placed it back where it belonged. He came back to her, took her dainty hand in his rough one, and led her out of the carriage house door, taking a few steps over, and opening the garage door.

Uncle Bertram's motor coach sat there, clean and shiny. It looked as if it had recently been polished. She looked at the car and then at him. "Are you saying...?"

"Why not?" Ezra asked, still holding her hand.

"I haven't the foggiest idea how to drive it," Meg reminded him.

Ezra laughed at her, and at first, Meg was offended, but when she saw his smile, she couldn't help but join in. "I'll drive," he finally managed.

"You know how?" she asked as he released her hand and approached the vehicle.

"Oh, yes. My father taught me. He wanted to be sure I knew how to drive in case your uncle or mother ever needed to get somewhere and he was indisposed." He was going about readying the vehicle, and Meg simply watched, not even sure where one was to begin. After a few moments, the engine was purring. Ezra went around to the passenger side and held the door for her. "Are you coming?"

Meg knew good and well this was liable to get her in heaps of trouble if her mother or uncle found out. Ezra, too. On the other hand, she couldn't help but feel as if she would be in trouble either way. The feel of Ezra's hand on hers still lingered, and the thought of having him drive her around was both tempting and frightening. She'd been thinking about him more and more lately; surely he'd be able to see that in her behavior.

"Meg, your mother will never know, and your uncle is likely passed out at the tavern."

"It's not even noon."

"And?"

He had a point. Meg had been looking for adventure, and now, here it was before her. Without another thought, she climbed into the passenger seat, a grin on her face. Ezra smiled and patted her hand where it rested on the door before he shut it and went around to the driver's side.

"Hold on," he said, "this is going to be a wild ride."

That turned out to be an understatement. While Ezra was quite cautious while driving in town so as to avoid any undue attention, as soon as he made his way out into the country, he pressed the gas pedal down to the floorboard, and they took off. Meg couldn't imagine ever going so quickly in an automobile. His father only drove slowly and carefully. Ezra made the car do things Meg had no idea it could do, like take corners without braking and slide on the gravel. He even drove it through an open field, which made the sides all muddy, but going over the bumps was particularly exciting to her.

Meg had always known her sense of adventure was still inside her. She just hadn't been able to find it for so long. Now, here it was again. Ezra had brought it out of her in a way she didn't even know was possible.

Once they were several miles away from town and hadn't seen

another person or vehicle for at least fifteen minutes, Ezra pulled over. "Would you like to have a go?" he asked, gesturing at the steering wheel.

"Me? Drive a motor coach?" Meg asked, shocked.

"Why not?" he asked.

"Why, I wouldn't know the first thing."

"It's not difficult. I can teach you," he replied. Before she had the opportunity to decline again, he began going over all of the various parts, showing her how they worked.

When he'd finished, Meg decided it sounded simple enough. Deciding one only lived once, she shrugged and said, "All right then. Why not?"

They quickly switched seats, and once she was behind the steering wheel, she realized her hands were shaking. "We'll just take it nice and slow," Ezra cautioned.

Meg eased up on the clutch and put in the gas as he had shown her, and the automobile began to slowly move forward. She took the steering wheel in her hands, and guided it down the road. Ezra corrected her a time or two, but after a moment, Meg began to laugh. "I'm doing it!" she exclaimed. "I'm driving!"

"Yes, you are," he replied, laughing. "And not too badly, either I might add."

She never got the car anywhere near up to the speed that Ezra had been going, the brake becoming her best friend, but he taught her how to turn a corner and how to stop. Meg couldn't believe how relatively easy it truly was; she wished she'd learned how to drive earlier.

After a while, she realized they were fairly far from home, and her mother might be back soon. The last thing she needed after such a wonderful day was to get in trouble. "I think we should switch places and head back home," she said, slowing the vehicle.

"All right," Ezra agreed, still smiling at her. He showed Meg how to turn the engine completely off, and they both opened their doors to switch seats.

As she came around the front of the car, Meg was so proud of herself and so happy, she didn't realize Ezra was walking the same way. They collided into each other, but before she could fall, she felt his strong arms wrap around her. "Beg pardon," she said, looking up into his face.

He was still smiling, one hand on the small of her back, the other on her hip. "Are you all right?" he asked.

"Yes, of course," she replied, the smile slipping away now. She had never been this close to him, not in years, anyway. The sun was directly behind him, and from this angle, the rays of light formed a halo around his golden head.

He leaned in, and she didn't hesitate to bring her lips up to meet his. She had been thinking about this moment for years now, and once it was finally happening, she was not disappointed in the least. He tasted like warm vanilla and mint, and the smell of his leather vest reminded her of all the times she'd stared at him through the window as he'd worked in the back garden, his muscles rippling in the sunlight.

It also reminded her that he was a servant in their home, and this simply wouldn't do. After a moment, she pulled back away from him, untangling her hands from around his neck.

"Meg?" he asked, as if he was unsure whether or not she was upset with him. His hands shifted so that they rested on her hips.

"It's getting late," she reminded him, forcing a small smile, and then she placed just enough pressure on his hands to make him release her.

Nodding, he made his way around to the driver's side and she slipped in through the still open passenger door.

The ride home wasn't nearly as long as the initial drive since they were on the most direct route with no side excursions or pasture exploration. Meg said nothing, only looked out the window, her hands folded in her lap.

Ezra glanced at her a few times, she could feel it. But he didn't say anything either. Once they reached the garage, he pulled inside, and Meg attempted to let herself out before he had the opportunity to come around and open her door.

She wasn't quite fast enough, and by the time she'd gotten the door opened and managed to get her riding habit out of the vehicle, he was standing before her, the expression in his eyes showing both hurt and inquisitiveness.

"Meg, I apologize for overstepping," he said quietly.

"No, don't apologize," Meg replied, trying to step around him.

His hand was on her shoulder, and she came to a stop. "It's only... you are the most beautiful woman I've ever laid eyes on. I've thought so for as long as I can remember." Stepping around in front of her again, he added, "I know that you are promised to another, and that we could never be.... But that doesn't stop my mind from wondering what if."

Meg wanted to declare that she had thought the same thing a hundred times over, that she had dreamt of the feel of his arms around her and his lips on hers. But she knew it could never be. If her mother found out, who knows what she might do to him? She cared too much for Ezra to put him in that sort of a situation.

"I need to go," she said quietly. She removed his hand from her shoulder and began to make her way toward the house. He let her go this time.

Once she was a bit of a distance away and felt she was out of reach of his gaze, she called back over her shoulder. "Thank you, Ezra. I had a lot of fun."

"You're welcome, Meggy."

She felt his eyes on the side of her face and was glad she had not turned to look at him. Without another word, she hurried on her way, hopeful that, if her mother had returned from Mrs. Donaldson's, she would not have noticed the motor coach was missing. Although, she couldn't help but to feel that, even if she was to be punished, it would be worth it. This adventure would certainly go to the top of her list.

CHAPTER SIXTEEN

NEW YORK CITY

"As you can see, our workers are very busy," Max Blanck explained to Charlie as he showed him around the work floor of his textile company, Triangle Shirtwaist. "We employee over six hundred workers, most of them young women. We prefer recent immigrants, as we want to give them the opportunity to make something of themselves."

Charlie was interested in visiting other textile companies since he would be running one himself someday—or at least he thought he would be. He was looking to do some investing of his own, and Triangle was known around the city for being able to fill large quotas quickly. Charlie wanted to see how it was done.

As Mr. Blanck continued to talk up his establishment, Charlie couldn't help but notice the girls all looked tired and worn out. The factory was stuffy without a lot of ventilation. The area was also very crowded. "How much are their wages?" Charlie asked, cutting off the statement Mr. Blanck was making about the top-of-the-line equipment the young ladies used.

"Oh, uhm, well, we pay fifteen dollars per week," he replied, his head held high.

"Fifteen dollars per week?" Charlie repeated, stopping in his tracks. "You don't say?"

"Well, as I mentioned, many of the girls are young. They have the opportunity to make more. Once they become more skilled."

Charlie glanced behind him at the liegeman he had recently hired, a man by the name of Stephen Jenkins who, so far, was almost as unimpressive as Mr. Blanck's treatment of his workers. Expecting to catch Stephen's eye to signal that he needed an excuse to leave, Charlie found the young man eyeing some of the girls instead. Shaking his head in annoyance, Charlie turned back to his tour guide. "Well, Mr. Blanck, I thank you for your time..." he began.

Seeing that he was losing the opportunity for a possibly substantial financial investment, Max Blanck interjected. "Our process works, Mr. Ashton, I assure you. These girls are able to turn out an amazing volume of product."

"I'm afraid I can't be associated with someone who pays so little and works his employees so hard," Charlie explained, taking his hat from Stephen and placing it on his head. "Now, if you can show me to the nearest exit."

"Yes, sir, it's right over here," Mr. Blanck said.

They approached a side door and Max fumbled for a key in his pocket. It took him a moment, but eventually, he managed to get it unlocked, stepping back out of the way as he pulled it open.

"Locked doors that open inward?" Charlie couldn't believe his eyes.

"There are ample exits, I assure you. This one is only locked so that we may check the women's purses as they leave. Some of them have sticky fingers, it seems," Mr. Blanck replied, though his voice began to show annoyance with Charlie's reprimanding now that he was certain he wouldn't be getting any money from the millionaire.

Shaking his head, Charlie made his way down the steps, Stephen in tow. The eight floors to the ground floor were rather awkward since Mr. Blanck no longer seemed willing to try to sell his company to someone who was clearly disgusted, and Charlie felt no need to continue to point out safety hazards to someone who didn't care about his workers.

Once they finally reached the ground floor, Mr. Blanck walked Charlie and Stephen to the door. "Thank you for your time, Mr. Ashton," he said offering his hand.

Charlie took it and nodded, absently thinking he would need to find a sink so he could wash away any stains that may have transferred from Mr. Blanck's dirty hands. "Thank you," Charlie replied politely, though he couldn't force himself to say more.

He began to exit the building only to turn to find Stephen still standing inside staring off into space. "Stephen?" he shouted, startling the young man, who nodded at Mr. Blanck and then grabbed the door from Charlie as he walked through.

His next meeting was only a few blocks away, and as he made his way up Washington Place, he considered what to do about these two predicaments. Clearly, he needed to say something to someone about the operations inside the Triangle Shirtwaist Factory, although he wasn't sure who might listen. And then there was Stephen.

It had been almost three months since Charlie had graduated from Harvard. He'd taken Stephen on shortly thereafter. It seemed like he'd interviewed dozens of applicants, and none of them were quite what he was looking for. Stephen came highly recommended by a friend of his father who had employed him in just such a position but said he had needed to let him go because his nephew wanted the position. When John had complained to the friend about Stephen's inadequacies, the other man had simply laughed and said, "Yes, that seems about right." Charlie soon realized he'd only been handing off his problem to someone else.

"Stephen," Charlie called over his shoulder, "give me a rundown of this next factory we are about to visit."

"What's that, sir?" Stephen asked, struggling to keep up.

"The next factory. Remind me of what we are looking at," Charlie repeated, trying to be patient.

They stopped at a corner to let several automobiles go by. While Charlie owned a few of the vehicles, he preferred to walk whenever he could, especially around the city. He wondered how long it might be before everyone was zooming about, and no one got any exercise at all.

"Right, sir," Stephen muttered. He was carrying Charlie's attaché case and began to open it, right there on the corner.

"Stephen, what are you doing?" Charlie asked, turning to stop him.

"I need the notes," the young man replied.

Charlie let out a frustrated sigh. "You shouldn't need the notes. We certainly aren't getting them out here on the street corner. You must know something of Barnaby and Sons' Textile Company without having to flip through pages of documentation."

"I'm sorry, sir," Stephen stammered. "I'm afraid I'll need to look at the notes."

Charlie pressed the heels of his hands into his eye sockets, attempting to stop the enormous headache he could feel forming behind his eyes.

"Founded in 1875 by Benjamin Barnaby, he later brought on his sons, Jeremiah and Josiah. Originally located on Flushing, as the company continued to grow, Barnaby realized they'd need a new location with more room. In 1882, he moved the factory to its present location, here on Washington Place. While they are not the most profitable textile company, only bringing in about seventy percent of the revenue brought in by their largest rival last quarter, Barnaby and Sons' is known for paying decent wages and treating their employees with respect."

Charlie couldn't believe his ears. About halfway through the speech, he had realized that the stranger in the bowler hat standing next to them was answering his question and turned to face him. While other people were stepping around them to finally cross the busy intersection, Charlie stood staring at the shorter, slightly older man, not sure what to say.

"I'm sorry—I didn't mean to interfere. I just thought... if you really needed some information about Barnaby and Sons', well I could help."

"Do you work for Barnaby?" Charlie asked, still not sure what to make of this fellow.

He laughed. "Oh, heavens no. I am currently employed at the tavern down the street there, Henige's. No, I don't work at Barnaby or any of these factories. But I hear a lot, and I have a good memory. Is there anything else you'd like to know, Mr. Ashton?"

Charlie almost asked how this stranger knew his name, but then he realized practically everyone knew his name. "No, thank you," he replied, shaking his head to clear it.

"Very well, then. Have a nice day."

"You, too," Charlie replied as the other man began to cross the road. He turned and looked at Stephen who was staring at the building across the other intersection, not paying any attention whatsoever. He realized a few seconds too late that he hadn't even caught the other fellow's name. Turning to see where he might be, he saw that he had already made it across and was too far out of earshot to hear even if he might holler. Now, there were several motor coaches coming through and they would need to wait.

Sighing in frustration, Charlie pulled out his pocket watch. They had ten minutes and about three more blocks to walk. He was hopeful they wouldn't be late. He hated being late. As the traffic slowed and they began to walk across the street, he looked at Stephen and decided it was time to do something. He could no longer let this person who was supposed to keep him on target make him look foolish.

The meeting with Benjamin Barnaby Jr. went considerably better than the one at Triangle Shirtwaist Factory, and by the time he was done touring the facility, Charlie thought he might actually have found a good place to invest some money. What that stranger on the street had said about taking care of their workers was certainly true, at least in comparison to the last place, and Charlie felt that the Barnabys cared about their employees similarly to the way he and his father cared for theirs.

That being said, Stephen had tripped and nearly fallen into one of the machines. He had been unable to answer a single one of Charlie's inquiries, and he'd gotten his attaché case caught on a piece of equipment, and upon jerking it free, nearly sent it flying into a group of young ladies working at a nearby sewing station.

Something had to be done.

Once he'd bid Mr. Barnaby goodbye, Charlie pulled Stephen off around the corner of the building where there weren't quite as many people walking by. He was usually fairly understanding, but this day had gotten the best of him. "Stephen," he said, waiting a second until he actually had the young man's attention. "We need to talk."

"Yes, sir," Stephen said, a sheepish grin plastered on his face.

Looking into his eyes, Charlie wasn't sure he could see any signs of life at all. "Stephen, I appreciate the service you've provided over the last few months...."

"Thank you, sir." The smile widened.

"However, I'm afraid our arrangement simply isn't working out," Charlie continued.

There was a vague form of recognition now. "It isn't?" Stephen asked.

"I'm afraid not," Charlie replied, shaking his head. "I think it would be best if you went back to the office and collected your items."

"But, Mr. Ashton, I'm sure, if you just give me one more chance—I know I can do better."

"I am more than happy to give you a reference should you seek similar employment," Charlie concluded. "I will forward your pay to you."

While he wasn't generally quick to grasp anything Charlie said, he finally seemed to understand this. "Yes, sir," Stephen sighed, handing over Charlie's attaché case and the keys he had been given. "If you should change your mind, please let me know."

Charlie only nodded, and as the young man began to walk off, head drooping, he reached out and grabbed Stephen by the arm. The young man paused and looked at him with hopeful eyes. "The office is that way," Charlie said, pointing him in the opposite direction.

"Right," Stephen moaned, and then he went off headed back towards the office. He was hopeful he'd be able to find the factory on his own, but he wasn't sure. There was a good chance his personal effects would still be present when Charlie returned later that day. As for now, it was early afternoon, and though he was not one to spend a lot of time hanging out in such locations, Charlie needed to find a tavern.

Henige's was a nice little establishment, not too crowded, but a good mix of businessmen and blue collar workers. It only took him a moment to spy the face he was looking for tending bar, and Charlie made his way over to one of the empty barstools.

As soon as the barkeep spied him, he smiled, as if he were seeing an old friend. He finished serving the customer he'd been interacting with and made his way over. "Well, Mr. Ashton, what can I get you?"

"Whiskey, straight, please," Charlie replied.

"Coming right up." He went over and retrieved the drink and sat it down in front of Charlie who took a sip as he asked, "How was the meeting with Barnaby?"

"Good," Charlie replied, setting the glass down. "I think we might actually do some business."

"Glad that worked out for you," he responded with a smile as he slid away to take care of another customer.

Charlie overheard the older man ask for a scotch and refer to the bartender as Jonathan, so at least he had a name to go with the face now. He wasn't sure exactly how to broach the question he wanted to ask, but he felt compelled to do so. As Jonathan came back and refilled his drink, Charlie asked, "How long have you worked here?"

"Oh, a few years. Five or so. I never planned on tending bar, but one night the owner was shorthanded and I volunteered to help out. Now here I am."

"I see. And what were you doing before that?" Charlie asked, taking another sip.

Jonathan motioned for him to wait one second as he went off to help another customer. Everyone seemed to know and like him, which was impressive to Charlie. He certainly seemed to do his job well.

A moment later, he returned to answer the question. "I've tried my hand at lots of things over the years, but I finally decided to attend NYCC to get my business degree. Unfortunately, I wasn't able to make enough money working part-time to finish my degree. So... here I am!"

Charlie nodded, and as Jonathan went to greet another guest, he analyzed that answer. He was smart, likable, knew everyone, worked hard. Just the sort of fellow Charlie was looking for. When he came back by, Charlie motioned for him to come over.

Jonathan looked at his mostly full glass and then back at him with a questioning look, as if he wasn't sure what he might need. "How can I help you, Mr. Ashton?"

"You know that other fellow I was with earlier? The bumbling idiot who wanted to let my notes fly about all over Washington Place?"

Jonathan laughed and nodded his head. "Yes, I noticed he was no longer with you."

"I had to let him go," Charlie explained. "I could no longer afford to let someone else make me look ridiculous. I do just fine at that on my own."

"All right," Jonathan said, still snickering. "And precisely what does that have to do with me, Mr. Ashton?"

"I want you to replace him," Charlie explained. "Be my assistant —my liegeman—my right hand man."

"Me?" Jonathan questioned, clearly not sure he was hearing correctly. "Why ever would you want me?"

"You're obviously very intelligent. You're a hard worker. You're pleasant. And I suppose if I asked you to unzip my attaché case you would know not to hold it upside down as you did so."

The laughter was back now, and Charlie thought Jonathan might actually hurt himself he was laughing so hard. "But, Mr. Ashton, I've never been a second before."

"You'd never been a barkeep before either, but you've made that work for five years."

Jonathan shrugged, and as another customer motioned for him to come down to the other side of the bar, once again, he signaled to Charlie that he would be right back.

Charlie finished his whiskey, hoping that Jonathan would say yes and this arrangement would work out. Otherwise, he had no assistant and he probably just made himself look like a fool. The way his day was going, it was likely that there were several witnesses and at least one news reporter among the crowd to let everyone know Charles Ashton strikes out again—can't meet his own fiancée, can't get a barkeep to be his assistant.

"Mr. Ashton," Jonathan said, as he sauntered back over. "I appreciate the offer, but..."

Charlie steeled himself for yet another rejection.

"I can't leave the bar tonight. It's just too busy. Would you mind if I started tomorrow?"

Charlie broke out into a huge grin, and jumped up, taking Jonathan's hand in his and slapping him on the back with his other. "Yes, of course. Tomorrow would be just fine. Come in in the afternoon if you'd like, after you've gotten some rest."

"Tomorrow morning should work," Jonathan assured him.

"Well, all right then," Charlie agreed, still smiling. "I'm looking forward to working with you, Mr...."

"Lane—Jonathan Lane," he replied.

"Well, Jonathan Lane, I believe this is the beginning of a beautiful friendship."

"A beautiful friendship indeed," Jonathan agreed, nodding his head, smiling almost as widely as Charlie.

Charlie grabbed his case and slipped some money on the counter to cover his drink and a tip. "You know where the factory is?"

"Yes, of course," Jonathan said, taking the money and nodding in thanks.

"I'll see you tomorrow then."

"Very good, sir."

As Charlie made his way out of Henige's, he finally felt that perhaps things were starting to go his way. Perhaps if he could talk the barkeep into being his assistant he could convince his fiancée to marry him--or to at least send him a photograph. One small step at a time....

CHAPTER SEVENTEEN

SOUTHAMPTON

R uth was growing into quite the curious little child, and though Patsy kept her most of the time during the day while Kelly and Daniel worked, Meg insisted on letting her stay from time to time so that she could spend the day playing with the little one.

At nearly two, she was in constant motion, always getting into things and running about. Meg liked to take her outside and push her in the pram. Ruth often had a better idea and would climb out and play in the flowers. She seemed to like the lilacs and oleander the best, too, but Meg was always very careful to make sure she never put any of the plants in her mouth. She knew that oleander was extremely poisonous.

Ruth had fiery red hair, the same color as her mother's, which curled up at her neck. Her vocabulary was immense for such a small child, and she kept Meg on her toes answering inquiries and explaining what different items were. She loved to look at picture books, particularly of animals, and Meg felt that she spent a good part of the day "moo"ing.

One day, while they were playing in Meg's study, Ruth managed to pull open a drawer to an old bureau, one Meg hadn't looked in for as long as she could remember. There, in the bottom lay one of her old dolls, the one she had called simply, "Dolly." As Ruth gasped in delight and reached for the plaything, Meg gathered both the little girl and the remembrance into her arms, sitting down on the rug as Ruth wiggled and shouted, "Baby!"

"It is a baby," Meg agreed. "It was my baby a very long time ago." Looking at the doll reminded her of happier times, when she used to play in the garden. She'd received this doll from St. Nicholas for Christmas one year when she was just a bit older than Ruth, though she suspected her father had actually picked it out. She'd spent hours in the garden pushing her around in a toy pram.

"Eyes broke," Ruth said, pointing at Dolly's eyes. "Baby ouchy."

"Oh, I see," Meg replied, noticing for the first time that the doll's eyes were broken. One of the blue orbs was cracked and the other was missing entirely. She had no idea how that had happened, but she suspected it might have had something to do with that awful Ms. Strickland. She never liked for Meg to play with toys. She also wondered if the woman might know what happened to her other doll, Lilac, which was nowhere to be found.

"Baby night night," Ruth said, snatching the doll from Meg's hands and carrying her across the room to rock her in one of the chairs that sat by the window.

"Is it time for baby to take a nap?" Meg asked.

"Shh!" Ruth insisted, covering her mouth with a chubby little finger. "Baby night night!"

"I'm so sorry," Meg replied, stifling a giggle at the cuteness.

"What are you doing?" Kelly asked, walking into the study and spying her child rocking the baby.

Ruth showed her mother no mercy. "Shh!" she said, even louder this time. "Baby night night!"

Kelly looked at Meg, and they both had to cover their mouths to keep from laughing aloud at the little child's antics. Ruth only liked to be laughed at if she was laughing, too, so they knew if they were caught, they'd certainly be scolded by the small tyrant.

Kneeling down next to her daughter, Kelly whispered, "Did you find a doll?"

Ruth nodded her head up and down vigorously.

"Do you know this doll used to belong to your Aunty Meg?"

Ruth's eyes went to Meg, and then she nodded again.

"I believe her name was..."

"Dolly," Meg supplied.

"Oh, yes, Dolly."

"Dolly's eyes broke," Ruth informed her mother.

The dolls eyes happened to be closed since she was sleeping, and since Kelly didn't want to wake the baby and upset the little mother she took her word for it. "That's too bad," she whispered.

"Maybe your daddy can fix them," Meg said shrugging.

Kelly turned and looked at her. "Oh, we can't take Dolly," she began.

"Of course you can," Meg said, sliding closer to them on the rug. "Who am I to keep a loving mother away from her baby."

"Oh, but Meg, this was one of your favorite toys. Didn't your father give her to you?"

"Yes, and now I'm giving her to Ruth," Meg smiled.

"Well, maybe one day, when Ruth is older, she can give her back to you—if you have a little girl who might like to play with her."

"NO!" Ruth interjected, no longer concerned that the baby was sleeping. "Ruth's baby."

"Oh, well then," Meg said, trying not to laugh, "I think that answers that question."

Kelly was clearly trying to hold back a giggle as well. "Thank you, Meg," she said leaning over and putting her arm around her friend. "You are so kind to my little lady."

"You're quite welcome," Meg replied, hugging her back. "Your little lady is very special to me," she said, patting Ruth's chubby little leg.

"What do you say to Aunty Meg?" Kelly whispered to Ruth.

Eyes wide, Ruth looked from her mother to Meg, a questioning expression on her face. Kelly whispered in her ear again, and then Ruth said, "Thank you, Aunty Meg!"

"You're welcome, darling," Meg said, leaning over to kiss her head. "I love you, my sweet."

"I wuv you, too!" she said, letting go of Dolly with one hand so that she could hug her aunty back.

"Come on, Ruth. Daddy will be home soon," Kelly said as she rose and plucked her child up off of the chair.

As Meg watched them walk out into the hallway, she wondered if she would ever be so lucky as to have a child of her own. She pulled herself to her feet and glanced out the window. Ezra was there, working in the yard. She sighed at the memory of the adventure they'd had, stealing her uncle's motor coach. Would it be possible to take Ezra with her to America? Could they have a family there? Could she really be a loving mother, like Kelly?

She wasn't sure if any of those things were possible, not after what her uncle had done to her and not with the predicament she was in with Charles Ashton. One thing was sure, however. Meg wasn't willing to let go of her happily ever after without a fight.

CHAPTER EIGHTEEN

NEW YORK CITY

"I really think that celluloid is the way to go," Charlie said, his feet resting on the edge of his desk, a stack of research sitting next to them. "I think it's the wave of the future."

"All of the evidence points that direction," Jonathan agreed with him. "It's just a question of how much you're willing to put in."

"Right," Charlie nodded. That was always the question. How much of his money should he invest in whatever new business, new project, new technology was coming out next? So far, he'd made some very wise investments with the small sum his father had given him to start off with and the wages he'd been earning working for his father since he graduated from Harvard the year before. He knew, however, it may take quite a sum to re-establish Westmoreland Textiles, and that was always in the back of his mind.

"I think you should go with the full amount. The numbers seem solid," Jonathan shrugged, looking over the top sheet again.

"You think so?" Charlie asked, sitting up and putting his feet on the floor. Jonathan never said to go with the full amount requested by these budding entrepreneurs. "That's quite a bit."

"I know, but I feel like this one will surely pay off. Just look at the progress Eastman has made already, and his funding has been relatively low so far. I'm not saying give it to him all at once, but I'd consider setting the full amount aside."

Charlie listened carefully to everything that Jonathan recommended. So far, in the year or so that they'd been working together, Charlie had been nothing but impressed. Jonathan was always one step ahead of everyone else, and his mind was like an encyclopedia, full of facts and relevant information. As Charlie looked back over the proposal sent to him earlier, he was convinced celluloid was the way to go. "Very good then, Jonathan. I'm sorry to keep you at the factory so long, particularly on a Saturday."

"Nonsense," Jonathan said, "as if I have anything better to do."

"You're free to go out this evening if you like," Charlie offered, beginning to straighten his desk. "I'll be spending the evening with my parents." He had recently bought a home closer to the factory, but on the weekends, he still liked to visit his mother and father.

"I think I might stop by Henige's and see if the old crowd is in. It's not quite five in the afternoon, but that's never stopped that crowd from drinking," Jonathan chuckled.

"Very good," Charlie replied when he realized he smelled something odd. At first, he couldn't place it, but after a few seconds, he knew what it was—the worst smell one can encounter in a factory: smoke. "Do you smell that?"

Jonathan was on his feet before Charlie even finished the question, clearly a step ahead of him—as usual. He stuck his head out into the hall that ran past the offices and oversaw the factory floor. They didn't run machinery on Saturday, so the factory was relatively quiet. "It doesn't seem to be coming from in here."

As he turned around, his eyes fell on something out the window, and his expression changed to sheer horror. Charlie turned to see what Jonathan was looking at. The entire sky seemed to be filled with smoke, and a few blocks over, they could see a dark plume reaching up into the New York sky. "Dear, God!" Charlie whispered. "Where is it coming from?"

"One of the other factories must be on fire," Jonathan replied.

Without another word, they both took off, down the stairs, and out the door. The air around them was smoky and bits of ash and debris floated about as they made their way towards the fire. A few moments later, they heard people shouting and the sounds of a fire brigade approaching. While some were running away in a panic, several others were hurrying to the scene, like Charlie and Jonathan, to see if they could help.

Charlie looked up at the building, and once he realized where he was, rage welled up inside of him. "No!" he shouted, pushing past some people to get closer. Jonathan was behind him.

"What is it?" Jonathan asked, coming up behind him and grabbing his shoulder.

"Triangle Shirtwaist Factory. I was here—last year. I told the owner it wasn't safe. I even wrote letters to the commissioner and the mayor. Now—if there are people in there, they won't be able to get out."

Even as the words left his mouth, they heard screaming from the eighth floor on up and realized the workers were trapped. There also appeared to be people on the roof. The ladies in the windows were shouting for help, but no one seemed to be coming out of the building. The fire escape lay mangled and charred on the sidewalk with several bodies twisted around it. A group of people huddled behind the police line with smoke and ash on their clothing appeared to be escapees of the blaze, but since he'd arrived, Charlie could not see anyone else exiting. The people atop the building were jumping across to the neighboring rooftop and safety.

Charlie remembered the doors being locked. He also remembered that they opened in. If there was a rush to the exits, people would be trampled before they could pull the doors open, even if they had a key.

The firefighters were working a ladder up the side of the buildings as the shrieks from inside grew louder. The women shouted, "Help us please!" soon followed by screams of, "She's on fire!" and "We can't breathe!" Eventually, the ladder was next to the building, and the men began to extend it.

Charlie held his breath, looking up at those anguished faces, praying that the firefighters would make it in time. However, as the ladder reached its full extension, they all sighed in frustration and grief; it only reached the seventh floor.

A firefighter began to climb anyway as others pulled out a net, but the workers had waited long enough, and the crowd watched in horror as, one by one, they began to fling themselves out of the window, landing hard on the sidewalk some 150 feet below. Few onlookers or first responders ran to try to assess the victims to see if they were still alive because the bodies continued to fall. Even the net was not helpful. Three girls jumped at once and ripped right through.

At first, those who faced the open window, looks of terror in their innocent eyes, and flung themselves to the cold concrete below clearly did so out of fear of the growing flames. However, as Charlie continued to watch the macabre parade, the young workers who plummeted to their deaths did so as human torches, their clothes and hair already ablaze. Though the firefighters were doing their best to gain control, the fire continued to rage on until the stack of bodies on the ground was several deep.

Eventually, Charlie could handle it no more and had to pull his eyes away from the carnage. He couldn't imagine what it must be like to stand before certain death and have to choose between burning and flinging oneself out into the open air and the waiting concrete below. He hoped that, should he ever be faced with a similar situation, he could be as brave as these young factory workers had been today.

And he would do everything he could to make sure the owners of the Triangle Shirtwaist Factory and other abominations like it were brought to justice for the despicable way they treated their employees.

CHAPTER NINETEEN

SOUTHAMPTON

Meg awoke to the sound of voices coming up through the radiator pipe. She blinked a few times and then looked at the time. It wasn't even eight o'clock yet. Who could her mother possibly be speaking to?

Slipping on the pink robe her mother had given her for Christmas last year (possibly the only gift her mother had ever given her that she actually liked), she crept over to have a better listen.

She could clearly recognize her mother's voice, but the man's seemed foreign to her. She tried to piece together the conversation the best she could to determine who he was and what he might be doing there.

"There's no way out, I can assure you," he was saying. "I've spent years trying to come up with something... anything... but it's legally binding."

"Perhaps there's another attorney we can speak to," her mother replied.

"I've spoken to lawyers this side of the Atlantic and the other,

Mrs. Westmoreland. The will must be carried out as specified by your late husband, and you are running out of time."

"Out of time?" Mildred questioned, and then Meg heard that distinct guffaw her mother made whenever she thought she was cleverer than whomever she was speaking to. "We have all the time in the world."

"No, you don't, Mrs. Westmoreland. You have read the contract closely, haven't you?"

"Yes, of course I have." Her voice went up both in octave and in volume.

"Then you'll remember that paragraph twelve specifies that if the marriage hasn't taken place by the time Mary Margaret is twenty-one...."

"What are you doing?"

Meg jumped, nearly hitting her head on the pipe. She turned to see Kelly standing in the doorway, a puzzled expression on her face. She shushed her and nestled her ear back against the pipe, hoping she hadn't missed anything important.

"Well, naturally I didn't know that or else we would have gone through with it years ago," her mother said, her tone showing she was completely put out now.

Kelly tiptoed over and stood next to Meg, also listening intently.

"All I can say is," the man continued, his tone also showing he was more than a bit perturbed, "I suggest you get this done sooner rather than later. Otherwise, you'll get nothing."

"Very well, Mr. Steele," her mother said, and Meg caught Kelly's eyes, finally knowing who her mother was talking to, though she had nothing to associate him with. "I shall talk to Bertram and we will make the necessary arrangements."

"She's nearly twenty now. That gives you about a year...."

"I am aware of how old my daughter is!" Mildred spat. "Now, Mr. Steele, Tessa will show you to the door."

"Good day, Mrs. Westmoreland," Meg heard him say, but in

response she only heard her mother shouting at Tessa to walk Mr. Steele out.

Hurrying over to the window that faced the front of the house, Meg peered through the curtains so that he wouldn't notice her and watched as a thin man in his mid-forties climbed into a horse drawn carriage that was waiting for him on the street. He gave a signal, and the driver took off.

"Odd that an attorney doesn't have a motor coach," Kelly mused.

"Well, if his other clients can afford what my mother can, it's no wonder," Meg responded, crossing her arms over her chest.

"Whatever is the matter?" Kelly asked, noticing her expression.

Meg didn't answer. Instead, she crossed over to her armoire and pulled a box down from the top shelf, bringing it over to her bed. She sat down next to it, and opened the lid. Curious, Kelly followed her and sat down on the other side.

A discarded hat and scarf, along with a pair of gloves later, and Meg pulled out her treasure—a hand full of bills and enough change to cover the bottom of a wishing well.

"What's all this?" Kelly asked. "Where did you get all of that?"

"I've been saving it," Meg replied as she began to count the bills. "Forever."

"It's quite a lot," Kelly muttered.

"Yes. Last I counted, I had nearly two hundred pounds," Meg agreed. "But that's been at least a year and a half ago."

"Two hundred pounds? Goodness! If your mother knew about all this...."

"She doesn't. She can't," Meg cut her off. Once she'd finished counting the bills, she set them back inside the box, looking at the coins, and determining there was no need to count them at the present moment, she put the other effects back on top. "Kelly—I'm done waiting to see what my mother may or may not do. I'm leaving."

"You're leaving?" Kelly echoed. "What do you mean?"

"I've been saving so that I can go to America. Now is the perfect time. Why wait any longer? I have enough for you and Daniel and

Ruth to go with me. We'll have to go second or third class, but that is all right. We probably should anyway—so that I am not recognized."

"Oh, Meg," Kelly began, slowly shaking her head. "America? Now?"

"Yes," Meg reassured her. "You've always said you wanted to go. Why not now?"

"But Meg," Kelly began, leaning back away from her friend a bit, "Daniel and I had been saving. But then, when Ruth came along, well, we couldn't save as much."

"It's all right," Meg assured her. "I've got enough saved to get us started. Once we get there, we can find employment. I can find work. Of some sort."

"I'm sure you could," Kelly replied. "But Meg, Daniel and I can't expect you to take care of us."

"I won't be. Consider it a loan then."

"Besides," Kelly continued, "there's something else.."

Meg was busy putting the lid back on the box and didn't see the expression on her friend's face. Once she realized she'd paused, she looked up, expectantly.

"I'm going to have another baby."

"Certainly you are. Have another baby. Have lots of babies. Have them in America."

"No, Meg. You don't understand. I mean I'm going to have another baby soon. In the fall, actually. Late fall, early winter."

Meg stared at Kelly as if she had just revealed she was actually a giant talking tomato with legs. "You're what?" she asked, shock and a bit of outrage in her tone.

"I wanted to tell you..." Kelly stammered. "It just never seemed like a good time."

Shaking her head, as if she were trying to clear away the obstacles, Meg said, "Well, have the baby in America. How far along are you? It's not as if passage takes months anymore."

"It's not that," Kelly sighed, shrugging her shoulders. "It's just that I've promised my mother we'd stay here until the baby is born.

She wants to see the child, and I owe that to her. Who knows when we might see my mother again."

"Why can't she come with us?" Meg asked, still trying to solve the problem.

"Oh, no. My mother would never come to America. My brother and his family are here. As well as her sisters. And her mother is close enough in Ireland that she can still go and visit every year or two. She won't be around much longer. Oh, no. There's no way my mother would ever go."

Meg let out a loud sigh and leaned back against the headboard. After a few moments of acceptance, she asked, "Well, when do you think you might be ready?"

"I'm not sure," Kelly admitted. "The spring perhaps."

"By then, my mother might have already married me off to Mr. Ashton." She remembered how the lawyer had insisted the marriage take place before she turn twenty-one, though she had no idea why.

"If worse came to worse, perhaps you could go over and wait for us," Kelly suggested, shrugging her shoulders again.

Meg considered the possibility. The thought had occurred to her more than once, particularly at times when Kelly had made her more than a bit unhappy. She'd also thought of taking Ezra with her. Maybe he would want to go. If that were the case, they could potentially be together. Though it had been over a year since their joyride out into the countryside, and she'd hardly talked to him since, she saw the way that he looked at her and knew in her heart he wanted to be with her still.

Kelly continued to look at her as if she was waiting on a response, so Meg finally managed, "All right. That's a possibility, though I'm not sure I could make it on my own in New York City for very long on what I'll have left after purchasing passage."

"Well... that's actually not all the money you have," Kelly replied, her voice just above a whisper.

"What's that?" Meg asked, leaning forward, her expression guarded.

Kelly let out another sigh and readjusted. Her eyes focused on her hands folded in her lap. "My mother wanted me to tell you some time ago, but I hesitated, because I was afraid you might do something foolish—like take off unaccompanied as a child."

"Kelly?" Meg prompted.

"You have a bank account in your name, Meg. At the National Provincial over on High Street."

"A what?"

"On the night of your father's death, he told my mother. He made her promise to let you know, should anything ever happen to him. It was as if he knew.... Anyway, she doesn't know how much it is, only that he opened it for you. So the money should still be there."

"Kelly!" Meg admonished. "Why didn't you tell me?"

"I told you; I was afraid you might leave. Also, if your mother found out, she might take the money from you."

"Still... I needed to know."

"Yes, and I'm sorry. I almost told you a few times before, but I just never found the right time."

"I certainly sound very unapproachable today," Meg muttered. She took the hat box back to her armoire and slipped it under some other boxes on the top shelf, including the one that held Charles Ashton's letters. Looking through her dresses, she found one that would allow her to move fairly freely and began to gather the other garments she would need to get dressed.

"What are you doing?" Kelly asked.

"Going to the bank," Meg replied. "I need to know if I have enough to start over."

It hadn't been difficult at all to sneak out the back door. Her mother and uncle were in the study having a heated conversation, and Meg could only assume they were talking about her. She couldn't worry about that right now, however. She was on a mission.

She found Ezra outside in the carriage house with Charlotte, who was petting the horses as Ezra fed and watered them. As soon as Charlotte saw Meg, she pulled her hand away from the horse and headed for the house, mumbling about having work to do. Meg paid her little mind. After all, she couldn't care less whether or not her mother's employees did their job.

Ezra placed the bucket he'd been using back on a peg that hung near the barrel of oats and smiled at her, shoving his hands into his trouser pockets. "Good morning, Meg."

"Good morning, Ezra," she said with a nod. "Are you busy this morning?"

"I'm never too busy for you," he replied, his eyes showing the sincerity of his words. "What can I help you with."

She stepped closer to him, looking around to ensure no one was listening, and then said quietly, "I have an errand to run, and I'm in need of a driver."

"My pleasure," he said with a smile. "Where are we off to?"

As he stepped over to grab the keys and ready the vehicle, she followed him. He always kept the motor coach pristinely clean, and Meg couldn't help but think it still looked rather nice for an older vehicle. "I can't say exactly where I need to go, but it's on High Street."

Ezra nodded and pulled the passenger side door open for her. "Hop in," he said making a sweeping gesture with his hand, and Meg climbed inside, glad not to have to sit in the back like he was her chauffeur instead of a friend.

They made their way across town, filling the void with a bit of small talk. It had been a long time since they had carried on a conversation, but it seemed like very little of substance had happened in that time. Meg mentioned a few events she had attended but didn't dwell on them since it seemed rude to talk about places Ezra wasn't allowed to go, and while he filled her in on the work he'd been doing in the back garden, not much remained to be said. Luckily, the ride did not take too long, and when Meg could see they were only a few blocks away, she asked him to stop the automobile.

"I will need about twenty minutes or so. Could you go drive about town and then pick me up here when it's time?"

"Certainly," Ezra replied, "but are you sure you want to go alone? Are you certain you'll be safe unaccompanied?"

"I'm only going a few blocks in the broad daylight. I'll be just fine," she reassured him. Before he could get out and open her door, she stepped out onto the narrow walk way, and he smiled and waved before he rejoined the meager flow of traffic. She waited until she was certain he'd driven on past the bank before she began to head in that direction.

Meg had never been in a bank before, and she wasn't quite sure what one was to do. When she walked in, she saw a teller behind a counter talking to another customer and a few other workers scurrying about. She decided the intelligent thing to do would be to get in line behind the other person and wait her turn.

It only took a moment for the other gentleman to finish his business before Meg found herself looking into the smiling face of an older fellow who wanted to know how he could help her. "Good day," she began. "My name is Mary Margaret Westmoreland, and I am of the understanding that my father, Henry Westmoreland, may have opened an account for me before his death. It's been several years ago...."

Before she could finish, the teller was nodding. "Oh, yes. Miss Westmoreland, it's very nice to meet you. Please wait one moment while I go and retrieve the president, Mr. Rogers."

Meg nodded, and the fellow stepped away. She watched him disappear down a hallway off to the side of the counter, thinking of how that was much easier than she had expected it to be.

Within a few moments, he was back, followed by a middle aged man with graying hair, spectacles, and a kind smile. "Miss Westmoreland?" he asked.

"Yes," Meg replied, offering her hand, which he took. "How do you do?"

"Quite well, thank you, miss. And you?"

"Just fine, thank you."

"Won't you follow me this way?"

Meg followed him down the hallway to what appeared to be a row of offices until they reached one that said, "Marvin. T. Rogers, President" in bold letters on the glass. He held the door for her, followed her in, and motioned for her to have a seat.

"We were wondering when you might be in," he began, sitting down in a seat across the desk from her. "Your father gave us specific directions to contact you upon your twentieth birthday if you hadn't visited us yet. That's coming up, isn't it?"

"In September," Meg answered, curious as to why her age seemed to be of such concern to everyone else today.

"Shortly before your father passed, he came to pay us a visit, Miss Westmoreland. He said he wanted to open an account in your name that you—and you alone—may access. He said that, if anyone else came with you, we should deny having any knowledge of the account. I see that you came in alone today. Were you aware of this stipulation?"

"No, sir," Meg replied. "There simply aren't too many people I can trust."

"Indeed," Mr. Rogers nodded, as if he fully understood what it was she spoke of. "You do have a substantial account with us, and we would be happy to continue to look over your affairs for as long as you should like."

Meg cleared her throat, not sure what to make of that. After a moment, she asked, "How much... how much is substantial?"

Mr. Rogers stood and retrieved a ledger, which sat atop a book-case behind him. Bringing it over to his desk, he flipped far into the book, and running his finger along the list, he finally reached her name. He followed the row across with his finger. Then, drawing a slip of paper and pencil from the corner of his desk, he wrote down a figure and another number before closing the binder.

"Our calculations go through the end of last month, so this is the figure with interest until that date," he explained as he slid the slip of paper across the table to her.

As Mr. Rogers stood to place the binder back on the shelf, Meg picked up the paper. She could hardly believe her eyes. She had known her father had amassed quite a bit of wealth in his time and that he always intended to look after her, but she couldn't imagine the figure would be nearly this high. Once Mr. Rogers had returned to his seat and she could find her voice, Meg asked, "Twenty-two thousand, four hundred, eighty-eight pounds?"

"And fifty-seven pence," he assured her.

Meg nearly fell out of her seat. She couldn't believe—all this time when she'd been worried about the lights being turned off, when she'd had her stockings re-darned several times, when she'd struggled to adapt last year's gowns—she was sitting on a small fortune. "May I have some water?" she stammered.

"Of course," he replied, leaving her for a moment to fetch the beverage.

Meg wished she'd worn a hat so that she may use it as a fan. She began to wave her hand in front of her face to try to catch her breath. Once Mr. Rogers returned with the water, she took a drink and nearly choked, sputtering all over the place. He handed her his handkerchief, and she wiped the water droplets off of her gown, embarrassed by her actions, yet still unable to comprehend that any of this was real. After handing back the damp handkerchief, she tried again, and this time she was able to keep the liquid down.

He was back in his seat, and after a moment, she realized he was speaking to her again. "As I said, we'd be happy to keep the account here for as long as you may like."

"Yes, thank you," Meg nodded, certain they'd love to continue to have her business. "As you may know, I am to marry soon. Once I've relocated to New York City, how will I be able to access my funds?"

"That other number that I've written on top of the slip of paper is your account number. No one else knows that number, except for you and me. I suggest you keep it that way. Once you've moved to New York City, we are happy to wire your money to you via another bank. Of course, we'd prefer if you continued to keep it here indefinitely and request a wire as you may need it. But should you choose to withdraw the remaining balance and deposit it in a bank closer to your new home, we will be more than willing to oblige."

Meg nodded along, certain she understood all that he was saying. "And may I access some of the funds today?"

"Of course," he replied, though she sensed a bit of hesitancy in his voice, as if she may try to take the entire sum. She doubted he even had that much money on hand. "How much would you like to withdraw?"

She considered the question, not really certain what she should do. If she took too much and her mother found it, she'd be forced to explain. That wouldn't do. Yet, the thought of going shopping, of purchasing gifts for those she loved, of buying something pretty for herself, was all very tempting. After careful consideration, she said, "One thousand pounds, please."

Unable to tell if his sigh was of relief or consternation, Meg watched as he nodded and rose out of his chair to go and retrieve the funds. She couldn't help but shake her head in disbelief. Perhaps the universe was happy with her again.

He returned shortly, and sitting in his seat, he proceeded to count out to her the one thousand pounds. Most were in hundreds, but he had brought her some smaller bills as well. Once he was finished and she had carefully placed the money in her purse, he asked if there was anything else he could help her with.

"No, thank you," Meg replied. He wrote down her new balance on another slip of paper, and Meg tore up the old one, tossing it into the waste bin. Though she wasn't good at math, she could have figured that sum herself; she supposed it was bank policy.

Once he had shown her out, and she had thanked the teller for his help, Meg made her way back to the place where Ezra had dropped her. On the way, she memorized the numbers to the bank account, tore the slip up, and tossed the new one as well. No one else needed to stumble upon that number by accident.

A few hundred yards from the meeting location, she saw her uncle's auto coming down the street and couldn't help but smile. Ezra pulled it to a stop and sprung out, running around to open the door for her. "Your chariot, my lady," he laughed.

"Why, thank you. And just in time as well."

"One never keeps a lady waiting."

Meg smiled at him, and staring into those shimmery eyes, she couldn't help but feel it was time to make some changes. That old Meg Westmoreland, the frightened one, the one afraid to take a chance, was gone. "Ezra, how would you like to go shopping?" she asked.

"Shopping?" he echoed.

"I believe you could use some new trousers."

He glanced down at his pants and then, with a crooked smile said, "Miss Westmoreland, I'm not sure why you're trying to get me out of my trousers, but I'm willing to find out."

Her eyes widened in shock first, but then Meg broke out into a fit of laughter, and as Ezra took off, she began to feel that freedom wasn't quite out of her grasp yet.

CHAPTER TWENTY

SOUTHAMPTON

April 7, 1912
Meg

The dress was light pink, flowing, in a soft chenille. The bodice was fitted and adorned with rhinestones that shimmered in the light. Her hair was pulled up off of her neck in a tight roll with ringlets framing her face. The shoes were silver with a faux-diamond-decorated clasp. As she gazed at herself in the mirror one last time, Meg took a deep breath, hoping God would give her strength to go through with this—if there was a God who heard the cries of young ladies trapped in worlds to which they were certain they didn't belong.

"You look lovely," Charlotte said, smoothing her gown in the back.

"Thank you," Meg replied. Kelly was out for a few days, so Charlotte had been called upon to help her dress for Alise's ball. Her mother and uncle were no longer attending such events, mostly because her uncle was seldom invited after the scene he'd caused so many years ago at Christina Edgebrook's ball, though Meg was fairly certain the real reason her mother did not permit her uncle to go to this particular ball was because she was certain he would say something awful to Charlie, who was also invited, and her mother wanted to appear to still be high society.

The money Charlie had been sending had helped with that, but it was getting more and more expensive to keep up the façade, and Meg couldn't come up with enough excuses for him to send payment. She had spent a bit of the money her father had saved for her, but she had to be careful because her mother might ask where she had gotten a certain item. Most of her money had gone to gifts for Kelly's family, including the new baby, Lizzie, who was born in October.

And of course she had spent a bit of money on Ezra. That day when he had driven her to the bank had been the first time she allowed herself to truly embrace the feelings she had for him. Ever since, she had spent many evenings in the solace of his arms, seeking refuge from a world in which she knew she did not belong.

Now, he was waiting in the garage for her and would be taking her off to start a new life.

Charles Ashton had also been invited to Alise's ball. She knew that they had mutual friends in Alise and her older sister Beatrice, but she had only just discovered a few days ago that Charlie would be attending. That's when she realized now was the time to take her future into her own hands.

Meg descended the stairs, clutching her pocket book, expecting to see her mother in the parlor, but when she turned the corner, the room was empty. She didn't hear or see her anywhere, which seemed rather odd; she was certain she'd want to see her off.

Walking into the kitchen, she saw Tessa straightening some of the items on the counter. "Where's mother?" Meg asked.

"Oh, she's gone to bed, miss," Tessa explained. "You look absolutely breathtaking, Miss Mary Margaret."

"Thank you," Meg said absently. "To bed?"

"Yes, she said her head was hurting."

"And Uncle Bertram?"

"Haven't the foggiest, though, if I were to guess, I'd say likely the tavern. It's only nine."

"Right," Meg muttered. "All right then. I guess I'm off."

"Shall I have Mr. Bitterly pull the motor coach around?"

"No, Ezra is driving me. Mr. Bitterly is also feeling poorly. I'll just go out the back."

"In those shoes?"

Meg smiled at her but didn't bother to answer. "Good night, Tessa." She looked at the older woman fondly for just a moment and then slipped out the back door.

He was waiting for her in the carriage house, and as soon as she saw him, a warm smile spread across her face. Standing in the lamplight, his hair gleaming golden, he looked like an angel, the angel that had come to save her.

"Oh, Ezra! Can you believe this is really happening?" she asked, as she flung herself into his arms.

"Meg, you look like a dream," he said, finding her mouth with his. He only pulled away long enough to tell her just how much he loved her.

"I love you, too, Ezra," she said, returning his kisses, her hands locked around his neck. After a moment, she pulled away, realizing they needed to get going so as not to arouse any suspicions. "Is my bag in the car?"

"Yes," Ezra replied, but he clearly had other things on his mind and pulled her back in, his kisses becoming more passionate and more eager, his hands beginning to roam her body.

"Ezra," Meg whispered as his mouth explored the curve between her neck and shoulder. "We need to be going."

With his arms still tightly wound around her, he released her neck, breathing her in. "Meg, I want you. Now. Let me show you how much I love you."

Her eyes widened, not sure how to respond. She planned to book a room under an assumed name for the next few days and then set sail on the next steam liner heading to America, which was leaving port on April 10, also under a different name. Kelly and her family would meet them at the hotel the next day. Though the plan was only a couple of days old, they had discussed it at length. Ezra would drive her to a hotel near the docks and then ditch the car. She couldn't imagine why he would want to change the plan now. Finally, she smiled and said, "Ezra, we'll be in a hotel together posing as husband and wife in just a bit. If you are serious, then, we can talk about it more once we are safely away."

"No, Meg," he said his hands caressing her hips. "I want to make you mine before we go. I need to know that you really love me, that you honestly want to be with me."

"You know I love you, Ezra. I have for years," she reminded him. As proof, she pulled him to her and kissed him, which only served to excite him even more, and several more minutes passed as they stood beneath the lamplight entangled in each other's arms.

"Come on, Meg. Come with me," Ezra insisted. He took her hand and began walking toward the ladder that led to the hayloft.

Meg glanced behind her. The lights were out on this side of the house except for the one in the attic, which must be Tessa. Surely no one could see them or would pay them any mind. His father's quarters were on the other side of the carriage house, in the back, and he was likely asleep.

Though she had reservations, she loved Ezra, and she was certain that he loved her as well. He had agreed to go to America, to leave his ailing father, and to run away with her. He'd kept all of her secrets—about the money and not wanting to marry Charlie--but also about her uncle. She'd cried in his arms after attacks, while he swore to get vengeance, but she made him promise not to. She couldn't bear to see another friend hurt because of her.

Climbing the ladder in those shoes was difficult, but he carefully helped her up, and when she reached the top, she could see that he had given this some thought. A blanket was spread atop the thinly strewn hay, surrounded by higher bales, forming a kind of cocoon. He had even sprinkled flower petals everywhere, and Meg could smell the heavenly scent of oleander and lilac.

"Ezra..." she barely whispered. Tears filled her eyes. Such thought and preparation had gone into this night; clearly the physical declaration of their love to each other meant a lot to him.

"Meg, you are everything to me," he said, standing before her, his hands encircling her waist. "I want to show you how much I love you, and I want this to stand as a promise that we will be together always."

He began to kiss her again, and Meg surrendered to his embrace. She soon found herself tangled in his arms on the moonlit blanket, their scent mingling with the perfume of the flowers.

CHAPTER TWENTY-ONE

Charlie

It was half past nine, and Mary Margaret still hadn't made her appearance. Charlie slipped his pocket watch back inside of his jacket and took another sip of his drink. Surely, she'd be there soon. What could possibly be keeping her?

"It's not like her to be late," Alise mentioned, sliding up next to him.

"She said she'd be here at nine," Charlie sighed. "You're certain she's not here?"

"I don't see her," the debutante replied.

"At least you know what she looks like," Charlie muttered.

"I told you. She's tall with blonde hair and a witty smile. She'll light up the room as soon as she walks in, and half a dozen young fellows will trip over themselves scrambling to have their turn to spin her around the dance floor. She dances like a ... a swan."

Charlie couldn't help but chuckle at the description. He'd always liked Alise, even though she was much younger than him.

"I'll let you know when she gets here, I promise. Even if it means

I have to cross the ballroom unaccompanied!" She made an "O" shape with her mouth and covered it with her gloved hand, as if doing such a thing was the worse atrocity one could commit.

"Thank you," Charlie replied, still laughing. "Well, I suppose your dance card is quite full, on this festive occasion. But if you have a spare line, I should like to sign it."

"Why, Charles J. Ashton, I thought you'd never ask," Alise replied with a demure smile.

Once Charlie decided to dance with Alise, and several other girls, he decided that Mary Margaret was the one who was missing out and determined he would have as much fun as possible, with as many other young ladies as he wanted, hoping word would reach her that not only was she horribly rude for not showing, she was the one who looked like a fool.

CHAPTER TWENTY-TWO

Meg

She'd always thought this moment would be frightening because of the trauma she'd been through, but it wasn't. Ezra was gentle and kind, and though it wasn't quite what she had expected it to be after hearing Kelly's description, she felt certain that Ezra loved her. She was ready to start her new life with him.

He helped her clasp the row of buttons that ran up her spine, and after she'd slipped into her shoes, he kneeled to buckle them, a smile plastered on his handsome face. As he stood and wrapped his arms around her she said, "I suppose I don't look half as polished as I did when I came in."

"You always look beautiful, Meg," Ezra assured her, kissing her again.

Eventually, she pulled away and gestured at the blanket and flower petals saying, "I guess we should clean this up so they don't know what happened and get on our way."

"Oh, I'll get it in the morning," Ezra said, nonchalantly, finally releasing her.

"In the morning?" Meg questioned. "Ezra, we won't be here in the morning. We're running away. Tonight. Remember?"

He stood before her, looking down at his shoes, one hand in his trouser pocket, the other running through his hair. "About that, Meg, I don't think I can go tonight. I need to stay here and say goodbye to my father."

Meg could hardly believe her ears. "What?" she asked, taking a step forward. "But... you said, if I proved my love to you, we would go. And I did."

"And it was wonderful," he assured her, stepping forward and clasping both of her hands in his. "We will go. First thing in the morning, I promise."

"No, we won't," she shouted, pulling her hands away. "Ezra, we have to go now. If my mother finds out that I didn't go to Alise's ball she'll... she'll kill me."

"She'll never know."

"She may already know! I was expected there well over an hour ago. It's quite possible someone's come looking for me."

"If that were the case, they'd have come back here to ask if I took you, and clearly no one has. Meg, we'll get up early, before your mother rises, and we'll leave then."

Inhaling sharply, she held her breath for a long moment, trying to calm herself. "Why can't you just tell your father goodbye now?"

"Because he's sleeping, and I don't want to wake him. He's very ill. He might even be dying. Isn't it enough that I've agreed to leave him to run away with you?"

"Fine. Then take me to the hotel and then you can come in the morning."

"Your mother will know that I've taken you somewhere. She'll get it out of me."

"You'd tell her?"

"I'm not a good liar, Meg," Ezra replied. "Listen, just go back in the house. Get some rest, and then, early in the morning, I'll come for you. I promise. We'll leave. I love you, Meg. Surely, you trust me."

Meg could hardly believe what she was hearing. She considered taking the car and driving away herself, but she didn't think that she would be able to do it; she'd only driven once and that was years ago. She wasn't even sure how to start it. She could try to walk to the hotel, but it was fairly far, and she'd be walking near the pier at night. Sighing in frustration, she finally said, "Fine. I guess we'll have to change our plans. But I'm telling you, Ezra, my mother will find out that I wasn't there, and when she does, she will likely kill me."

"I will never let her—or your uncle—harm you again, Meg, I promise," he said, taking hold of both of her arms and pressing his forehead against hers.

"All right," she finally acquiesced. "Where's my pocket book?"

After a careful search of the floor, Ezra finally found it behind one of the bales of hay and handed it back to her. He went down the ladder first, careful not to let her fall, and before she headed off to the house, he took her in his arms one last time, kissing her longingly, declaring his love, and promising to see her early the next morning.

Meg was able to sneak back into the house undetected. Once she reached her room, she couldn't help but let the tears flow down her face. She was so frustrated that Ezra was able to talk her into showing him her love but then wouldn't agree to leave. She cleaned herself up with water from the washbasin and pulled quite a bit of straw out of her hair before slipping into her nightgown and attempting to get some sleep.

Thoughts of what might be happening at the ball and of what her mother would say when she discovered she hadn't gone prevented her from resting. She even wondered what Kelly would do when she realized she hadn't left home. Would she make it to the hotel before the O'Connell's? What would Ezra do if her mother attempted to punish her in the morning? She knew for certain he would protect her, but she couldn't imagine him actually fighting her mother or uncle.

She also recalculated precisely what Kelly had told her about what time in a woman's cycle she could get pregnant. Meg was fairly certain she couldn't possibly need to worry about that right now, but the thought had crossed her mind. She was never good at math, but she thought she could manage the easy calculation this problem demanded.

She finally began to doze off just before the sun came up, wondering how much longer it might be before Ezra came to wake her. Would he be able to sneak in undetected? Surely, it would have to be soon. Otherwise, everything would be ruined. Her last thoughts before she finally drifted off were of freedom—freedom for herself and Ezra, and freedom for Charlie Ashton who would no longer be forced to wed a woman he'd never even met.

CHAPTER TWENTY-THREE

SOUTHAMPTON

April 8, 1912
Meg

"Miss? Miss? Get up!"

Meg felt the jostling but could hardly pry her eyes open. Where was she? What time was it? Who was shaking her? After another hard jerk, she opened her eyes, and realized it was Charlotte.

"Miss, your mother is asking to see you in the parlor," the younger woman exclaimed. "She's quite put out. Hurry! You should dress."

It took Meg a moment to realize that she was still in her room—but that she shouldn't be. A glance at the clock on the wall showed her it was half past nine.

Ezra had never come.

Her mother knew.

Charlotte scurried about the room, grabbing clothing items,

219

hurrying her to take her night clothing off, and forcing her undergarments and gown on. She tossed some slippers in Meg's direction and then, before Meg could even stand, threw herself on the bed and began to pull her hair up into a bun.

I don't think I've ever seen her work so quickly or so hard, Meg thought. She, on the other hand, was in no hurry at all. She was quite certain her mother would end her the second she walked into the parlor.

"All right. Go," Charlotte ordered as she finished with her hair.

Meg thought she should grab her pocket book from the night before. She had about one hundred pounds inside, which she planned to use for her trip. She'd given some money to Daniel the day before to purchase their tickets. Other than the money she had in the bank, that was all the cash she had in the house, and if she decided to run away from her mother, she might need it.

"Hurry!" Charlotte insisted, and since Meg didn't see the bag anywhere, she decided to go. What were the chances she would actually take off? Surely, her mother would just scold her and send her to her room.

She took the steps slowly, noticing that Charlotte did not follow. Once she reached the parlor, she found her mother and uncle seated there. A noise from the adjoining room caught her attention, and she caught a glimpse of golden blond hair and wondered if he had come to defend her or if her mother realized what had happened and had brought him in to punish him as well.

Having Ezra nearby gave her strength, so, as she stood before them, Meg held her head high. "You wanted to see me, Mother?"

"Mary Margaret," Mildred began, "how was the ball?"

She knew her mother well enough not to fall for her bait. "I'm not sure, Mother. Did Mrs. Donaldson report to you this morning? Or someone else?"

Mildred stood, crossing the two feet between them rapidly. "Mary Margaret Westmoreland, where were you last night? Why did you not attend Miss Townly's ball?"

"I didn't feel well," Meg replied, keeping her chin up.

"That is an outright lie! Charles Ashton came all this way to meet you, and you stood him up! Do you have any idea how insulting that is?"

Meg could hold back her anger no longer. "Oh, no! What if that means he breaks of the engagement, and you can no longer blackmail him for his money?"

"How dare you!" Mildred spat, her hands turning into fists. "After all I've done for you—we've done for you. You insolent child!"

"Done for me? You've done nothing for me, Mother! The only person you ever think about is yourself. And I won't have it anymore! I'm leaving!"

Meg turned to walk away, but her mother caught her arm. "You're not going anywhere, young lady, except for back to your room. I expect Mr. Ashton will show up here soon, and when he does, you will apologize!"

"No, I won't mother! I won't apologize, and I won't marry him!" Meg spat, pulling her arm away.

"Oh, yes you will," her mother said, her voice gravelly and deep, each word calculated. "You will do exactly as I tell you."

Though she was surprised her uncle had been quiet so far, Meg saw him leaning forward in his seat and knew that, if she tried to get past him to the dining room, where Ezra still stood, he would grab her. She was wondering why Ezra had not stepped in yet. Perhaps he needed a cue. "No I won't mother! I love Ezra, and we're going to leave this place and start over together!"

"Ezra?" her mother asked, her eyes widening.

Meg still stared at her defiantly. Only the sound of her uncle standing nearby drew her attention away, and her mother used that flicker of a distraction to strike. The first blow hit Meg right in the cheekbone, the clasp on her mother's ring tearing into her skin near her temple. Gasping in shock, Meg lost her balance and nearly fell, but just as she caught herself, her mother struck again. She slapped her so many times, Meg quickly lost count, and once she stumbled into the wall behind her, and began to sink to the floor, Mildred finally let up.

"Is that where you were last night? With the gardener? You ungrateful little bitch!"

"Ezra!" Meg began to scream. "Ezra! Help!" Her head was ringing and her face stung and her head felt fuzzy. Why wasn't he coming to help her?

Before Meg even realized what was happening, she found herself being hoisted into the air, rough hands tossing her over a boney shoulder as insults and accusations filled with curses littered the air.

Her uncle's arm had her pinned so that her own gown was a prison. She couldn't break free from him. Though he was old, he was spry and strong, and he managed to haul her up the stairs, even though she struggled against him, all the while screaming for help. But no help came, and once she was on her bed, Meg realized that this monster attack would be different and the most terrifying of all.

CHAPTER TWENTY-FOUR

Charlie

"Well, how was the ball?" Jonathan asked, handing Charlie a cup of coffee as they sat on his hotel room balcony overlooking the ocean.

"It was actually quite fun," Charlie admitted. "That Alise Townly is a character. And the English certainly know how to throw a party."

"That's good to hear," the liegeman replied. "So why the long face then? Was Miss Westmoreland not quite the beauty you had anticipated?"

Setting his coffee cup on the table between them, Charlie replied, "I wouldn't know."

"What's that now?"

"She didn't attend."

Jonathan nearly choked on the liquid he was swallowing. "How's that? Did you say she didn't attend?"

"That's correct."

"At all?"

"Unless she came and left before I got there at nine, then I'm assuming not at all."

Clearly puzzled, Jonathan was quiet for a moment. Charlie assumed he was wondering how this could have happened. After all, in the nearly two years that Jonathan had worked for him, almost everything had gone perfectly according to plan. It was a gift of his—he knew just how to make everything work so that Charlie was very nearly always happy, on time, and impressive. Now, Charlie was certain he was wondering where he had gone wrong. At last, Jonathan muttered, "I honestly didn't see that coming."

"Nor did I. After all, she sent a telegraph the day before I embarked saying how excited she was to see me. I've traveled all this way, and she can't spare a few hours to attend a dance?"

Jonathan was shaking his head. "Well, at least you kept your promise to Alise. That's something."

"Yes, I would've come anyway. But the opportunity to finally meet Mary Margaret was the driving force behind this trip. She is supposed to be my wife soon—before September--and I have never even seen her in person."

"And the last photograph you received, she looks so young, I highly doubt you'd even recognize her if you ran into her on the street," Jonathan added.

"Indeed. I've half a mind to just get on the next ship and sail right back to New York."

"You know your father would disapprove of that," his liegeman reminded him.

Charlie sighed, knowing he was right. "I could always try again in a month or two."

"Or you could just go to her home. Perhaps she fell ill and couldn't send word. Or perhaps she tried but her message wasn't delivered."

"Or perhaps she's joined the circus," Charlie mumbled.

"Come now, Charlie. You may as well pay her a visit. The next ship to leave isn't scheduled until the tenth, and we are supposed to be here nearly two weeks. You have meetings scheduled with several factory owners—including Bertram Westmoreland. You can't just run away."

"Run away?" Charlie echoed, a bit put out. "Jonathan, I've been trying with this woman practically my entire life! I stood next to my college buddy as he wed the only other woman I've ever had any feelings for because this was the right thing to do. She can't even stop by and say good evening?"

"I didn't mean it like that," Jonathan assured him, patting him on the arm. "I just meant—give it another try. You're here. You may as well."

Charlie considered what he was saying. He did understand how much this meant to his father, and he didn't want to let him down. If he went to visit her and was unable to see her, then he'd sort out what to do next. "Fine," Charlie finally agreed. "I'll pay her a visit. But if she isn't there or can't see me, I want to go back to New York."

"Fair enough."

CHAPTER TWENTY-FIVE

Meg

H er body ached all over, her head throbbing with each beat of her heart, which had finally returned to normal after she came to; she wasn't exactly sure when she had blacked out, but everything seemed fuzzy. She was certain she had seen her mother there in the doorway and that she'd done nothing to help, nothing to stop him.

There were voices downstairs. She recognized her mother's, but she didn't know the other one. It was a soft tenor, and though he sounded upset, there was a calmness about the way he spoke that made her feel at peace—something she wouldn't have felt possible at this point in time.

Wanting to find out who was in her home, Meg rolled over, pain radiating through her body as she did so. She managed to sit up and then push off the bed to stand, shuffling across the floor to the radiator.

"You can imagine my consternation, Mrs. Westmoreland," the stranger was saying. "I've come all this way expecting to meet your daughter, and when she wasn't there, well, it was quite upsetting."

"I can only imagine," her mother said in the most sympathetic tone Meg had ever heard come out of her mouth. "I sent word with a family friend of Mary Margaret's illness. I regret that it never reached you."

"Mrs. Westmoreland," the voice that must belong to Charles Ashton replied, "I would like for you to be quite frank with me. I've invested years of my life in courting your daughter. For years, I've honored my father's agreement with your late husband, thinking only of her. Now, if you are not planning to follow through with the arrangement, please let me know. I understand you've dropped your lawsuit and have officially accepted that the agreement is legally binding. But if you want out... well, just say so. I will speak to my father and see if he is agreeable."

"Mr. Ashton...."

"Charlie is fine."

"Yes, Charlie," her mother repeated, "I assure you that my daughter has every intention of becoming your wife. We couldn't think of a finer young man or a finer family to join together with. Mary Margaret is a bit... frail, I'm afraid. I think she will do quite well once she reaches America. It's only a temporary setback, I assure you. She will become your wife this summer."

As Meg pondered her mother's ridiculous statement that she was sickly and frail, Charles Ashton said something that made her gasp. "That's good to hear, Mrs. Westmoreland, because I've envisioned your daughter as my wife for so long, I couldn't even dream of finding another."

Tears began to slide out of Meg's eyes. Tears for this young man whose life she'd unknowingly ruined, tears for all that she'd suffered, tears for her father who wanted to protect her but couldn't. How could Charlie say such a thing? If he had any idea what the woman standing above him had done, the horrible choices she'd made, he would realize that she had done them both a favor by choosing to be set free from their obligation.

She heard her mother assure him that her daughter should be

well by tomorrow if he'd like to come by then, and as footsteps echoed through the parlor towards the door, Meg slowly made her way to the front window.

Pulling the curtains back just a crack, Meg peered through the rain covered glass at the front walkway. She could no longer hear anything, but she waited for just a moment as they said their respective goodbyes and then watched as Charles Ashton made his way down the path toward the street. As if he could feel her gaze, he turned and looked up at her window, and while her first instinct was to drop the curtain and hide, she couldn't take her eyes away from him. His green eyes were beautiful, and he wore his sincere heart on his handsome face. He was tall and lean, graceful, and well-dressed. He was clearly concerned—about her, about the arrangement, about keeping his promises. And she had thrown it all away. In that instant, she both loved and hated him at the same time. Loved the promise of what they could have had together if she had only honored the agreement; hated that someone so perfect and kind could ever think that she deserved a life with him.

Meg made her way back to her bed and hid under the covers. She knew now that she could never be Mrs. Charles Ashton. She'd made at least one too many mistakes for that. Resolved to do what she must the next day, Meg finally fell asleep, dreaming of a new life, of freedom, of America.

CHAPTER TWENTY-SIX

SOUTHAMPTON

April 9, 1912
Meg

Meg's dreams had morphed into nightmares, as if her unconscious mind wanted her to remember the events of the day before. She dreamt of her mother standing in the doorway screaming at her, saying she'd ruined everything, of the awful things her uncle had said, and finally of sinking in ice cold water, spindle fingers grasping at her ankle. When she awoke, the sun was already up, and Kelly was sitting on the edge of her bed, a worried expression on her face.

"What time is it?" Meg asked, her eyes not yet focused.

"Nearly nine," Kelly said, a bit of relief washing over her countenance. "I tried to wake you, but you wouldn't budge."

Meg yawned, but stretching hurt too much, and she didn't want Kelly to see her wince, so she sat up carefully. There was no reason for Kelly to know what had happened, not yet anyway, and since she was already feeling much better than she had the day before, she was hopeful she could pull off the charade. "When did you get back?"

"A few hours ago," Kelly answered. "I was due back, and since you never showed up yesterday, I was beginning to worry. What happened?"

There was no way she could answer that question without bursting into tears, so Meg sidestepped it instead. "Ezra wanted to say goodbye to his father. So he did. And then, my mother found out I had missed the ball."

"Oh, no!" Kelly interjected. "Is that where that bruise came from?"

Meg's hand instinctively flew to the side of her face. "Is it bad?"

"No, it's mostly in your hairline, but I noticed," Kelly said. She slid over on the bed and forced Meg to turn her head so she could look at it. "Did she hit you with something?"

"I think her ring caught," Meg replied, finally pulling away. "Anyway, everything is ruined for sure now. We need to just slip out and go."

"What about Charlie?" Kelly asked, the expression on her face giving voice to her hesitation.

"He stopped by yesterday, and my mother told him to come back today. Kelly, I can't be here when he arrives. My mother and uncle would like nothing more than for me to marry him so that they can have his money, and I won't be their pawn."

"But doesn't Charlie want to marry you?"

"I don't know. But if he knew what he was getting, he wouldn't," Meg replied. "Besides," she added, her mind slipping to thoughts of happier times, "Ezra does, too. I'm disappointed that he didn't help me yesterday when I got into it with my mother and uncle, but perhaps he was just frightened."

"No, I don't think that's it," Kelly said, shaking her head.

"Kelly, he really does love me. I know he wants to go with us so that we can be together. He just doesn't understand exactly what it entails yet to be a proper husband. I'm sure, once we get to America, he can learn...."

"He's gone."

Meg froze, mid-sentence. "He's what?"

"Gone," Kelly repeated, dropping her eyes from Meg's shocked face.

"How can that be?"

"I don't know. I came in this morning, and Tessa said that he had lit out of here last night. Told his father goodbye and left."

Unable to believe her ears, Meg stared down at her hands for a moment, trying to wrap her mind around what Kelly was saying. Certainly, she'd been upset at him for not helping her. She wasn't even sure she loved him anymore. But she was willing to give him another chance. After all, they'd pledge themselves to one another, and that meant everything to her. Tears began to fill her eyes, and not wanting Kelly to see her cry, she wiped them away before they could even roll down her cheeks.

"I'm so sorry, Meg," Kelly said, wrapping her in her arms.

"No, it's okay," Meg said, wiggling free. "I'm just... surprised. That's all."

"Well, there's more," her friend began, her voice still cautious. Meg looked at her expectantly, and Kelly continued. "He took Charlotte with him."

Dumbfounded, Meg stared at her friend's freckled face for a long bit before she finally muttered an expletive under her breath.

"I know," Kelly agreed. "If I ever see him again, I'll kick him in the privates so hard, he'll be peeing out his eyebrows."

Even as irate as she was, picturing such a thing made Meg giggle, and then her laughter turned to tears of anger and frustration, and Kelly held her for a long while as she cried in exhaustion and disbelief.

After a bit, Meg finally pulled herself together and said, "Well, we still need to go before Charlie gets here. Is my mother about?"

"When I came up, she was out and your uncle was allegedly at work," Kelly replied. "Where's the bag? The one with my old dress in it?"

"I left it in the motor coach," Meg realized.

"That's a problem," Kelly muttered, her hand resting on her chin in thought.

"Why is that?"

"Because Ezra stole the car."

Meg could only shake her head. "Don't you have another dress in your room I could borrow, once we get to the hotel?"

"Yes, I suppose so," Kelly nodded. "I do believe we should all be third class passengers, though. You know there will be a lot of high society people on this maiden voyage."

"I know. All right. Help me put on a traveling gown for now. The boat doesn't leave until tomorrow. Surely, we can hide out in a hotel for one day without being caught."

"I should hope so," Kelly replied as she helped Meg get dressed. She did her best to make her look simple and plain so as not to draw any attention to them.

Once she was dressed and ready to go, Meg asked, "Do you see my pink pocket book anywhere? The new one?"

Kelly helped her look for the bag for quite some time before they finally found it on the floor under the dresser. Meg wasn't surprised to find that it was empty. "I wonder if Charlotte stole my money this morning or if Ezra took it when we were in the carriage house?"

"Either way, it's gone," Kelly shrugged, almost as disappointed as Meg.

"I have all of those coins," Meg remembered. "Perhaps we can find a place to trade them in?"

Kelly helped her draw her hatbox down from the top shelf, and as she did so, all of the letters from Charlie fell to the ground. While Kelly collected the coins, Meg stooped and picked them up, looking at each of them, and wondering what her life might have been like if she'd agreed to be Mrs. Charles Ashton. Now, she would never know.

"All right, love, we're all ready to go," Kelly said as she dropped the last of the coins into a bag along with a few necessities Meg might need.

She carefully placed the letters back on the shelf and then stepped out of the way so that Kelly could put the hatbox away. Her pink robe caught her eye, and for a moment, she remembered the Christmas her mother had given it to her. She'd thought, perhaps, that day had opened a new chapter for them, that they would be proper mother and daughter from that point on. Even though that had not worked out, the robe was a reminder of what might have been, and Meg picked it up and shoved it into her bag.

Meg took one last look around her room; she wouldn't miss it one bit.

CHAPTER TWENTY-SEVEN

Charlie

Charlie had learned from business to always trust his gut. He knew when he was being treated fairly and when he was about to be made to look like a fool. Even though he was quite certain that this was not the day that he would meet Mary Margaret Westmoreland, her mother had asked him to return, so he intended to comply.

While he was off paying his visit, Jonathan was trying to find out if there was more to this story. He had a very hard time believing that Mary Margaret was actually sick the day before. If there was information to be found, Jonathan Lane would find it. Of that, Charlie was certain.

Arriving at the Westmoreland residence, Charlie found the household in a bit of an uproar. Servants were scurrying about, and Mrs. Westmoreland was sitting in the parlor, red-faced and wiping her nose with a handkerchief, as if she had been crying. He was shown in and took the same seat he'd been in only the day before.

"Oh, Mr. Ashton, it's just terrible!" she began as soon as she recognized him. "Someone has absconded with my daughter!"

"What's that now?" Charlie asked, on the edge of his seat. "Are you saying she's been taken?"

"Yes! She's simply vanished."

Charlie found this story quite difficult to believe. "Are you certain she didn't just go for a stroll?"

"No, I'm certain. She was taken. You must know, Mr. Ashton, Mary Margaret would never leave without my consent. She is very obedient. There's evidence that she's been kidnapped. Why, I've even filed a report with the authorities."

"Evidence? What sort of evidence?" Charlie asked.

Mildred Westmoreland began to sob. "Oh, Mr. Ashton, I can't possibly discuss it again. I love my daughter with all of my heart. The idea that something might have happened to her is more than I can bear!"

Though something about this situation did not seem quite right to him, Charlie offered his condolences to the grieving mother, standing to put his arm around her as she cried into his jacket. "What can I do to help?" he offered.

Pulling away, she looked up at him. "Well, we are a bit low on funds," she said through her sniffles. "I am sure I could organize a search party if we had a few thousand pounds."

Charlie's gut was certainly telling him this was a ploy, and as much as he wanted to shake the woman and accuse her of being a gold digger, he composed himself. "I haven't any cash on my person just now, Mrs. Westmoreland," he replied.

"Perhaps you could send a wire transfer?"

Her tears seemed to have dried up for a moment, and as he appeared to consider her request, she began to wail again. "Perhaps," he replied. "For now, I will go and speak to the detectives and see if there's anything I can do to be of service."

"Oh, they've assured me they have Southampton's finest on the job," Mildred replied, wiping at her tears. "There's no reason for you to trouble yourself with that."

"Very well then," Charlie said, shaking his head, and stepping back away from her. "I shall return to my room. If you should hear anything, please send notice. I'm staying at the Harbor Hotel."

"Yes, of course, Charlie," Mildred said. "You will come back and check in tomorrow, then? Perhaps you shall have some funding you can spare for the search by then?"

"I am scheduled to meet with Mr. Westmoreland tomorrow," he reminded her. "I shall seek an update from him."

"Do say a prayer for my Mary Margaret," Mildred said, tears streaming down her face, as she signaled for a servant to show him to the door.

"I hope she is found safe," Charlie nodded, following the older woman to the front entrance. Yesterday, when he had left, he couldn't help but feel as if he was being watched. He felt compelled to have one last look at the home before leaving. Today, he walked out of the Westmoreland residence fully resolved never to look back.

Less than an hour later, he was sitting on his balcony next to Jonathan, staring at the vast ocean, wishing he could instantly be back on the other side, home in New York, away from this nightmare of a town and this nightmare of a family.

"My understanding is that a servant boy is missing as well," Jonathan explained. "I'm not sure that's the full story, but I don't think that Miss Westmoreland was actually taken against her will."

"You don't say?" Charlie asked, sarcasm dripping from his voice. "I'm quite certain this is just another of the Westmoreland family's plots to get more money from me."

"Perhaps when you meet with Bertram tomorrow, he'll be more forthcoming."

Charlie shrugged. He'd been made a fool of so many times in the last few days—by the same woman—he could hardly stand it anymore. "I don't think I will be meeting with Mr. Westmoreland tomorrow,

Jonathan. I think I shall return home, explain things to my father, regroup, and see what he would like to do next. In all honesty, I think this might be the end of my courtship with Miss Westmoreland."

Jonathan nodded. "I think that's fair. I can't blame you for being upset—and put off. I'm sure your father will understand."

"I should hope so," Charlie agreed. "He's a stubborn man, but he won't like seeing our name dragged through the mud any more than I do."

"Very well, then," Jonathan replied. "Shall I go book us a trip home for tomorrow then?"

"Yes," Charlie said. "The faster the better. I'm ready to be back in New York City away from the madness of the Westmorelands. Honestly, I hope I never see any of them again."

CHAPTER TWENTY-EIGHT

April 10, 1912
Meg

The excited crowd waiting to board the ship seemed to vibrate around them as Meg waited with the O'Connell family for it to be their turn to pass through inspection and gain passage aboard the steamship that would take her to America.

Traveling Third Class was quite different than the First Class treatment she was used to, but she didn't mind. She would no longer be the high society debutante she was before. In New York, she would start over, become someone else, and leave this place far behind her.

She was wearing a dress she'd borrowed from Kelly, and while the fit was unusual, it was quite comfortable. Without the corsets and undergarments she was used to, she felt free. And freedom was always a good thing.

While the entire day before she'd been nervous that her mother or uncle would find them, or that she would be recognized by someone on the streets, as they crowded aboard the deck to wave goodbye to the people standing near the pier, she began to believe this was really happening, that she had actually escaped. No longer would she live in fear. No longer would she carry the burden of belonging to someone else. Once she was in New York, she would be her own person at last.

Ruth was bubbling over with excitement as her father held her up to wave at the crowd. She was shouting, "Goodbye! I love you!" over and over, even though she didn't know a single soul in the throng below them. Meg could see the relief on Kelly's face as well as she stood next to her holding baby Lizzie. She'd been carrying the burden of Meg's predicament for almost as long as she'd carried it herself. Meg was thankful to be giving her best friend some liberty, too.

Once the ship began to pull away from the harbor, Meg breathed in the fresh salt air and exhaled all of her cares and worries into the wind. At last, she felt perfectly safe and happy. Nothing could harm her aboard the RMS *Titanic*.

CHAPTER TWENTY-NINE

Charlie

Standing on the First Class balcony, Charlie looked out at the vast ocean and was thankful that he was aboard one of the fastest ship that had ever been built. He couldn't wait to get back home to New York City and leave the ghosts of Southampton behind him.

Still stunned by Mary Margaret's actions, Charlie had hardly slept the night before. While he would certainly discuss how to proceed with his father, he knew in his heart he could never forgive her for the way she had treated him, particularly if what Jonathan had found out about the servant boy was true, and chances were that it was; Jonathan's information was rarely wrong.

He was resolved to leave off courting and engagements for a good long while, and yet, as he peered over the side, a young lady on one of the decks below him caught his eye. She had beautiful blonde hair that hung around her shoulders in waves. When she turned and he could see her profile, he noticed how her complexion looked flawless, almost like porcelain. Her eyes were a stunning blue. She was possibly the loveliest creature he'd ever seen, and he couldn't help but hope somewhere between Southampton and New York City he would have the opportunity to meet her, to see if her personality was as sparkling as those eyes.

Jonathan pulled his attention away, insisting that they move to get a better look at another ship that was about to collide with the *Titanic*, and within a few moments, Charlie had lost sight of her. But he wouldn't forget those eyes. Even though he had sworn off women, he couldn't help but hope that fate would intervene and he would bump into that woman again before they reached New York. Despite his destiny being chosen for him so long ago, Charlie had always believed in fate, and now he began to consider, perhaps he was meant to be aboard the maiden voyage of the *RMS Titanic*.

The End

MEG AND CHARLIE's story continues in *Titanic: Ghosts of Southampton Book 2*

A NOTE FROM THE AUTHOR

Thank you so very much for reading *Prelude*. I hope that you enjoyed reading about Meg and Charlie, who are characters near and dear to my heart. Please consider leaving a review. Meg and Charlie's story continues in *Ghosts of Southampton: Titanic*.

With the success of *Ghosts of Southampton: Titanic*, which I wrote before writing *Prelude*, I determined that the rest of Meg and Charlie's story needed to be told. I decided to do a prequel, which is what you have here, and I'm happy to announce that Book Three: *Residuum* will be out in early 2018. It tells the story of what happens when the survivors reach New York and how difficult it is to live on after bearing witness to the devastation aboard *Titanic*.

While a few readers have expressed to me that they find it difficult to read Meg's story, I want to express how important I believe it is for our society to continue to have conversations about the types of uncomfortable topics explored here. Did you know that according to The National Center for Victims of Crime, one of every five American girls is sexually abused? The number is one in twenty for boys.

245

These statistics from 2010 are unbelievable, and we must do everything we can to create a society where our children are safe. I created Meg's character in part to bring light to this subject and to show that abuse knows no bounds—regardless of one's circumstances, all of our children, unfortunately, are at risk. I hope that you found my handling of the events in this story tactful but that their inclusion will cause more awareness so that whenever we see signs of abuse, we can reach out and help spare other children the trauma that Meg went through.

For more information, please visit:

http://victimsofcrime.org/media/reporting-on-child-sexual-abuse/child-sexual-abuse-statistics

Would you like to subscribe to my newsletter to hear about upcoming releases? You can read *Leaving Ginny* for free when you sign up on Instafreebie here: https://claims.instafreebie.com/free/Eypqj

ALSO BY ID JOHNSON

Stand Alone Titles

Deck of Cards

Cordia's Will: A Civil War Story of Love and Loss

The Doll Maker's Daughter at Christmas

Beneath the Inconstant Moon

The Journey to Normal: Our Family's Life with Autism (nonfiction)

The Clandestine Saga series

Transformation

Resurrection

Repercussion

Absolution

Illumination

Destruction

A Vampire Hunter's Tale (based on The Clandestine Saga)

Aaron

Jamie

The Chronicles of Cassidy (based on The Clandestine Saga)

So You Think Your Sister's a Vampire Hunter?

Who Wants to Be a Vampire Hunter?

How Not to Be a Vampire Hunter

My Life As a Teenage Vampire Hunter

Ghosts of Southampton series

Prelude

Titanic

Residuum

Heartwarming Holidays Sweet Romance series

Melody's Christmas

Christmas Cocoa

Winter Woods

Waiting On Love

Shamrock Hearts

A Blossoming Spring Romance

Firecracker!

Falling in Love

Thankful for You

Melody's Christmas Wedding

Reaper's Hollow

Ruin's Lot

Ruin's Promise

Ruin's Legacy

For updates, visit www.authoridjohnson.blogspot.com

Follow on Twitter @authoridjohnson

Find me on Facebook at www.facebook.com/IDJohnsonAuthor